INTRODUCTION

Ret. US Air Force pilot Jackson (Jax) Reed's FBI career is just beginning, but when he's called to find a stolen US Air Force drone, he must confront the people who forced him into retirement. When he discovers more to it than a stolen drone, Jax will hunt and be hunted by the people who cost him his wings.

With a few weeks until the inauguration of a new President, Jax must look into the highest branches of government. Racing across the country, he'll discover that treason is ripe in America. His findings may shatter the American government and push him to the brink of losing the one person who stood by his side.

DISUNION BY FORCE

A JACKSON REED NOVEL

JACKSON REED
BOOK 1

BRIAN B. BAKER

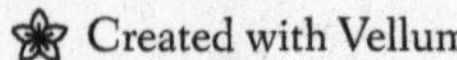 Created with Vellum

For a fourteen-year-old who found solace in these kinds of books.

Disunion by armed force is treason.
   Andrew Jackson

CHAPTER ONE

THE AIRCRAFT SAT on the tarmac.

Its black surface reflected the desert surroundings. The two small armaments along its wings with their US Air Force logos blacked out could almost be seen in the sunlight reflecting off the aircraft's fuselage.

The dark color enhanced its sleekness. A new variant is used for more recent drones, like the Raven. The aircraft was the same size as other drones, but its engines were similar to those on the F-35. They were quickly maneuverable and allowed the drone to work more like a fighter than its predecessors.

As it taxied down the runway, inside a small reconfigured railcar, Lieutenant Jared Phillips stared at his heads-up display. The desert floor extended beyond the nose of the aircraft. Jared glanced behind him as he throttled up, and the Raven rose off the tarmac and into the blue sky. Major Webb had come in moments before, and the man stood directly behind him.

"Had any issues with it lately?" Webb asked.

"No, sir, the bird is perfect. I thought that new update might throw it off, but it's still clean."

"Very well. I will see you later," Webb replied.

"Anyone able to get ahold of Dickson? This was her ride this morning."

"We've called, but there have been no answers."

"Okay, I'll finish the flight, but I need to be out of here as soon as possible. Ultrasound is today." Jared said, but Webb had already walked out of the box.

"I guess he had things to do," the Box Sergeant said.

Jared, who had been flying the aircraft the whole time and talking simultaneously, turned the aircraft to the right. It banked and passed over a small berm, dipped low into a valley, and Jared pulled hard on the stick. The aircraft screamed into the sky as it rocketed in a full climb.

Jared wondered what it would have sounded like if he'd been around to hear it.

"Don't push it too hard. It's not service ready yet."

"It's as service ready as it's going to get," Jared replied.

The sergeant didn't reply. Jared brought the aircraft out of the climb, dipped it down into the valley, banked it left, climbed over a small mountain, and finally dipped into the next valley.

"Be careful in there. They don't like people flying these things around there."

"Groom is no problem. They tested this thing there. They know all about it."

Jared dipped the aircraft, dusting the desert floor, and pulled up.

His hand jiggled, and the aircraft dropped.

"You're losing it," the sergeant said.

"No, I'm not," Jared said, flipping switches and buttons. The camera on the aircraft showed the desert floor rushing to meet the aircraft.

The stick moved, and the aircraft corrected itself.

"There, you got it. I thought."

"No, I don't. I don't know who does, but I'm not flying this thing." Jared informed him.

The aircraft dipped down, rose, and did loops.

"Whoever it is, they're good."

"Should I scramble an aircraft from Nellis?"

"No, I'll try and get it back," Jared said.

The aircraft rose again, drifted to the right, and came over a rise, hovering in the air.

Jared glanced from the screen to the Sergeant behind him.

The aircraft and whoever controlled it throttled up, and Creech Air Base came into view. Then the drone rose, moving on to another part of the base.

Jared stared at his controls.

A small warning popped up on his screen, '**System Armed.**'

"Shit," Jared said.

The payload on the aircraft streaked across the midmorning sky. It struck the box as Jared and the Sergeant reached for the door. The sudden blast rocked the base, and the aircraft, still hovering beyond the base, turned right and took off into the morning sun.

* * *

Director of National Intelligence Williams stared at the folder on his desk.

Project Raven stood out in bold letters.

"So you're putting the project on hold?" Williams asked.

The man across from his desk shuffled in his chair.

"Look, Aaron, with the recent developments, we feel the money would be better put on hold until we find out why the drone crashed." Speaker of the House, Miles Frank, said.

"You know, Miles, I don't like this. This project was a chance to save lives. American pilots' lives." Williams said.

"I understand that, but with the loss of one drone, we feel that until the investigation is complete, the money should be put on hold," Frank replied.

Williams stared across his desk at the other man but didn't flinch.

"If I knew the answers, I'd go directly to the FBI and OSI," Williams said.

"Aaron, this is a big deal. We have the inauguration coming up. This needs to be solved by then. If it's not, there will be a push to remove you as DNI. The President-Elect Franklin is undecided on what she's doing with you. If I'm being frank, I will also push for your removal."

"You're lucky to have kept your job after how badly the party was trounced in the last election. I'm still stunned you kept the majority in the House." DNI Williams thinly retorted.

"So am I, but with the incoming administration and the loss of the Senate, along with the large margins in the EC as well as the popular vote, the President-Elect is running on a mandate from the people. I'm not happy about our losses, but they are what they are."

The Speaker of the House paused.

"Look, we'll hold onto the funds as long as possible, but it has to be withdrawn in the next quarter. It goes somewhere else if we don't appropriate that money for something. You know that, Aaron."

He did know that. Over the last few years, he'd been on the hill numerous times in closed and open-door sessions. He thought it would be easier than the DNI, but he was wrong. He was just another rung on the ladder of bureaucracy.

"I have a meeting with the President-Elect and her people

later today. I know they will ask me to stay until they find a replacement. I'll stay on until they do, but I need the funding for this project. You've seen what that aircraft can do, Aaron."

"I have, but I also know one of them crashed. Can you imagine if that leaked to the press before the inauguration? Thompson would be livid."

"They're fucking vultures. They circle any carcass no matter how fresh."

"There's some truth, at least for some of them. This project is dead until the investigation is over."

Frank stood and walked to the door, stopped, and turned back.

"I'm sorry, Aaron. I know how much this project meant to you."

You have no idea.

Miles Frank walked out of the room, and Williams pressed a button on his desk.

"Yes, Sir," the man on the other end replied.

"Get me the AG," he said.

"Right away," the man replied.

He stared out the window at the trees and to the landscape beyond.

His phone buzzed again.

"His secretary says he's out for the day. Would you like me to call him at home, Sir?" the man asked.

"No, I'll get ahold of him later in the week. Mark, what time is my meeting with the President-Elect?"

"It's at four," the man replied.

DNI Williams glanced at the clock on the wall; it told him the time was one.

"Okay, I need something to eat before then. Can you have some food sent up?"

"Of course, Sir. The usual?" the man asked.

"Yes," Williams replied.

He stared out the window a moment longer and picked up the phone.

"It's me. I need to talk."

CHAPTER TWO

JACKSON REED SAT in front of the TV, his game controller in his hand. His daughter Elizabeth sat next to him, her controller in her hand.

He pressed a button on his controller; his daughter's aircraft on the screen exploded.

"Daddy, that's not fair," she said.

"Sorry," he said.

"You're not supposed to blow me up every time. Let me blow you up, okay?" she said.

Jackson laughed.

The morning had been quiet, and although she'd opened all of her presents, the litter of wrapping paper still lay strewn around the floor. Her biggest present was the game system. She'd wanted it 'most of all,' as she'd told him numerous times on her visits to his apartment in Georgetown.

They'd eaten pancakes for breakfast; hers loaded with chocolate chips, his covered in maple syrup. It was the one thing he'd wanted to do when his ex-wife, Sarah, agreed to let their daughter spend the holidays with him.

He'd picked her up the previous afternoon. She'd opened all

her presents from her mom and Tom, her mom's boyfriend. But there was no game system. She'd been told by Tom that there wasn't a Santa Claus six months ago. Even though it had been mainly over the phone or video calls over the last few years, Jax looked forward to celebrating Christmas with his daughter and was angered by this.

During this time, he and Sarah agreed he should have her over the holidays.

When they'd arrived at his house the night before, there were no presents under the tree.

Lizbeth's stare had shifted from her dad to the tree.

"Dad, where are the presents?" she'd asked.

"Santa hasn't come yet," he replied.

"Dad, you know there isn't a Santa," Lizbeth replied.

"I know that's what Tom told you, but I will find a way to prove it to you." He said.

She smiled, carted her My Little Pony carry-on to her room in the back of his apartment, and returned with a present.

"Mom helped me pick this for you." She stated proudly.

"I'll open it tomorrow," he said.

She frowned at his response.

He had opened it on Christmas morning with Lizbeth staring at him.

The watch she'd given him sat on his wrist. It was silver. The face bore two silver wings around the outside with the United States Air Force emblem in the center.

Jax stared at it as Lizbeth started up a new game of After-burner. It was the only game she'd wanted. Jax had beaten her most of the rounds, though he'd let her win a couple of the dogfights because she'd become increasingly frustrated with it.

His watch read noon.

"How about some lunch?" he asked.

"Okay," she replied but gazed absently at the game load screen, and he wasn't sure if she'd heard him or not.

Jax entered the kitchen, got out the bread, and his phone buzzed on the counter.

He picked it up and stared at the incoming call on his screen.

Lizbeth noticed and watched him intently."I thought you didn't have to work?" she asked.

"I'm supposed to be off," he replied and answered the phone.

"This is Jackson Reed," he said into the phone.

"Jax, it's Decker."

"Sir, I have time off until the new year."

"I understand your time off, but this came from the DNI."

Jax pulled his phone away and glanced from it to Lizbeth, whose eyes were still on him.

"Why would the Director of National Intelligence want me?"

"Jax, you know who DNI is? I know you were around each other before you retired from the Air Force. They have a problem at Creech, and your name came up. They've asked for you to handle this."

Jax knew better than to question his boss. He'd only been with the FBI for the last three years, and he continued to feel like he was a rookie. Being in his late thirties, it was a difficult thing to deal with.

"Yes, Sir," Jax said, "I'll make the arrangements with Sarah."

"I don't know the particulars, Jax, but you'll be briefed when you get there. There is a plane leaving in a couple of hours. Can you make that?"

"I believe so," Jax replied.

"Good, Jax," Decker said, "I hope you have a safe flight and keep me updated on what's going on."

"Yes, sir," Jax said and ended the call.

He set the phone down and looked up.

Lizbeth wasn't in the living room, the TV was off, and the game controller sat on the couch.

"Lizzy?" he called.

"I'm in here," she said from what sounded like her room.

Jax hurried down the hallway.

She sat on her bed, wiping her eyes.

"What's the matter?" he asked.

"You have to work. You promised you didn't have to work."

Jax got on one knee next to her bed and glanced around the room at the near barren walls.

As if she knew what he was thinking, she spoke, "We were going to get posters for my room this week. Now you have to work. I hate your work."

Jax could only listen.

"We were supposed to do fun stuff. See the art museum and the airplanes. Tom took me to see them with mom, but he doesn't know them. He had to look at the signs. You know the planes."

"I'm sorry. I was supposed to be off, but they called me. I have to go back to Las Vegas for something."

She wiped her tears and smiled, "Can you get a flamingo?"

"What?" he asked, wondering if he'd heard her correctly.

"A flamingo," Lizbeth said, "mom said they had them at a hotel in Las Vegas."

"One of the hotels has a whole garden of them. You want a stuffed flamingo?"

She nodded, sniffed, and put her arms out.

He hugged her. She was almost ten, and he noticed how much she'd grown since the last time he saw her. The cute little face was gone. She's leaned out and stretched so she looks more like her mom. A fact that tugged at his heart.

"You get your stuff packed. I have to call your mom."

Jax stood up, the muscles and tendons in his legs making noises similar to popcorn, and left Elizabeth alone to pack her things.

He took a breath, picked up his phone, stared at the ring on his finger, and dialed Sarah.

"Jackson, what's wrong?" she asked.

"I have to work," he said, waiting for the inevitable sigh.

It came, then there was silence on the other end.

"I thought you had the week off?"

"Something happened at Creech. I was asked for."

"Creech? What could happen there that they want you?"

"I'm not sure yet, but I must leave in a couple of hours. I need to bring Lizbeth back."

"Jackson, Tom, and I had plans," she said.

"I'll drop her off at the nearest bus station then. She should be safe until the CPS shows up."

The sigh and silence on the other end caused him to glance at the phone, ensuring she hadn't hung up.

"Okay, I guess there's no other option. I'll tell Tom."

"I'll be over in a little bit." He said.

Jax walked to the window and glanced out. Snow covered most of the roads below, and he wondered how long it would take to get Elizabeth home.

He walked to his room and packed what he'd need for the trip. All of his items went into a rolling carry-on. He wore a suit, fixed his hair, and trimmed his beard. It was short, something it had to be as an FBI agent. His firearm went into its holster, and he opened the door.

Elizabeth sat on the couch. Her carry-on rested next to her.

"Daddy, it's snowing. Will we be okay?"

He smiled.

"We'll be fine." He grabbed his coat and hers from the

closet, helping her to put hers on. It was those things he missed more than anything.

Jax shook his head, clearing it, and glanced around the apartment. His phone was in his pocket. At his feet, his laptop was in his carry-on, and Elizabeth stood in the hallway waiting for him.

CHAPTER THREE

JAX PULLED in front of Sarah's house, his old house, and stared into the backseat. Elizabeth's brown eyes stared back at him.

"You okay," he asked.

She nodded, but he saw the mistiness in her eyes.

The snow came down increasingly quicker as they drove from his apartment. Reaching Sarah's and his old house in Virginia felt like it took forever.

He helped Elizabeth out of the car and grabbed her carry-on. The ponies on it appeared to stare at him accusingly. He ignored them, grabbed Elizabeth's hand, and led her up the drive to the house. It was a small two-story, with white beams running across its front. It was similar to the rest of the houses on the street.

Elizabeth rang the doorbell, and they waited in the falling snow.

Sarah came to the door. She looked as if she'd hurriedly put her clothes on. Tom stood on the stairs, his clothes messy as well. He nodded at Jax, who nodded back.

"Take your things upstairs," Sarah said to Elizabeth.

"I'm sorry. I had no choice."

"Sure you did. You could have told them no."

Jax frowned. Old feelings of regret bubbled up, and he sighed.

"DNI Williams asked for me to be on this."

Sarah stared at him.

"Why would the Director of National Intelligence ask for you?"

"I worked out there for a long time. They know me. That's all I have."

"Can you at least tell me what's going on?"

"I don't know anything yet."

He glanced behind her as Tom led Elizabeth up the stairs.

Jax frowned, and Sarah glanced back at what he was looking at.

"He does a good job. He's trying. It's hard for him."

"I know what that's like."

Sarah glared at him. Her dark brown eyes saw straight through him.

"Jax, it just didn't work out the way we thought it would. After you resigned, everything changed."

"I thought that...."

"Thought what?"

Jax sighed, "It's Christmas, and I don't want to fight. I have a long flight ahead of me."

He raised his left hand and waved at Elizabeth as she stared at him and Sarah.

Sarah stared at the ring on his left hand.

"Jax, look, I'm having the papers drawn up. They'll be at your apartment by Monday."

"You were going to serve me divorce papers while Lizzy was over?"

"Let's not have this argument now. With your schedule, it's

the only time I knew you'd be home. Unless you'd rather me have you served at work?"

Jax thought about that for half a second.

"No, I don't need that headache." He paused, "Okay when I get back, I'll sign them."

"What about that?" she asked, pointing to his ring.

"I'm still dealing with that."

"Jax, it's been two years."

"I know."

Jax paused before continuing. "I'll call Elizabeth when I get settled in Vegas."

Sarah glanced at the snow falling around them. "Have a safe flight."

Jax nodded as he hurried to his car.

He watched the door close, then stared at the light in the top left bedroom.

Elizabeth came to the window and waved.

He waved back, though he wasn't sure she could see him through the falling snow.

Jax started the car and drove to the airport.

Pulling into the long-term lot, he parked his car and ensured everything was locked before walking away with his bag.

The terminal was quiet. He stopped to study the flights on the monitors. One was leaving in an hour. The TSA line was short, and he walked to the airline check-in counter.

He pulled out his badge, ID, and credit card.

"I need to book myself on the flight to Las Vegas, leaving in an hour."

The girl behind the counter popped her gum and smiled at him.

"Well, there is one seat. It's in the back of the aircraft, so you won't have much leg room."

"That's fine," Jax replied.

"When will you be returning?" she asked.

"I'm going there for work. I'm not sure when I'll be back."

"What kind of work do you do?" she asked, typing in his information.

He tapped the badge he'd put in front of her. "I'm a federal agent."

"Well, okay," the ticket agent said, "I will bump you up to a better seat then."

"That's not necessary," Jax replied.

"Not a big deal. You'll be in the emergency exit row with plenty of room."

Jax nodded. She printed his boarding pass, and he slid his card across.

"Thank you, Mr. Reed," she said.

Jax took his card and the boarding pass.

He showed his badge again when he reached the TSA. It would make his firearm less of an obstacle. He was waved through security as a man and woman behind him were stopped for more intensive checks.

"Hey, why does that guy get to go straight through?" the man loudly asked.

Jax stopped, turned, and walked back to the man. He wore a watch that would pay for a few semesters of college for Elizabeth. The woman wore earrings that would add a few more years.

Jax leaned forward so only the man could hear him, and his shoulder holster was visible.

"I know you weren't purposefully trying to bring attention to an Air Marshall, so I won't make you go through more extensive security. You and your bottle blonde should be careful."

The man dropped his gaze from Jax to the sidearm.

"Sorry," the man muttered sheepishly.

Jax continued, hurrying down the concourse to his gate. It

was still snowing, and he wondered if the flight would be canceled.

The door to the plane opened, and Jax stood up.

When he reached his seat, he sat down and watched as the same man and woman boarded the plane.

They avoided his looks and shuffled past his seat to wherever they were sitting.

Jax pulled out a book from his carry-on. Before boarding, he'd forgotten to grab one from home and bought it from the airport gift shop. He'd also purchased a bag of snacks.

He buckled his seatbelt and waited for take-off.

The plane lifted off from Reagan International at three in the afternoon.

He dove into his book, wondering about what lay before him in Las Vegas.

It had been four years since his retirement, and while he thought about flying often, he was grounded from flying any aircraft.

Jax stared out the wing of the 737 as the city's lights came into view.

The white beam of the Luxor announced the aircraft's closeness long before they entered the valley. Though Jax was in his late thirties, his eyes continued to be perfect.

The plane touched down, and once they'd reached the gate, Jax waited until everyone had deplaned before grabbing his bag from the overhead bin.

Hurrying to the rental car counter, Jax picked an SUV to drive around. It was big, black, and looked like an official vehicle.

He drove to his hotel, checked in, and put his bag in his room. He sat at the desk in his room, pulled out his laptop, and called Decker.

"So, what's going on?" Jax asked.

"I'm sending you a file to your email. Go through that, and I'll talk to you in the morning. Have a good night's rest. You'll need it."

Jax fired up his VPN program, opened his email, ran the decrypt, and read the email.

So they'd lost a drone? What's the big deal? Drones crash quite a bit.

Jax turned off his laptop, stuffed it in his bag, and glanced at the clock on the nightstand.

It read eleven, and he hadn't eaten, besides the airplane food and his snacks, since that morning with Elizabeth.

He stopped, and after concluding it was too late to call, he went to the casino.

The place was empty, just as he'd remembered Las Vegas being the week before New Year.

When he walked into the cafe, he gazed at all the open booths.

"Take a seat wherever you like," the hostess said; Jax glanced at her name tag, Mary.

"Thank you, Mary," Jax replied.

The woman smiled, and Jax walked to an empty booth on his right. The menu was in a holder in the middle of the table.

Mary came over with a notepad a few moments later.

"What can I get you?" she asked.

"Doing two jobs tonight?"

"Yeah, one of the waitresses called off."

"Sorry," Jax replied.

"It's OK. I'll make a little extra tonight.

"Nice," Jax said, "I'll have the steak and eggs."

Mary wrote it down as she glanced at the ring on his finger.

Jax noticed her eyes and smiled.

She rolled her eyes and walked away.

He didn't look forward to the next day and being back at

Creech. The thought caused him to stop and stare at the walls in the cafe. When his food arrived, it was delivered by a different waitress. The one who'd seen him to his table was nowhere in sight. It wasn't like he would make a move. He thought of himself as married, even if Sarah had moved on.

After his meal, he returned to his room to rinse the smell of the airplane and the day from his skin.

When he fell asleep, he tried not to think about how he'd failed his family, but mostly how he'd failed Elizabeth.

CHAPTER FOUR

THANKS to the early morning Las Vegas traffic, it took Jax an hour to reach Creech Air Force Base. He rolled up to the gate, his badge ready.

The guard stopped him, then waved him forward.

"What can I do for you, Sir?" the guard said.

He was in his mid-twenties, his hair cut short. His eyes were clear, his tone direct.

"I'm here to see the base commander," Jax replied, handing his badge over.

The guard studied the badge, smiled, and handed it back.

"I'll alert the Colonel that you're on your way. It's good to see you home, Captain," the guard said.

"Thank you, Airmen," Jax replied.

"You remember the way?" the airman asked.

"I do," Jax replied.

"Very well, Sir," the airman saluted.

Jax, who knew the protocol, did not salute. He knew which boundaries he could cross and which he couldn't.

He pulled his SUV through the gate and headed towards

the base commander's office. There were more guards along the fencing than when he'd left four years ago.

Two guards, one with a dog and the other with a rifle, walked along the front fencing. They could be on patrol anywhere, but seeing the patrol along the fence made Jax wonder what had happened.

He pulled up to the base commander's office.

Jax glanced at the base as he reached the steps of the commander's office. It appeared he'd brought the storm with him. Black clouds hung along the eastern side of the ridge beyond.

When he stepped inside, a woman in a crisp and pressed uniform smiled at him.

"You must be Jackson Reed?" she asked.

"I am," Jax confirmed.

"Colonel Smith is waiting in his office. Right this way, please," she said.

Jax followed her past a group of offices along a hallway. They ducked inside one of them, and Jax was suddenly facing the man whose orders had resulted in him being forced into retirement.

Colonel Rex Smith got up from his desk, a big smile on his face. The man was five-nine, though he looked taller. His body resembled a younger man's, and his uniform looked tailored to his frame.

"Jackson Reed, as I live and breathe. I never thought I'd see you out here again." Colonel Smith said.

"Neither did I, Sir," Jax replied.

Colonel Smith glanced at the woman next to Jax.

"I assume you've met your liaison with OSI?" he asked.

Jax reevaluated the woman on his right.

"My what?" Jax said.

"Jax, this is Lieutenant Vanessa Griggs. She's been assigned to you during your work."

"For what purpose?"

"Let me show you," Colonel Smith said. He exited the room and waved for Jax and Griggs to follow.

Smith walked to a door at the end of the hallway, unlocked it, and entered.

Jax and Griggs followed him. A round white table with white chairs lay in the middle of an empty white windowless room.

A slight whooshing sound filled the room as Colonel Smith closed and locked the door.

Jax stared at Smith.

"A secure room? I thought it was just a downed drone?"

Smith ignored him as he stepped up to a panel along the wall.

A slight buzzing noise was emitted, then cut out.

"Please sit. What I'm about to tell you is classified as top secret, and I had to have both of you cleared by your COs, or in your case Jax, the AG. The AG does not know the particulars, and DNI Williams didn't give him any. Anyway, what I'm about to show you does not to leave this room. If you discuss it with anyone outside this room that has not been cleared, it will cause a shit storm unlike anything seen in the branches since Abu Ghraib. Are we clear?"

Jax glanced to his left, where Griggs sat.

"Yes, Sir," Jax and Griggs said in unison.

Smith pressed another button, and a projector lowered from the ceiling while a screen rolled out in the front of the room.

A video started from inside of a drone control box.

"That's a new box," Jax said.

"Please, hold any comments until the end," Smith said.

Jax and Griggs watched as the video shifted from the flight box's interior to the drone's video.

As the video ended, Jax stared across the table at Smith.

"Did I see what I thought I did?" Jax asked.

"You did. The pilot, Jared Moseley, and the operations sergeant were killed in the explosion."

"What type of drone is that?"

"They're calling it the Raven."

"So the actual drone was stolen?" Griggs asked.

"That is affirmative."

"Why did you call me in for this?"

"I didn't like how it went down. I knew you were the only one who could do this. When I discovered you were an FBI agent, I sent a message up the chain. It reached various people, but DNI Williams decided you should handle this."

"Why?"

Smith glanced at Griggs.

"It's a long story, but he felt bad about what happened to you both times. He told me he feels responsible."

"I dropped the bombs, though," Jax replied.

"Look, let's get this taken care of. I think you can find something with the crew."

"I noticed something about that. Where is this flight area? I didn't recognize it at all."

"We've expanded the base into the hills. There is a runway for this aircraft. It's away from the rest of the base."

"How many of these Ravens are there?"

"There are only two. One is gone. The other is grounded."

The projector retracted into the ceiling, as did the screen.

Jax and Griggs stood up from their chairs and moved towards the door.

"Jax, this is a big deal. This drone had things on it that were top secret. This was a new project we were doing."

"New how?"

Smith looked into the hallway.

"Go up the hill to the flight line, and the crew will explain it better than I can."

"How do we get there?"

"You'll reach a gate. I'll call ahead, so they know you're coming. That will lead to fewer hassles."

"Fewer hassles?" Griggs asked.

"We had a crew out here. They were doing a write-up for the Army Times. They got lost. Yes, they were in uniform, but you know how guards can get around."

"Right, so what happened?" Griggs asked.

"They ended up getting a new camera out of it."

"Oh shit," Jax exclaimed.

"Exactly, so be careful out there."

"Who is the commander of this crew?"

"Jax, it's Webb," Smith said.

"Well, fuck me," Jax said.

"I know it's not the best situation, but we need you for this. I need you to be clear-headed about this. Can you do it?"

Jax nodded, "Yes, Sir."

"Good, now head up there. I have to make a call."

Jax and Griggs headed out the door. Jax climbed into the SUV and stared as Griggs pulled on the handle to the passenger door.

"I'm coming with you," she said, her voice muffled through the door.

He relented and unlocked the door.

Griggs got in, and Jax started the vehicle.

"Look, I know you're not super keen on this, but we both have a job to do," Griggs said.

Jax smiled, backed out, and followed the road.

"What did Smith mean about Webb?"

"When I was out here, Webb was my CO. He had a little more seniority than I did. I dropped a bomb in the wrong place, and he swore he had given me the correct coordinates for the drop. When I went to find my papers, they weren't there. I could retire early or be court-martialed."

"So you retired?"

"I had no choice. It was the worst choice I could have made. It cost me my marriage."

Griggs stared at the ring on his finger, "And you've remarried since?"

Jax followed her gaze to the ring, "No, that's denial," Jax replied as they rolled up to the gate.

Three guards stood at the gate, two with dogs, while the other held a rifle at the ready.

The one with the rifle approached the vehicle.

Jax rolled the window down.

"You need to turn around and leave," the guard said.

"Colonel Smith called ahead for us," Jax replied. He handed his badge to the guard. The guard peered into the vehicle and stared at Griggs.

"He needs yours as well," Jax explained to her.

Griggs pulled her ID out and handed it over.

"I'll be right back," the guard said.

Jax nodded.

He returned moments later with their IDs and a mirror on a long stick.

Jax took their IDs and watched as the guard walked around their vehicle with the mirror.

Griggs stared at him.

"They're checking for devices?" Griggs asked.

"Yep, this place is locked up tight."

When the guard finished, he returned to the window.

"Follow the road until you see the hangar, then turn right. It will take you to the Boxes. Major Webb will be waiting for you."

"Thank you, Airmen," Jax said.

The guard waved his hands, and the two other guards with the dogs opened the gate.

The dogs and their handlers only stared as their vehicle went through.

"Well, that was intimidating," Griggs said.

"It was meant to be," Jax replied.

CHAPTER FIVE

JAX FOLLOWED the dirt road until he saw the hanger, turned right as he was told to, and stared as flight boxes rose out of the desert floor.

The boxes themselves were little more than modified train cars with big A/C units attached to them.

Jax studied the boxes as they approached. A blue tarp covered the ground near them.

"Is that from the other box?" asked Griggs.

"It is," Jax said.

Jax pulled the vehicle into a slot near the hangar and stepped out.

Two guards approached them.

"We're here to see Major Webb," Jax said.

"Wait here," the guards said.

The guards returned moments later with a man with olive skin, a small mustache, and a smile.

"Jackson Reed," the man said, "I never thought I'd see you out here again."

"Hello, Major Webb," Jax replied.

"I heard you went and got a job with the FBI, but I didn't believe it until the Colonel called me this morning."

"Believe it, and I'm here to do my job," Jax said.

"Fine, but let's not start up old rivalries," Webb said.

Jax smiled, but his jaw tightened.

"Who's your friend?" Webb asked.

"Liaison with the Air Force, Sir," Griggs said.

"Liaison? Why would they do that?"

"I'm just here to investigate. Then don't pay enough for those answers." Jax responded.

"Right," Webb said.

"Show me the impact zone," Jax said.

"Follow me," Webb said, leading them towards the tarp.

"So I saw the video. You left just before it happened?"

Webb stared at him, "Yes. I had some paperwork to finish and needed to check in with the flight crew."

"Is there any particular reason?" Jax asked.

"No, the aircraft flew great. There have never been any problems with it. It was a perfect bird."

"Flight crew have anything to say?"

"They were talkative about the aircraft. Said it was a perfect day for flying, too."

"What about the pilot?"

"Moseley? He was a good pilot. Knew his shit. Flew well. He was a bit young but earned his work. He moved up quickly. His wife went into labor that morning. You should talk to her. She'll know more."

Jax stared at the hangar. A sleek black aircraft sat in the middle with guards all around it.

"Is that the other one?" Jax asked.

"Yes," Webb said.

"Where's the pilot for that one?"

Webb looked away.

"Major, where is the pilot?" Jax asked.

"Jared Moseley was the pilot for that one."

Jax and Griggs glanced at one another.

"So, who was the pilot for the aircraft that crashed?" Griggs asked

"Airmen, what is your MOS?" Webb asked.

"I'm with the MP's at Nellis, Sir," Griggs replied.

"So you're an investigator?"

"Yes, Sir," Griggs replied.

"Hold on now," Jax said. "I'm the lead on this. I'm a civilian, but I know all this backwater bullshit. If you're going to harass those working with me, I can talk to the Colonel."

Webb, attempting to stare down Griggs, turned his head towards Jax.

"No, it's fine. The pilot is Sadie Dickson. She's been AWOL. We don't know where she is. She was supposed to fly this thing instead of Moseley. When flight time came, she didn't show up."

"So Moseley was her backup?" Griggs asked.

"Yes."

"And Moseley would be alive if she had shown up?"

Webb looked uncomfortable at that moment and nodded.

"So, when Dickson didn't show up, Moseley got the call. Have you sent anyone to check on Dickson?"

"I had Metro go to her apartment."

"And?"

"Nothing," Webb said, "her car wasn't there, and no one answered the door."

Jax glanced past Webb to the hangar. A group stood around as if waiting for their turn.

"That's the flight crew?" Jax asked.

"Let's go talk to them," Griggs said.

Webb glared at her.

"She's spot on. Let's have that talk." Jax said.

They walked into the hangar, and the flight crew muttered amongst themselves.

"Tech-Sergeant Gonzalez," Webb said, "this is Jackson Reed and First Sergeant Vanessa Griggs. They would like to talk with you and your crew."

Jax stared at Gonzalez. She was five-six. The sleeves on her uniform stretched the fabric around her biceps. Her uniform was clean, a stark contrast to Webb, whose uniform looked as if the Major picked it out of the dirty clothes pile.

"Captain Reed, it's a pleasure to meet you," Gonzalez said, saluting.

"I'm no longer in the service, but I appreciate it." Jax didn't return the salute.

"There is an office in the back if you need a place to talk?" Gonzalez offered.

"That would be perfect," Jax said.

Gonzalez walked toward the back of the hangar. Jax saw the office she spoke of. He thought it was probably what Webb used to keep an eye on his troops, but the blinds lining it made him pause.

Jax moved to follow her. Griggs followed behind him.

Jax turned and stopped her.

"I need you to speak to the crew."

"You'll speak to the female airman without another female present?"

"Griggs, I know we've only met, but ask anyone I served with, and they'll tell you I never screwed around."

"Okay," Griggs said.

"Ask them about anything odd in the days before the loss of the aircraft."

Griggs nodded.

Windows in the room looked out on the hangar floor. No doubt Webb could keep an eye on the crew from his desk.

Jax held the door, and Gonzalez entered and sat in a chair to the left of a desk littered with papers. Jax shuffled them to one side.

"Look, I'm not here to ruffle feathers. I'm only here to find out what happened to the aircraft. Hopefully, you can help me figure that out."

Gonzalez stared at him, "You know I'm the first woman to lead a flight crew for the drone program? It took a lot of work to get to where I'm at. I don't want to screw up my career."

"I understand. I know what it's like to screw up a career."

Gonzalez glanced up at Jax.

"I heard you were the best to fly a drone. Could make them do things the manufacturer never thought of, even."

"Where'd you hear that?"

"Around," she replied, "they talk about you like you're a myth. We know all about how you were run out of here by Webb. I don't much like him. He runs a good operation, although...."

"Although, what?"

"He has a thing for new people. He tries to get them on 'his side.' You know what I mean?"

Jax nodded. He knew exactly what she was talking about. It was one of the reasons he was no longer in the Air Force.

"So he's still up to that?"

"Yeah, is that why he worked to get you out of here?"

"Let's not talk about me. Let's talk about the aircraft."

"Do you have top secret clearance?"

"I wouldn't be here if I didn't."

"The aircraft was designed to take the pilots out of the aircraft. To limit the amount of exposure a pilot had, and to change how things are done in the skies."

"You mean using drones for everything?"

"I do," Gonzalez replied.

"Okay, let's talk about Dickson."

"She's quiet. She does her job and comes around before flight time to ensure the bird is ready before she heads to the box."

"But no one has seen her for a while?" Jax asked.

"Yeah, Webb said he sent Metro to her apartment. But there was nothing there."

"He told us the same."

"So Metro goes to her house and finds nothing there?" Jax continued.

"That's what Webb said."

"Where is her apartment?"

"The South side of the valley. There's this new apartment community off of Durango near I-215."

"Was there anything done recently with the guidance system?"

"Umm yeah, there was. How did you know that?"

"Lucky guess. Was it in an update package for the drone?"

"It was, but we only put it on the lost one. We kept it off the other one. I had to make sure there were no glitches."

"Have you had anyone look at the code for it?"

"I did. The code was weird. There were things in it I didn't understand. But it's been isolated from the other things. We're not allowed to send the bird up until the package is checked out."

"You know code?"

"Kind of a prerequisite for this job," Gonzales said, "I learned it in high school. But Webb said this package would make it fly more smoothly. 'Fewer bumps,' he said."

"Had that been a problem?"

"Only a minor one," Webb said, "the aircraft is top of the

line. It's capable of doing many things. We were told it was the future of flight for all branches. I wanted to make sure the aircraft worked properly, so with reservations. I uploaded it to the aircraft."

"How long after it was uploaded was the aircraft lost?"

"The next flight," she replied.

"But it wasn't put on the other one?"

"No," Gonzales replied, "all software updates are on hold until we find out what happened.'

"How did Webb react to the loss of the aircraft?"

She glanced at the door, then at Jax.

"He was furious. He's been over to talk to Jared's wife. She lost the baby, too. She has nothing right now. I've been over to talk to her too. We've brought her food. I even went over and made her dinner. She didn't want to come out of the bedroom."

"She's home then?"

"Yes, she was discharged from the hospital yesterday. She's trying to plan two funerals."

"I need to talk to her," Jax said.

"I can give you her address."

"That would be a lot of help."

Jax studied the tech sergeant carefully.

"I see your last name on your uniform. What's your first name?" Jax asked.

She stared at him and raised an eyebrow.

"Sorry, nothing like that. I'm married." Jax said.

"That's never stopped, Webb," she replied.

"So you and he...?"

"Hell no," she said, "I don't like that man much, but he's my superior and well...I don't."

"I understand. You don't have to say it."

"My name is Victoria," she said.

Jax watched her walk out the door and open the blinds.

Webb stared at him from across the hangar. Griggs stood close to him, talking to the flight crew.

Jax walked out of the office, turned the light out, and Griggs walked towards him.

"Find anything out?" Jax asked.

"A few things," she said, glancing back to the crew behind her. "Most of the crew doesn't like Webb. They love you, however. You're a damn legend to them. You didn't see how they looked at you when you walked into the office. It was like they were watching a rock star." Griggs continued.

"So I heard."

"Where to next?" Griggs asked.

Jax stared across the hangar at Webb. The man stood talking to one of the soldiers guarding the aircraft. Beyond him, a desert storm rolled across the tarmac through the open hangar doors.

The wind blew dust and tumbleweeds into the hangar. Webb ran to a panel on one side of the hangar as Gonzalez ran to another.

An audible alert sounded as the doors rolled together, sealing the breach.

Jax and Griggs walked through a small door and into the blowing air.

A drizzle of rain came down, and Jax pulled his coat closer.

"Got cold all of a sudden," Jax said.

"You have been gone for a while. This is typical desert weather."

Jax walked to the car and stared back at the hangar and Webb. The doors were closed, but Webb stood outside them, watching him and Griggs.

Griggs glanced back to see what he was looking at.

"He doesn't like you much," she said.

"The feeling is mutual."

The rain intensified, and they hurried into the car.

Griggs got in and stared at him.

"So," Griggs said, "you think he had a hand in it?"

"I don't know," Jax said, "but after what happened to me, I wouldn't put anything past him."

He pulled out of the slot and drove down the road to already open gates.

The two guards with dogs stood on one side while the other stood inside the guard shack.

"Huh," Jax said.

"What?" Griggs asked.

"I think Webb called ahead and said we were leaving."

"He wants us out of here?" she asked.

"Probably," Jax replied.

"Where are we going first?"

"Dickson's apartment," Jax said.

The rain continued to beat down. It turned the dirt road leading away from the upper part of the base to mud. His SUV had four-wheel drive, so he slipped into gear. When they reached the lower part of the base, an inch of water covered the road.

"I'm going to let you get your car. I'll meet you at Dickson's apartment," Jax said, stopping in front of Colonel Smith's office.

"I can get my vehicle later. Let's get this done now."

Jax stared at the clock in the car. It read two.

"You sure? It's going to be late when we get back," Jax said.

"I'd rather get this done now."

Jax pulled away from her car, and they drove out of the gate and onto I-95 towards Las Vegas.

It took almost two hours to reach Dickson's apartment with the weather.

The rain continued to pour down, and Jax pulled into a slot, but the parking lot was full.

"That's her building," Jax said, pointing to a building with the letter "C" on it.

* * *

Jax stared at the address Tech-Sergeant Victoria Gonzalez had given him.

Griggs glanced at the paper in his hands as they stared at the apartment.

"What's the other address?"

"It's Jared Moseley's wife's address. We'll probably go there later today or tomorrow." Jax said.

Jax stepped out of the car, put his suit jacket over his head, and ran for building C. He glanced behind once to make sure Griggs followed.

She had put her cover over her head, but in an almost comical way, had also thrown her hands over her head to try and cover herself as she ran.

Jax smiled at her when she reached the sidewalk.

"What?" Griggs asked.

"Nothing, let's find her apartment," Jax said.

He glanced at the marker on the side of the building. Apartment 307-C was on the third floor. Jax hesitated at the metal stairs and swallowed hard.

"Not used to the physical stuff?" Griggs asked.

"I've been behind a desk or on foot for the last few years at the Bureau."

They walked up the stairs, stopped at apartment 307, and Jax knocked.

The door across from them opened.

"Who are you?" a woman in pink shorts with a tight pink t-shirt stared at them.

Jax pulled out his badge, and she gasped.

"What has Sadie gotten herself into?"

"That's why we're here," Griggs said.

"She hasn't been home for a few days."

"Did you talk to the officers who came to check on her?" Jax asked.

The woman raised an eyebrow, "There ain't been nobody over there, especially not Metro."

"You sound like you knew Miss Dickson?" Jax asked.

"Yeah, we partied a few times," she said.

"When you say partied, you mean...."

"We fucked a few times," the woman said, cutting Jax off.

"I see. When was the last time you saw her?"

"A few days ago," the woman said, "she'd just come home. I wanted to come over, but she said she was tired. I haven't seen her since."

"Has there been anyone else over to see her?"

"There was this guy she's been hanging around with. I thought she changed teams, but she told me he was her new roommate. I knew she didn't need a roommate, but that's what she said."

Jax and Griggs stared at each other.

"This guy, what did he look like?" Jax asked.

"Big guy, bald head, white dude. It looked like he could kick some ass."

"Anything else about this white guy?" Griggs asked.

"He's been coming and going all night. I saw him last night. I thought it was Sadie. He looked startled when he saw me."

"What's your name?" Jax asked.

"Sirese," the woman replied.

"Thank you," Griggs said.

Sirese closed her door. Jax put on some gloves and turned the handle to unit 307. The door swung open.

Jax handed Griggs another pair from his pocket.

"Put these on," he said.

He pulled a set of booties from another pocket, slipped them over his shoes, and handed a pair to Griggs.

"Put these on, too," he said.

The smell struck them in the face, and Griggs made a noise.

"You better not puke," he said.

"I won't. Not yet," she replied.

"Call Metro, but wait a few minutes." He said.

Jax stepped into the apartment, following the scent of death.

He stopped in the living room.

"Found out why she didn't show up," Jax said.

Griggs stared at the body. Her stomach lurched.

"I said don't you puke in here. Go outside."

Griggs's boots echoed as they thumped down the stairs, shaking the whole building, or at least it felt that way to Jax.

Jax turned his attention to Lieutenant Dickson.

She sat in a chair. Bruises covered her wrists, ankles, and face. A single bullet wound was on her left temple. There wasn't much left on the right side of her face.

Griggs returned, and Jax stared at her.

"You okay?" he asked.

"Yeah," Griggs muttered.

Griggs's color gave her away. Her warm brown skin was now ashen, and her eyes looked bloodshot from the force of her vomiting.

"She wasn't killed here," Jax said.

"How do you know?"

"There are no brains on the ground. There should be brain matter and blood. It looks like it was a decent caliber. Flies and hatchlings covered most of the damage."

Griggs made another noise.

Jax glared at her.

"We need to search as fast as we can," Jax said.

They hurried down the hallway. Jax glanced into the bathroom, opened the medicine cabinet, and studied the labels. He took a picture and put his phone away. He rummaged under the sink.

Griggs returned.

"Find anything?" he asked.

"A few receipts," she said.

"Show me," Jax said.

They moved into the bedroom, and Jax stared at a set of receipts on the dresser.

"Where are the banks?" Jax asked.

"Bulgaria, Caymans, and Turkey," Griggs said.

"What do you want me to do with them?" she asked.

"Take pictures of them," Jax said.

She pulled out her phone and snapped a few pictures.

An open suitcase sat on the bed, but clothes were strewn about the room.

A newspaper sat next to the papers on the table with pictures of the President-Elect and the current President. Jax knew it was from a meeting the two had a week ago. He'd read the article.

"Maybe she was trying to leave and was caught in the act?" Griggs asked.

"But we don't have an airline ticket."

"When you were in the bathroom, did you find a box of tampons?" Griggs asked.

Jax stared at her.

"It's not for me," she replied.

"Yeah, I did. Why?"

Griggs walked out of the room, and Jax followed close behind.

Griggs walked into the bathroom, pulled out the box, rummaged inside, and pulled out an airline ticket.

"Holy shit," Jax said, "I would never have found that."

"I know. It's a trick my grandmother taught me."

"Where was she going?" Jax asked.

Griggs checked the ticket.

"Eastern Europe," Griggs said.

"So we have an idea about why she was killed. She was trying to bail on something. Maybe the drone?" Griggs asked.

"But who did it?" Jax asked.

"Maybe it was the bald guy?"

"Maybe, but there's also the fact that Webb lied. He never sent Metro. Which means he knew something was wrong."

"Right," Griggs said.

"Maybe, but we better call this in," Jax said.

Griggs put the tampons away but kept the airline ticket.

Jax pulled out his phone and dialed 911.

CHAPTER SIX

JAX AND GRIGGS sat on the curb as Metro's CSI unit worked inside the apartment.

"So you didn't think to call Metro when you got into town?" Detective Abrams asked.

He'd been one of the first Metro Detectives to show up.

Jax and Griggs had already given their statement to the uniforms.

"Look, I was investigating something at Creech. It didn't have anything to do with Metro until we found Miss Dickson."

"Okay, fine," the detective relented.

Abrams was around six-two; his skin was the color of obsidian. His freshly pressed shirt clung to his body, and his shoes reflected the blue and red police lights around them.

Jax immediately respected the man based on his appearance and how he'd effortlessly taken control of the crime scene.

Abrams stormed off.

"He's pissed," Griggs said.

"He has every right to be. It's above his pay grade, and he'll probably be doing paperwork all night."

"I bet he was a tough beat cop," Griggs said.

"I'm sure he wouldn't take any shit from anyone."

Jax got up and walked over towards Abrams.

"Are we free to go?" Jax asked.

"Yes, but I'll want to ask more questions later, so don't go leaving town without giving us a heads up."

"I understand. When do you think the ME will be able to get to our victim?"

Abrams stared at him.

"It will be a couple of days. This being just after Christmas, there are usually many bodies in the morgue. But she should be able to get to it by New Year's Day."

"I'd like to sit in on the exam," Jax said.

Griggs turned green and glared at Jax.

"Does this have something to do with your case?"

"Maybe, but I want to cross the t's and dot the i's."

"Fine, I'll let you know when she can get to it."

Jax handed Abrams one of his cards, and they walked to their car as Jax glanced around.

"What?" Griggs asked.

"I think whoever did this is here," Jax said.

Griggs glanced around at the people gathered beyond the police tape. They'd gathered quickly once the police arrived, as did the various news crews. Jax and Griggs had sat away from the light of the cameras.

He was immediately glad he'd parked the car where he had. It was just inside the police tape, and while the news crews would be on them once they drove through, they probably wouldn't be able to get a decent shot because of the rain. He didn't want to be seen on the local news since he knew Sarah still looked at the Vegas news.

Jax drove to the edge of the police tape, and the patrol officers stared at them. One of them lifted the police tape enough for them to navigate through.

Jax peered into the darkness beyond their car for anything that would make him think otherwise, but he believed whoever killed Dickson was in the crowd of people.

They pulled onto Durango, and Jax glanced at the clock on the dash. It was almost midnight. It had taken most of the night for them to clear their names and get assurances from Jax's and Griggs's bosses at AFOSI(Air Force Office of Special Investigations) and the FBI in Washington.

Jax's boss didn't like the late call but understood.

As the car moved along Durango, a tall man with a bald head watched it disappear down the road.

He walked away from the scene, his head covered with a Vegas Golden Knights ball cap.

CHAPTER SEVEN

THE MAN in the Knights cap, Malcolm Drake, walked a short distance to his car, got in and drove along Durango, turning into the Lakes.

The Lakes, a manufactured community created so rich people could spend their time sunning themselves along the shores of a fake lake, lay on the western side of Las Vegas.

It's own small community of mostly older, retired people. Drake pressed the button on the visor of his car, and the large metal gate opened.

He turned right and drove to one of the smaller homes along the shoreline of the fake lake. He pulled into the garage, got out, and went upstairs.

His target would still be in bed, but he knew the call would come.

He walked into the house; he ran through all the moments of the past few days. His eyes darted to the corner of the room. He'd been able to clean up the blood and brains, though that had been easy since he'd covered things in plastic.

He pulled out a small earring from his pocket. He'd taken

both of them off her ears but only kept one—the other lay in a storm drain.

Drake went up the stairs and stared at the computer monitors in front of him. Each monitor showed the house across the lake from where he was. The man in the bed next to the dark-haired woman rolled over, his face becoming apparent on the monitor.

"I hope you have a pleasant morning, Major Webb," Drake said.

The woman stirred slightly, but it was the man who piqued his interest. He'd interacted with the man a couple of times.

He opened his phone, set the alarm for four, and laid down on a cot in the corner.

Drake slept for a few hours before his phone rang.

"Yes, I know they found her. We knew they would." Drake said.

"Drake, this is a big deal. We didn't want civilian interaction."

"They're going to do her autopsy and find out she was beaten, but they won't find anything else."

"You're sure?" the voice asked.

"Positive," Drake replied. "This will give our friend a little scare. I'm sure he's freaked with the FBI and OSI involved."

"Be careful, and take him if you need to. What is he doing now?" the voice asked.

Drake glanced at the monitors. Major Webb had sat up in bed.

"He's just getting up."

"Okay, keep an eye on him," the voice ordered.

Drake had never met the voice. Their interactions had been restricted to over the phone and through secure email and text.

"I'm doing all I can, Sir," Drake said.

"The first test flight is tonight. We can't have anything screw this up." The voice said.

"I'll cover my end," Drake assured him.

"That's what we're paying you all of this money for," The voice said, "and if this goes well, I'll make sure you get more money."

Drake heard the words, but his interpretation was different.

He heard, 'you'll be dead if you don't do what we're paying you all this money for.'

"Yes, Sir," Drake said.

The call ended, and Drake set his phone down and stared at the monitors.

Major Webb had moved into the shower while the woman, one Drake had seen before, hurriedly put her clothes on. Her uniform would not be as crisp and clean for duty as it had been the day before.

She entered the bathroom, where Webb stood in the shower and pulled on the shower door. They kissed, and Webb tried to pull her into the shower.

"I have to go," she protested.

The microphone was one of many Drake had placed.

Webb shrugged. The woman hurried out of the house.

Drake walked towards a window in the room that looked out over the road. He watched the woman get in her car and drive away.

Webb stood in the shower a few minutes longer. He stepped out, pulled his uniform out for the day, set his boots to the side of it, and his phone rang.

Drake stared at the screen as Webb picked up the phone. He could only listen to one side of the conversation, but the words he heard made him smile.

The call ended, and Webb stood in the middle of his bedroom.

Webb picked up his phone again and called into the base to say he wouldn't be able to make it in. The death of Dickson shook him.

Drake laughed as the man scrambled around his room. He hurriedly looked out the window, got dressed, grabbed something under his bed, and ran down the stairs and out the door.

Drake watched as Webb pulled out of the garage and drove away.

With Webb gone, he walked over to the man's house, opened the door the woman had left unlocked and hurried up the stairs.

He'd seen something on the video he didn't like, and he wasn't sure how he'd missed it.

When he reached under the bed, he found a small box. He glanced around the room and saw what he'd been looking for.

A video from a small pinhole camera relayed the feed to a box under the bed. Three hard drives connected to it, but Drake surmised that only one would be the feed. He grabbed the bag he'd brought, plugged the device into the hard drive, and wiped it clean.

The door from the garage to the house opened, and Drake froze.

How had he not heard the garage door open?

He finished what he was doing, placed the recording device under the bed, and listened as Webb's feet stomped up the stairs.

Drake hurried into the closet, buried himself under a pile of clothes, and froze.

The closet door opened, and Major Webb peered in.

Drake barely breathed as the man stood before him, rummaging through clothes on hangers.

Webb closed the closet doors and left the room. His shoes

echoed in the living room as Drake slowly opened the closet doors and stepped out.

Fuck, that was close.

He walked to the sliding door next to the bed, opened it slowly, and slid out. Drake closed the door, dropped to ground level, and glanced at the door that led from the living room to the deck and a small boat on the water.

He could see Webb beyond the glass sitting at his kitchen table, a cup of coffee in his hand.

Drake hurried away from the house, crossing the gaps between houses with one or two bounds until he was in the yard of the house he had come from.

Once inside the house, he watched the monitors. Still, Major Webb only stared at the home around him with a worrisome, vacant expression on his face.

CHAPTER EIGHT

A PHONE RANG, and Jax picked it up.

"This is your wake-up call, Mr. Reed," the voice said.

"Thank you," Jax replied.

He sat up and stared at himself in the mirror across from him.

"Another thing you've gotten us into," Jax said to his reflection.

He picked up his cell phone and stared at the messages.

Two were from DC area codes, another from Virginia, and another from Las Vegas. He knew the DC and Virginia numbers but not the Las Vegas ones.

Jax showered and dressed, making sure he lined up his suit. It was an old habit, but he'd stuck with it since leaving the Air Force.

He dialed Sarah's number and waited for her to pick up.

"I tried calling you last night," she said upon answering, not hello or anything else.

"I've been busy. Is Lizbeth where I can talk to her?"

"Hold on," Sarah said.

"Lizzy, it's your dad on the phone," Sarah called.

"Hi, Daddy," Elizabeth said.

"Hi, Princess, what are you doing?" he asked with a smile.

"Just playing in my room," Lizbeth replied, "where are you?"

"I'm in Las Vegas. Did you still want the pink flamingo?"

She giggled into the phone, "Of course."

"Okay. I'm sorry I had to leave. I hope you know that."

"When you get back, can we continue our game?"

"Yep, I'll be back in a few days, but I'm still working. I'll drop off the flamingo when I get back."

"Okay, love you, Daddy," she said.

"Love you, too," Jax replied.

Jax smiled to himself, and Sarah picked up the phone.

"Jackson, she was upset you couldn't stay," Sarah said.

"I know. So was I. There was nothing I could do about it."

"So, what's going on out there that they requested you specifically?"

"I can't talk about it, but it's a big damn mess," Jax replied.

"Right, well, I'm sorry you had to go back," she said.

"Me too," Jax said, "it was difficult driving through those gates without a uniform on."

"I'm sure. You have a partner on this one?" she asked.

"They assigned someone from OSI. She's stationed at Nellis."

"She?"

"Yeah, young kid. She's trying hard to impress. I think she wants to move up and out."

"Why do you say that?"

"Just a feeling," Jax replied.

"Well, I have to get Lizzy ready to go. We're going to Georgetown for lunch."

"Okay," Jax said.

"Bye, Jackson," Sarah said and ended the call.

Jax stared at the phone for a minute.

"Sorry," he said to the silence.

His phone buzzed, and a Las Vegas number called while he was sleeping.

"This is Agent Reed," Jax said into the phone.

"It's Detective Abrams with Metro. We're going to be able to get to your vic sooner. Don't eat lunch first."

"Thank you, Detective," Jax said.

The call ended, and Jax dialed Griggs. The phone rang a couple of times, and a tired Griggs answered the phone.

"Griggs," she answered.

"It's Reed. We have our shot with the ME today. Are you coming?" he asked.

A groan stretched out on the other side of the phone. Jax pictured her holding the phone away and contemplating the idea of seeing Dickson's body opened up, "Yeah, okay. What time?"

"Abrams said afternoon, so one."

"Fine. I'll meet you there." Griggs said.

"I could come and get you. That way we don't have to take two cars. I know the drive back killed you last night."

Another groan filled the other end, "Yeah, it did. Come to my house. Bring food and coffee."

Jax stared at his phone for a minute and laughed.

Jax dialed the DC number and waited.

"Decker," the voice said on the other end.

"Just checking in," Jax said.

"How are things out there, and how is my daughter doing?"

"Your daughter? Who's your daughter?" Jax asked.

The other end grew quiet.

"Griggs is my stepdaughter, but how is she?"

"Is this how she got assigned?"

"No, I checked with her CO. She was on the rotation already. She didn't mention it?"

"No, but I'm sure it would have come up sooner or later."

"So, how are things?"

"They've grown complicated. I don't want to talk about it over the phone, but it's more than a downed drone." Jax said.

"Send me an encrypted, and I'll get back to you."

Jax pulled his laptop close to him and turned it on.

"I'm turning my laptop on right now," Jax said.

He opened a secure folder, typed in the encryption password, and typed what he knew while Decker stayed on the line.

"Okay, I sent it," Jax said.

The line went quiet, and Jax listened to the clicking of keys from Decker.

"Holy shit. Please tell me this is a joke?"

"I wish it were," Jax replied.

"There is a bright spot in all of this," Jax said.

"What's that?" Decker asked.

"Your daughter is a hell of a detective."

"I'll let her know you said that."

"Okay, but please wait until after we're done with the case."

"I will," Decker said.

"So what happened to her old man?" Jax asked.

The other end went silent.

"It's okay. I'll ask her," Jax said.

"Please don't," Decker said, "he was shot down over Iraq. He was one of those captured by Al-Qaeda in Iraq."

"Oh, so they—"

"Yes, so please don't bring it up," Decker said.

"Okay, I must get up and bring her some food."

"We'll chat later, and if you need anything, call the office in Las Vegas. They know you're out there, but they're a little pissed that one of them didn't get this call."

"I can understand that. Any idea why the DNI wanted me on this?"

"I don't, but others are watching how this plays out if he did. I'm sure with the inauguration, President Thompson doesn't want the press to get wind of this."

"Right, well, they did last night."

"Is that what is going on in Las Vegas?"

"It is," Jax said.

"Okay, try and stay out of trouble, Jax."

"Doing my best, Sir," Jax replied.

Decker ended the call, and Jax stood up.

He checked to ensure he had everything and walked out of the room into the hallway, nearly bumping into the housekeeper's cart.

"Sorry," a housekeeper said.

"It's fine," Jax said.

"Sir, did you need anything?" she asked.

"Could you have my room made up for me?"

Jax glanced at the clipboard resting on top of the cart. She had two more floors to do after his, and he felt terrible about asking.

"Yes, sir," she replied, "I will after finishing this room," she stared down at her clipboard, "Mr. Reed."

"Thank you," Jax said and held out a ten.

The woman took the ten, stuffing it in her pocket.

Jax hurried down the elevator and got his car from the valet.

CHAPTER NINE

JAX STOOD on the stoop outside Griggs's house.

When he pulled up, he thought it was the wrong address.

The house was on the western side of the valley, as close to Red Rock as possible, without actually being inside the canyon.

Five years ago, there hadn't been any houses that close. Their gradual encroachment of the canyon frustrated Jax.

He rang the doorbell, and Griggs opened the door, "Oh, thank you, God," and waved him inside.

He glanced around at the room beyond and stared as windows stretched up one wall while French doors lay at the back of the house leading to a pool. Jax stared at the cover on the pool.

"It's too cold for that," Griggs said.

Jax set the food on the counter and handed her the coffee. She took a sip and smiled.

"I hoped that would work," Jax said.

"It does."

Jax opened the bag of food, handing her a burger.

"Coffee and burgers?"

"It works," he said.

She took a bite of her burger, then sipped at the coffee. Griggs frowned.

"You must have some weird taste buds."

Griggs pushed the coffee aside and dug into the burger.

Jax glanced at his watch. It was 11:30.

"We better eat and get over to the ME's office." He said.

"Chill a minute. We'll get there." Griggs said through a mouthful of burger.

Part of it slipped from the bun onto the wrapper, and Jax stared at her.

Griggs shrugged. "Give me a break. I haven't eaten since yesterday."

Jax ate, but more quietly and with less mess.

He glanced around again.

"Nice, right?" Griggs asked.

"How are you able to afford this?"

"It belongs to my brother and his wife. While stationed at Nellis, I had trouble finding a place at first. They work on the Strip. I use their house. They have two others."

"They must charge a lot for it?"

"Not really," Griggs said, "they bought it when the economy turned. My brother and his wife make good money and could afford to give me a break."

"I see," Jax said.

They finished their food, and Jax grabbed his coffee while Griggs tossed the garbage from the meal.

She retrieved her coffee, and they went out the door.

They took Summerlin Parkway towards the I-15, took the Alta exit, and drove a few blocks to the ME's office.

Jax and Griggs walked in, gave the clerk their information, and stood in the hallway waiting.

"How many of these have you done?" Griggs asked.

"A few," Jax said, "they've done the exam work. I want to see the wrist and ankle wounds.

"You still think she was killed somewhere else?"

"Definitely," Jax said, "we need to know why she was killed somewhere else and returned to her apartment."

The door opened, and Griggs glanced up.

Detective Abrams stood in the doorway, the light flooding into the darkened hallway.

"Glad to see you made it. I trust you slept as shitty as I did?"

Griggs groaned a response while Jax only nodded.

"Glad to hear it. I was up until five filling out paperwork on your vic. The ME got to her quickly."

"Any idea why?" Jax asked.

"My Chief received a call this morning. The call pushed your vic to the front of the line." Abrams said.

Griggs and Jax glanced at one another.

"Who made the call?" Jax asked.

"I wasn't told, but it ruffled some feathers. I hope you don't mind that the ME is a little pissed. They made her get up to work on this at seven this morning."

Abrams walked past them, and they followed behind him into a large room.

The room had an almost industrial aesthetic. Steel tables and chairs glittered under bright overhead lights.

A woman stood next to a table.

"This our vic?" Jax asked.

The woman glanced up. She was in her mid-fifties. The size of the bags under her eyes looked as if she were going on an around-the-world trip.

"I'm sure Abrams has already talked to you, but let me explain something. I wouldn't say I like waking up to a fresh corpse on my day off. I understand it's my job, but I was looking forward to spending time with my husband today."

"Reed and Griggs, this is our ME," Abrams said, "Dr. Janice Barkov."

"Yeah, glad to meet you," she said.

Jax wasn't sure if her tone was mocking or honest; he thought it was likely the former.

"Afternoon," Jax said, "I understand you have a few things for us?" Griggs said.

"Sorry for whoever called you in. We'd planned on waiting a few days before someone got to her." Jax said.

"That's what Abrams told me, but here we are."

Abrams cleared his throat.

"Let's get to it," Abrams said.

"Right then," Dr. Barkov said.

Jax and Griggs moved to the side of the ME as she pulled the cloth down.

"There are multiple abrasions on her wrist. They are consistent with restraints, possibly wire. There are similar markings on her ankles."

"What about these bruises around her face?" Jax asked.

Dr. Barkov knelt next to Dickson's body and pointed with a metal stick.

"There are major injuries to her orbital. Whoever beat her caused enough damage to her orbital cavity that had she lived, she would have been blind in one eye."

Jax stared at the abrasions on Dickson's face. The bruising and damage on what was left of her right side were more severe than on her left side.

"Was the person right or left-handed?"

Dr. Barkov smiled, "The person was left-handed. They'd have bruises around their knuckles and the palm of their hands. There is nothing to indicate that they wore gloves."

"Why's that?" Abrams asked.

"She's exceptionally clean. When I started working in the

ME's office in the '80s, they had me working on mob cases. I never saw a body this clean. They cleaned under her nails and may have washed her hair."

"Why do you say that?" Jax asked.

"The exit wound has trace amounts of residue from washing. I couldn't find out what type of shampoo, but it is a cheaper brand. This would make it near impossible to find where it was bought."

"So it was professional?" Jax asked.

"The red marks on her skin are consistent with some type of cleaner."

"That's all weird as hell," Griggs said.

Barkov turned to her.

"Yes, but every killer has their kink or fetish."

"What else?" Abrams asked.

"I read the reports, and she was moved. The scene was empty of blood or brain matter. Whoever did this moved her to her apartment. I think they wanted her to be found."

"Thank you, Dr. Barkov. If something else comes up, please call." Jax said. He set his card on a side table.

"Thank you," Dr. Barkov said.

They left the room, and Jax stared at Abrams.

"So, what do you think?"

"I think someone tried to get information out of her or set it up to scare someone else."

"Why do you think that last part?"

"Why would they move her? They could have just dumped her anywhere, but they put her back in her house. They didn't stage the scene, so they didn't care much about that. They knew she'd be found and that it would reach the right people. That right person or persons would run, scared." Jax said.

"I guess you two have some work to do?" Abrams asked.

Jax nodded.

Abrams went to shake his hand, but Jax waved him off.

"I don't do that anymore," Jax said.

"I understand. There are a few in our department who lost people to Covid. They're not doing that either."

"If you find anything else, could you call me?" Jax asked.

"Of course," Abrams replied.

Jax and Griggs walked out of the dark corridors of the ME's office into the sunlight.

Jax shielded his eyes.

"Damn, that's bright," he said.

"Where to next?" Griggs asked.

"We need to talk to Moseley's wife."

"For what reason?"

"If Dickson was working on the drone thing, then she was getting paid for it... but maybe whoever paid her asked Moseley first."

"Right," Griggs said.

CHAPTER TEN

WILLIAMS STARED at the woman across from him who would be President in less than a month. She wore her hair short, and there was a look of intelligence behind her eyes that scared the hell out of him.

Williams watched her rise. Her strength made him wary.

"Madame President-Elect, I would like to stay on if that's in the cards?" Williams asked.

She leaned in and smiled, "I would like that. We've done a lot of work towards finding a replacement in case we don't work well together. When I was in the house, I remember our discussions. I thoroughly enjoyed your candor on issues."

The Vice-President Elect sat next to her. The man was twenty years her junior but had a drive that others in his party lacked, save for the President-Elect. He knew what he wanted. Williams had seen that in the debates early. He wanted to be President, and being Vice was a stepping stone to that goal.

Former Army and Williams respected that, but he didn't vote for either. He wanted the world to stay as it was. None of the chatter from her camp sounded suitable for the projects he had in the pipeline.

"Yes, our discussions went well."

"We've read the intelligence about what's happening over-seas, but I would like to hear it from your mouth, not from the briefing sent over." The President-elect said.

"Of course," Williams replied.

He went through what had been in their briefing since they'd captured the nomination the previous August, detailing everything.

"I think what Madame President-Elect is asking for is something else," the VP interjected.

Williams glanced from one to the other.

"I've read the daily brief since I've had access to it. We both believe it should be read and studied. I would like to know if there are places in the world that you're worried about."

He smiled, "The Middle East is always a big one, but I think it's China and Russia and this supposed partnership. It scares me more than anything that could happen in the Middle East. It will always be a region we're wary of, but this new partnership with those other two countries scares the hell out of those in the field."

President-Elect Elaine Franklin leaned back on the couch and frowned, "What does each country get out of this new part-nership?"

"They're sharing intelligence on minor issues, but we're afraid there's a bigger plan in mind. Neither side does anything without a plan."

"The other two superpowers are sharing intelligence? To what end?" she asked.

"We don't know Madame President-Elect. There isn't much to go on. We noticed chatter about a joint operation six months ago. They carried that out a week ago."

"You're speaking of the military exercises?"

Williams nodded, "Their Navy's are coordinating with one

another in the Northern Sea. It was the largest amphibious exercise since D-Day."

"Holy shit," the Vice President-Elect said.

"Those were my words when I watched the video they released."

"How do we confront this?" Elaine Franklin asked.

"Madame President-Elect, there is no way to confront it. We can go to the UN, but both countries will say it was a training exercise. But we know from recent events with Russia, most notably Crimea, that anything the Russians do is a precursor to something in the future."

"Right, I remember the Russian's training exercises before they annexed Crimea."

"Yes, small drills along the border didn't cause any trouble. We called patrols for the safety of villages, and that's when they swept into Crimea," Williams said.

"Are there any agents that confirm it's a precursor?"

"That's not something I can discuss right now. Once you're in the chair, we can talk about it. There are ongoing things we don't want to be interrupted, and the slightest slip may cost lives."

"Understood," President-Elect Franklin said.

"Have you told President Thompson about this?" Vice President-Elect asked.

"He doesn't care. He's glad to be out of what he calls, 'that dirty old house.'"

Her jaw dropped, and he smiled.

"He's had his share of problems, and the economy took a nosedive after his last election and never truly recovered. I'm honestly surprised he didn't place the blame on someone else and resign." Williams said.

"You thought he would?" Elaine Franklin asked.

"Let's just say there was a betting pool, and the odds were leaning that way."

She sipped from a glass of tea that had been brought in.

"I would like to discuss this further when I'm behind the desk," she said.

"I would as well," he replied.

"Very well. I think that's it for this meeting," she said and stood up.

He went to reach for her hand; she waved him off.

"I don't do that anymore," she said.

"Even with the vaccine?" he asked.

"That was one virus. We don't know when the next one will come along," she replied.

"Yes, there's truth in that," he agreed.

"Thank you for meeting with me," she said.

"I serve at the pleasure of the President. I hope I can serve you as well as I have the current administration," he said.

She nodded.

Williams walked towards the door and stared as the Speaker of the House walked past him.

The man smiled at him.

ORIGIN ON AIR FORCE 63

CHAPTER ELEVEN

AMY MOSELEY SAT across from Jax and Griggs. She wore her blonde hair straight, but the makeup she'd had on when they'd arrived had run down her face.

Griggs handed her a tissue as she wiped at her eyes. She was maybe twenty-three but looked seventeen.

"Tell me what your husband did?" Jax asked.

"He flew drones for the Air Force."

"Did he ever talk to you about anything in particular?" Griggs asked.

"He kept his missions secret. He liked the idea of sitting in the box and playing with the aircraft. Then he got promoted to this new thing, and things changed."

She wiped her eyes again and smiled up at Jax.

"Changed how?" Jax asked.

"He was on base. He didn't tell me what he was doing, but the jump in pay was great. He thought it would lead to drone pilots taking on other duties."

"Did he say why?"

She stared at the floor.

"I understand all you've lost, but we're trying to find out what happened," Griggs said.

"What happened? They said a drone malfunctioned and crashed into the building. My mom said I should sue, and I could get some money out of it. I told her Jared wouldn't want me to do that."

Jax and Griggs stared at each other.

"My wife and I lost a baby when we were starting. It was early in the pregnancy, but I understand your pain. But we're trying to find out why the drone malfunctioned. If he said anything that could help us, it would be a big help."

She stopped and stared across the room. Her eyes moved to the door, then a pair of boots near it.

"What is it?" Griggs asked.

"Well, when he got this new position, he said someone offered him a lot of money to do something. He didn't give me specifics, but it unnerved him. He thought about talking to someone about it but didn't want to hurt his job. He said another pilot did that and was forced out."

Jax's eyebrows went up.

"Did he say who offered him this thing?"

"No, but it was someone on base. He said it would have given us enough money to put our daughter through college. Neither of us went to college, and we wanted that for her. He said he didn't want the burden of it on his head. His words scared me. Do you know what he was talking about?" she asked.

"I don't," Jax said.

She stood up, "I have to finish some things around here. My parents are flying out today. They're going to help me. Can you imagine living with your parents at twenty-three? I'm not looking forward to it, but I don't have anything else. The Air Force is paying for his body to be taken back to Tennessee, our daughter's too."

Jax's heart broke for the girl.

They got up and walked to the door.

"If you think of anything, give us a call," Griggs said and handed Amy Moseley her card.

The sky was blue, and there was no rain on the horizon, but Jax felt like he'd walked into a mud puddle.

"That poor girl," Griggs said after they had left.

"Yeah, " Jax said, "this is pretty fucked up. I hate to see anything happen to good people. It sounds like he got the same offer Dickson did."

"We need to find out who made that offer," Griggs said.

"That could be key to this," Jax said.

"Where to next?" Griggs asked.

"Back to Creech. I want to inspect the other aircraft and talk to the crew more. Could you call someone that could arrange that?"

"I could call my dad...er, Decker for that."

"That's another thing," Jax said, "why didn't you tell me who your dad was?"

"I wanted you to judge me on how well I worked, not that my dad was your boss."

"Okay, well, you call your CO. If that doesn't work, I'll call Decker."

Griggs pulled out her phone and dialed a number.

Jax got in the car to give her privacy.

She got into the car, all animated.

"We can go," she said.

"Really?" Jax asked.

"My CO got a call from the base this morning. Webb called off."

"Well, that's interesting," Jax said.

"You think he had something to do with this?"

"I do, and it's becoming more clear."

Jax started the car and headed in the direction of I-95 towards Creech.

The drive to the base was quiet as both processed what Amy Moseley told them. The thought of that woman dealing with this loss by herself upset Jax.

They pulled through the gate after security scrutinized their IDs more than on the prior occasion.

They reached the second gate above the base, where they kept the drone.

Gonzalez stood on the curb waiting for them as Jax pulled into the same slot he'd used.

"I hear you want to get a look at the drone?" Gonzalez asked.

There was a smear of grease on her face, another on her uniform, "That's right. I understand your CO didn't come in today?"

"He called off this morning. Said he wasn't feeling well."

Gonzalez glanced up as a drone flew over.

Jax also glanced up, noticing the split tails fins and motor on the tail section.

"Reaper?" Jax said.

"Yep, but it's the new model; and if we can keep this project going, it will be the last version they make," she said.

Her words startled Jax.

"Is this project that advanced?" Jax asked.

"This will replace all of them." She said, smiling.

Jax and Griggs followed her into the hangar. The drone sat in the middle with the crew around it, as well as the guards.

"What can you tell me about it?" Jax asked.

Her team stood around the aircraft.

"What are you doing to it?" Griggs asked.

"We're running a diagnostic on the flight systems."

Jax stared at the aircraft.

The tail section swept back into a V pattern, and the wings merged with it at the engines, which drew Jax's attention.

He hadn't noticed the engines the last time he'd been in the hangar. The guards had made it difficult; now, they stood to the sides as Gonzalez walked them around the aircraft.

"These look like the engines from the F-35," Jax said, pointing to the engines.

"They are similar. They move the same, but they're scaled down to accommodate the size of this aircraft." Gonzalez said.

Her crew watched Jax step closer to the aircraft. They were positioned under the drone, with a box on a cart that he didn't recognize.

The landing gear sat at the front of the aircraft and on the tips that angled the way a B-52's wings did, but the wings looked much more stable.

There were small holes near the front of the aircraft, and Jax knelt before them, staring into them.

A large-caliber machine gun rested within the holes.

"Holy shit, these are gun ports," Jax said.

"They are. I was wondering how long it would take you to notice."

"What does a drone need gun ports for?" Griggs asked.

"As I said, if this project continues, it will make having a pilot in the cockpit unnecessary. Think of things we can do with aircraft if we don't have to consider accommodations for the pilot. Gone will be the seat, the oxygen tanks, and then there are the maneuvers a pilot can do without worrying about g-force blackouts."

Jax stared at the sweep of the wings to its tail section.

"It's designed for dogfights," Jax said, "isn't it?"

"Now you understand why this project is so important," Gonzalez said.

"So, what happens to you and your crew if this project ends?" Griggs asked.

"We would get reassigned to another project."

"And Webb?" Jax asked.

"Look, I know you have it out for him. We all do but toss aside the bullshit he does, and he knows his shit. They took the design from records of pilots of drones and regular aircraft."

"Where did the aircraft get its start?" Jax asked, changing the subject away from Webb.

"It was officially flown at Groom but was brought here after it passed all their tests."

"They had this at Groom?" Jax asked.

"Yeah," Gonzalez said, "it's been in the pipe since you were flying."

Jax looked back at the aircraft.

"Do you know who the pilot was at Groom?" Jax asked.

"Yes," she said but only stood there.

"But you're not going to tell me?" Jax asked.

"'The projects at Groom are kept on a need-to-know basis. When we got this project, we were stunned at its capabilities. Sadie and Jared were mesmerized by the things they were able to accomplish."

"Is there still a box that can fly it?" Jax asked.

"Yes," Gonzalez said, "we've had them connected since the beginning. We were never allowed to have both aircraft up simultaneously, though."

"Could I fly one?" Jax asked.

"We were told to show you the aircraft, that's all," she said.

"Isn't that part of showing?" Griggs asked.

Gonzalez glared at her, "Look, I didn't want to show you the aircraft. If Webb knew, he'd be freaking out."

"We got authorization to inspect the aircraft, and I know

how to fly one of these. Sure, it's been a few years, but it's like riding a bicycle."

"The pilots go through a course for this aircraft specifically. The pilot from Groom was the one who taught them."

"Was?" Jax asked.

"Yes, it *was*. He was killed there last year, just after these were delivered to us."

"What was his name?" Jax asked.

"Milburn, Jonathan Milburn," she said, "He was the best pilot they had. I heard they almost shut the project down after he died."

"I've never heard of him," Jax said.

"He only worked on the black projects and only at Groom. From what I heard, he flew in every campaign. Desert Storm, Kosovo, Afghanistan, Iraq. Because of his knowledge, he was sent to Groom."

"I thought you wouldn't tell us anything about him?" Griggs asked.

"Why would a career pilot give it up to fly things at Groom?" Jax asked.

"I heard his CO was a problem. He wanted to keep flying, but he was old and wanted to retire. Then Groom stepped in. You've heard how they can be out there."

Jax nodded. He had heard rumors about how quiet they kept things. Just scuttlebutt among pilots, but he didn't know it was true.

"Who's supposed to train the new pilots for this project?" Jax asked.

"We don't know, though we've heard rumors in the last couple of days that the Navy may take over the project if the Air Force doesn't get their funding."

"You're sure I can't take it up?" Jax asked.

"Negative. The Colonel would have my ass."

"All right," Jax said, "if anything comes up, let us know." He handed her his card.

Jax and Griggs walked back to their car. The wind picked up again, but no clouds were on the horizon.

"What do you think?" Griggs asked.

"I think we need to talk to whoever was this Johnathan Milburn's CO at Groom," Jax replied.

"You think it's possible to talk to someone out there? It's like a Black Site," Griggs said.

"I may be able to get on that base because of my history," Jax said, "but they won't let you on."

"I have clearance," Griggs replied.

"I have to talk to someone high up to get in there," Jax said.

"Like who?"

"The person who put me on this assignment."

CHAPTER TWELVE

NO REAL ROAD leads towards the Groom Dry Lake Testing Facility, known by its other name, Area-51 or Dreamland. The only highway eventually joins Groom Lake Road and meanders through hills and canyons. Passersby wouldn't know it was there if they hadn't looked it up on the internet, of which there are many sites giving directions.

Route 375(deemed the Extraterrestrial Highway by the state of Nevada) goes past farms and a couple of gas stations, then is cut off from all human habitation until reaching Rachel., NV.

Along the sides of the road are dead animals, hungry coyotes, snakes slithering across the hot asphalt, and the occasional scorpion.

The Nevada Test Site and the Training Range, including the Groom Lake facility, lay in the desert beyond the road until one exits the switchback canyons. A mailbox marks it, but nothing else.

The road was sometimes called Mailbox Road, but Groom Lake Road is its official designation. It led directly to the base, though there was a heavy contingent of private security watching the base.

A large placard greets any visitor: **US Air Force Installation. It is unlawful to enter this area without the permission of the Installation Commander. While on this installation, all personnel and the property under their control are subject to search.**

Jax stared up at the sign. His call to DNI Williams had gone better than expected, and the man had made conditions for his escort to the Installation.

Jax watched as three jeeps rolled over the hill towards him. He'd tried to text Griggs that he'd reached the fence line, but there was no service.

As the jeeps drove towards him, he stepped out of his vehicle.

He knew the guards on the base were touchy about who was allowed on base, but he'd received authorization from DNI Williams to be on the base. Something he wasn't sure would happen, but he stood in the sagebrush, rocks, and dirt as the jeeps stopped.

"You Jackson Reed?" one of the guards asked.

He wore a black balaclava over his face and held a desert-colored Mk4.

The men in the other jeeps climbed out, rifles at the ready.

The guard said, "We don't want you here, but the boss got a call from up high. You will do what you're told. You will ask the questions you need to be answered; then, we will bring you back to your car. Is that understood?"

"It is," Jax replied.

The guard who spoke handed his rifle to another. All of them wore desert balaclavas.

He approached Jax and pulled a hood from his pocket.

"You will wear this," the guard said.

Jax nodded, and the hood went over his head.

They moved him roughly into one of the jeeps.

The drive was rough, though he anticipated it would have been worse.

Jax knew they'd reached the actual perimeter when the jeep stopped, a few voices were heard, but they didn't come from within the jeep he rode in.

It was another half an hour, possibly longer, before the jeep stopped, the engine went off, and cool air poured in on his sides.

He sat waiting, the heat of his breath moistening the hood over his head.

They pulled him out of the jeep and jerked the hood off.

A man stood in front of him. He was possibly sixty-five by the lines on his face, but from how the man fit into his uniform, Jax was unsure.

"I am Colonel Black. I run this installation. Why are you here?" the man said.

"Thank you for meeting me. I know that my coming here is...."

"No, shut up. This is not the time for bullshit. You will tell me why I received a phone call from the Director of National Intelligence?"

Jax stared at the man, then at the guards who'd gathered around. All of them were covered, while this man showed his face to Jax. He looked around the room. It wasn't a hangar, more like a large warehouse. There were vents around the perimeter, which he reasoned was where the cool air came from.

There were no windows, and Jax surmised he was underground, but he didn't remember the jeep stop. Had they put something in his mask to make him sleep?

"Where the hell am I?" Jax asked.

Colonel Black was becoming frustrated because he tapped and fidgeted with his hands.

"You are where you asked to be," the man said, "now, ask your questions. It took a lot for me to get here."

The armed guards around Black fidgeted with rifles, and Jax wondered if they were waiting for the kill command.

"Okay. You had a pilot out here working on drones. He died. Is there anything you can tell me about him?" Jax asked.

The man pondered his question.

"You're talking about Milburn?" Black asked.

"Yes, Sir," Jax replied.

The Colonel smiled at the show of respect.

"I know who you are and how you were screwed over. I have respect for you, but Milburn died. Those switchbacks can be a nightmare late at night. Johnny was heading home. He'd been out here for a month. I decided he needed a break. Being isolated from the world does funny things to the human mind. Some people deal with it well, others not so much."

"I take it John Milburn was the latter?" Jax asked.

Black nodded, "I sent Johnny back to Vegas. I thought about sending him on a bird, but he said he'd be fine."

"Do you think he died in the crash?" Jax asked.

"Now that's an interesting question. It would help if you started with that question. You think the best pilot I've ever seen could lose control of his car and burn up in it?"

"Are you saying—"

"I'm saying what I said. There is more to be said about it. He had money trouble, which may have sent him to do things. Maybe the service clocked him out, and he found a way to set him up."

"Do you know of anywhere I could look for him?" Jax asked.

"In his coffin," Black said, "if that's empty, he has a friend that works out at Creech. You should talk to him."

"What's his friend's name?" Jax asked.

"David Webb, Major David Webb," Black said.

Jax almost choked but kept it down.

"Thank you," Jax said.

Black nodded, "Now, get the fuck off of my installation."

Jax glanced around the hangar. There were two aircraft under a black tarp. One looked like a drone, while the other was much bigger. Two men stood underneath it, working on something Jax couldn't see.

Before he could figure it out, the cloth went over his head.

"Good luck, Reed," Black said.

Jax smiled under his hood, "Yes, Sir," Jax said.

They shoved him into a jeep. The ride was quiet, which gave him time to think about all that Black had told him.

He stared out at the sky as they pulled him out. They'd put something inside the covering to knock him out. His head pounded, and he was confident that the building had been underground.

"Now, get out of here," the guard said, shoving Jax towards his car.

A dust cloud rose in the distance. A big blue bus rolled through the fence line.

Jax took out his phone. There were no bars.

"Shit," he said to himself.

He turned his car around and drove back to Vegas.

CHAPTER THIRTEEN

JAX PULLED into the driveway of Griggs's house and got out.

He knocked, and she came to the door. He'd tried calling her as he drove back, but there had been no service until Jax reached I-15, so he waited.

"Come in," Griggs said.

Jax walked in and sat at the counter.

She was making something. Jax couldn't tell what, but the house smelled fantastic.

"So, what did you find out?" she asked.

Over the next twenty minutes, Jax relayed all that Colonel Black had told him.

When he was done, Griggs stared at him.

"Holy shit," she said, "you mean Webb, our Webb? The one you've thought all along had a hand in this?"

"Yes, the same," Jax said.

"So, what do we do now?" she asked.

He shook his head and stared at the pan of food on the stove.

"It's a stir fry. I haven't eaten much since we started, and I like to cook. I thought it would be just me until you showed up."

"Sorry," Jax said.

"It's fine. I made enough for both of us." She reassured him.

She stirred in some rice with the vegetables she'd been sautéing. The smell of sesame oil filled the kitchen as Griggs drizzled it over the food.

"I've been thinking about a few things," Griggs said.

"Okay," Jax said, suddenly nervous.

"Why would they put you on this case? There are tons of agents in Vegas."

"I wish I knew. I expect it has something to do with my familiarity with Creech, drones, and all of that, but I could be wrong."

"You have a history with Webb too."

"I think that's secondary. I wanted to stay home with Lizbeth. This place dredges up too many memories."

"Good ones, I hope?" Griggs asked.

"A little of both," Jax said, "take this house. It's similar to the one Sarah and I lived in a while stationed at Creech."

"I'm sorry," she said.

"It's okay. But there are little things like that. I like this city, I do, but there are a lot of bad memories here."

He stared at the ring on his finger and spun it with his other hand.

"Is that why you still wear that?"

"I don't know why I still wear it. Sarah made it clear she was done. She's sending the papers over when I get back. She's going to marry that guy."

"Then it's all over, and you're having difficulty saying those words."

Jax nodded and stared at the floor.

"I guess so. When I was offered the chance to resign, Sarah thought I should fight it. But I knew how it would look on my officials. After that, we had a big fight; I got the job with the FBI.

I thought I'd redeemed myself, but then I started working. I was away from home a lot—more than when we were in Vegas. I hoped we'd work it out for Lizbeth, but sometimes people change, and there's nothing you can do. Now I watch her with him, and part of me breaks."

"Are you talking about your daughter or your wife?" Griggs asked.

Jax raised his head, and a tear ran down his face, "Both. This shit is hard. I try to be a good dad and husband. I moved my family away from things. Then it just fucking fell apart. I still love my wife, which makes it harder, but she doesn't feel that way. She's told me that. I haven't been on a date since I moved out."

"You haven't dated in the two years you've been separated?" Griggs asked.

"Nope, not once," Jax replied.

Griggs smiled.

Jax frowned. There was tension in the air, and he knew he'd have to stop it.

"Your dad has a way of finding things out. He always has. It won't happen."

It was Griggs's turn to frown.

"How do you know him?"

"When I was stationed at Nellis for a little while, there was an investigation. He was the lead. I talked to him a few times afterward. I thought of leaving the service. Sarah wouldn't have it. She liked the 'military wife' life. Then I was discharged, and I gave him a call. I was older but made the cut. I worked my ass off for that shield."

"He was your reference?"

"He was one of them. I had a few others from my time in the service, but I believe he got me in."

She plated their food and handed him a fork.

Jax took a bite and stared at her.

"He doesn't always find things out," Griggs said.

Jax felt the tension skyrocket.

"Thank you for dinner. I have to get back to my hotel and call Lizbeth."

"You can stay here," Griggs said and leaned closer.

"That would be a bad idea."

"What are you afraid of?" Griggs asked.

Jax knew precisely what he was afraid of.

He grabbed his jacket and hurried out the door. He didn't look back, but he knew Griggs would be standing at the door.

CHAPTER FOURTEEN

DRAKE STOOD BY THE WINDOW, glanced at the monitors in front of him, then at Webb cleaning his firearm.

Drake knew as well as Webb did that Reed was getting closer, so he'd have to take care of things. Make it work to his advantage first, though.

Webb was one cog in the machine. He didn't know how many more there were, but the person he'd been reporting to would be interested in recent developments.

The visit to Groom Lake would hold special significance.

Drake walked down the stairs into the kitchen. Moonlight stretched through the big windows onto the walls. It illuminated the kitchen enough that he'd pulled the light from the fridge.

He grabbed the juice from the fridge, drank it straight from the carton, and set it down.

He dialed the number on his phone.

"Hey, so that FBI agent is going out to Groom asking questions," he said.

The other end went silent for a minute.

"Okay, I guess we're playing clean up. They will probably come and talk to Webb soon. Make something work. We can't have Webb talking, and Reed and that woman he's with are becoming a nuisance." The voice said.

The voice was all Drake ever called the person on the other end.

He'd been hired and brought in to take care of things. He'd been given the house to use, an unlimited bank account, and he knew it would all go away if he screwed up, just like he would 'go away.'

"Yes, sir, you want them all gone?" Drake asked.

"No, we take out an FBI agent, and we'll have a target on our backs. Figure something out."

"I understand," Drake said, ending the call.

CHAPTER FIFTEEN

ELAINE FRANKLIN STARED at the ceiling; it would be a busy day. She would meet with the cabinet members she wanted and her Vice President.

The bed she lay in was comfy, and though she worked her whole life to get to this point, she was not looking forward to giving up her mattress for one in the White House. She'd grown accustomed to how it fit her body. It gave her comfort, and she thought about it at the end of every day.

Robert, her husband, lay next to her. His soft breathing reminded her that he was there and healthy. She watched him breathe, staring at his thinning hair, his mouth moved, and his eyes twitched in a deep sleep she hadn't had that night.

She got up and walked into the bathroom.

"Elaine, you okay?" Robert called.

"I have an early day," she replied.

He laughed, and the bed creaked as he climbed out of it.

Robert's feet scuffed the floor as he walked. Old age was not for the faint of heart. Her mother had told her when she'd started to grow old. Now, as she sat days away from the White House, the memories of her mother brought her comfort.

Robert walked into the bathroom as she stepped out of her clothes.

He wrapped his arms around her, as he'd done numerous times.

"Well, I guess I'll see you tonight. I have a meeting with the First Lady. It should be fun." He said.

He sounded less than enthusiastic, "I know, all right. This is what we've both worked for. You've always pushed me. We wouldn't be here without those pushes."

He smiled at their reflection.

"You remember when we first started this? You were on the city council, and I was doing the law practice on the side." Robert said.

"I remember our little apartment. I think we had more roaches than you had clients at your practice. Things moved quickly after that. We won the Governor's Mansion, then the Senate. We've come a long way from that apartment."

"Yes, and you've earned all that we've achieved. I'm proud of you, Elaine," he said.

She stopped and stared at him for a moment.

"What is it?" Elaine asked.

"It all feels surreal, and I want to remember this feeling. Everything moved so quickly that I didn't always acknowledge it. I'm taking this moment to notice it."

"Okay, you had me worried. I thought you would say cancer came back or something."

"Nope, I had my checkup a couple of days ago. Everything is fine. This just all feels like we made it."

Elaine laughed, "Hell, I thought that way when we made it to the Governor's Mansion."

He laughed in response, "You know what I mean. Two kids from the Middle of Nowhere, Colorado. Did you think we'd make it this far?"

"I hoped we would."

He kissed her on the forehead and walked out of the bathroom.

"You don't want to sit and watch me shower?" she asked.

He smiled.

"I wish I could. I'll let you have your shower. I know you have a busy day. I love you, Elaine." He said.

"Love you too, Robert," she said.

He walked out, and she stepped into the shower. The conversation had unnerved her.

What's gotten into him?

CHAPTER SIXTEEN

WHILE THE NEXT President of the United States took her shower, Jax was in his room, silent as he stared across the room at his curtains.

He got in the shower, dressed, and called Sarah.

She picked up after the first ring.

"Where the hell have you been?" she asked.

"I'm working. Sometimes I can't call." He replied.

"That story about that dead woman in Vegas, I saw a picture of you at the crime scene. What the hell is going on?" she asked.

"I can't talk about it." He said.

"Okay, but I was worried," she said.

Jax smiled, "You were worried about me?"

"Don't be cute. I was worried for Lizzy's sake. She loves you. She was telling us about the game you two had."

"Oh," Jax replied.

"I've needed to talk to you, though."

Here it comes, "About what?"

"Do you know what Tom does?" she asked.

"I have no idea," Jax replied.

"He's going to be Elaine Franklin's Chief of Staff," Sarah said.

"Oh, no, I didn't know that," Jax replied.

"Well, he got tickets for the inauguration. I want to take Lizzy. Would that be okay?" Sarah asked.

"Yes, that would be fine. I should be coming back to DC in the next day or so." Jax said.

"Oh, she'll love to hear that. We've had so much snow; I hope your flight is okay."

"I haven't booked anything yet, but I'm sure it will be fine. Could I talk to her for a minute?"

"Of course," Sarah said.

The phone was silent, and he knew she'd set it down. He heard her calling for Elizabeth in the background.

Jax thought about their old bedroom when Elizabeth got on the phone.

"Hi, Daddy," she said.

"Hello, baby. What are you doing?"

"Playing on the computer," Lizbeth said, "Tom got me my laptop. He played a couple of games, showing me how to use them."

"That's wonderful, Lizbeth," Jax said, "I'm glad you found something to do. I'm sorry I couldn't be there."

"It's okay. Mom said you've been busy in Las Vegas."

"I am, but I will come home in the next couple of days. Then we can do something. Did you still want to go to the plane museum?" he asked.

"Yes," Lizbeth said, "Tom and Mom were going to take me, but he doesn't know the names of the planes."

"Okay, I'll see you in a couple of days. I love you, Lizbeth," Jax said.

"I love you too, Dad," she said.

"Jackson, there was something else I needed to talk to you about," Sarah said as Lizzy handed the phone back.

"Okay," Jax replied.

"The papers have been sent to your lawyer. When you get back, could you stop in and sign them?" she asked.

"What's the hurry," he asked but already knew the answer.

"Tom proposed," she said.

Jax pulled the phone away from his face and stared at the ring on his finger.

"Yeah, I'll do it when I get back," he replied.

"Thank you," she said.

"Yep," he said, fighting tears.

"I'm sorry, Jax," she said.

"Yeah, me too," he replied.

He ended the call and set his phone down because he didn't want to throw it.

It buzzed, and he picked it up again.

"Reed," he answered.

"Jax, it's Decker," his boss said.

"Yes, Sir," Jax replied.

"I haven't had an update for a few days. What's going on out there, and why did you need to go to Groom Lake?"

"Sorry, I've been busy. And as for Groom Lake," Jax said, "I was chasing a bread crumb."

"What kind of bread crumb takes you out there? I had some higher-ups very pissed off at that."

"I'm sorry, Sir. A question was raised, and the only place with an answer was out at Groom."

"How big is this thing you're chasing?" Decker asked.

"Well, sir, I will send you an encrypted about everything," Jax said.

"That would be great. The Director and someone from the AG's office called me. They were very pissed off. I didn't tell them what I knew, but they were under the belief that this was just a crashed drone."

"Well, Sir, when you see my email, you'll know it's much bigger. We're going to talk to someone today that should make everything more clear."

"I hope so," Decker said.

Jax ended the call, pulled out his laptop, connected to a secure server, and wrote up all he'd discovered. It took him forty minutes to get it all down. He sat and waited for Decker to call.

It only took ten minutes.

"Holy shit," Decker said when Jax answered. "So you think that Webb has a big hand in this?"

"I think that's become clear after my talk with the Colonel at Groom."

"Where do you think this is leading?"

"I don't know yet," Jax replied.

"Okay. Keep me posted. You and Vanessa, be careful out there," Decker said.

"Yes, Sir," Jax said and ended the call. He then called Griggs.

"You on your way over?" she asked.

"Heading to the car now," he said and closed the door.

CHAPTER SEVENTEEN

DRAKE STEPPED into the hallway and eyed the maid at the end of the hall.

He'd watched Jax leave, so he went to the room where the man came out.

He'd slipped some money to a front desk clerk when he'd arrived and had come up the elevator, seeing Jax as he walked into another elevator. He waited a few minutes in case the man came back.

Drake put on his gloves and walked toward the room.

The maid ignored him as he walked past but turned and glanced at him as he slipped the room key into the slot.

Drake walked in, studied everything in the room, and went straight for the laptop on the desk.

He opened it and beat the password program but found nothing else on the laptop. The security was tighter than he'd expected for an older FBI agent, and while he got through some things, most of the computer was locked up, which unnerved him.

He flipped through papers on the table and read through them, finding them to be only the rudimentary documents about the case. But there was nothing tangible enough to lead him in a solid direction.

He put the room back together and hurried out the door.

"What do you know about the man in that room?" he asked the maid, who still hovered outside the room.

The room attendant stared at him.

"He's been here a few days. There's nothing much to tell. His room is clean. He sleeps only on one side of the bed."

"Has he had any guests?"

"Not that I could tell. As I said, only one side of the bed is slept on. He must be married."

"Why do you think that?"

"Single guys sleep on the whole bed. Married men are used to their wife: They sleep on one side of the bed."

Drake handed her a ten.

"Thank you," he said and hurried to the elevator.

The maid stared at him leaving and wrote down what he'd looked like.

CHAPTER EIGHTEEN

JAX AND GRIGGS pulled up to the gate.

They scanned the screen for Webb's name but were only through the letter S when a car honked behind them.

Griggs stuck her head out the window.

"He forgot the opener," she called to the other car.

The gate opened, and Jax let the car behind them pass. He didn't want them to see where he was going.

The car's passengers waved as it passed and turned left through the gate.

Jax and Griggs pulled up to Webb's address and got out.

Jax knocked and stared as Webb opened the door.

The man was in his uniform and looked like he was headed out the door.

"Reed, what are you doing here?" Webb asked.

Jax watched the man. There was a nervousness to him Jax had never encountered before.

"We have a few questions," Griggs said.

"Oh, I thought you'd be done when you found Dickson?"

"Heard you called off work," Jax said.

Webb stopped and stared at him.

"Are we going to do this out here, or would you like to invite us in?" Griggs asked.

"Sorry," Webb said and waved them inside.

"How are you feeling?" Jax asked after they'd sat on the couch just beyond the doors.

"Still a bit of a sinus issue, but I'm okay. I was heading to the base."

"How close were you and Dickson?" Griggs asked.

"We worked well together. Sadie was a good pilot, but we weren't close."

"Why is that?"

"She had her umm...friends if you know what I mean," Webb said.

"So, she was gay?" Jax asked.

"Yes, it wasn't a secret."

"How does someone on your salary afford a place at The Lakes?" Griggs asked.

Webb stared at her.

"I made some money in the market. There were a few of these on a short sale. It's worth twice the prices I paid."

"Does anyone on your team have a problem with her?"

"Look, I have to get back to work, so if there is nothing else," Webb said.

"*Look*, I'm just doing my job. You understand," Jax said.

Webb nodded.

"Maybe you should talk to the woman who lived across from her. She works at a club. She might have some answers for you, or her girlfriend might."

"Which club was that?" Jax asked.

"Fire," Webb said, "it's on Industrial."

"Okay, we'll go do that," Jax said.

"Hey, there's one other thing. Do you know someone named Johnny Milburn?" Griggs asked.

Webb froze and stared from one to the other.

"I flew with Johnny. He was a hell of a pilot. I was pretty upset when he passed."

"Okay," Griggs said.

Webb led them out, and Jax and Griggs sat in their car as Webb pulled out of his garage.

"He was lying," Griggs said.

"Like a politician," Jax replied.

"Are we going to talk to Sadie's neighbor again?" Griggs asked.

Jax nodded and started the car.

CHAPTER NINETEEN

JAX AND GRIGGS stared up at the sign.

'Fire,' the sign read with neon flames pouring out the sides.

"Have you ever been here?" Jax asked.

"Not my type of place," Griggs replied.

"Nope," Jax replied, "me neither."

It was early and busier than Jax thought it would be.

A woman was on stage with her top off, and only a thin piece of cloth covered the rest of her.

He showed his ID to the doorman, who led them to the bar and picked up the phone.

"I'm Lawrence. I handle inquiries. What can I do for you?" a man asked as he approached where they waited.

He wore a clean suit and a freshly shaved face, and his arms looked bigger than Jax's head.

"We are looking for someone," Griggs said.

"That helps," the man said.

"She told us her name was Sirese," Jax said.

"Oh, that's Deva," he said.

"Diva," Griggs said and almost laughed.

"No, like this: D-E-V-A," Lawrence said.

"Where could I find her?" Jax asked.

"She's in the back. She's not on stage for a few minutes, but don't make her late." Lawrence walked them to the dressing room.

"I wouldn't dream of it," Jax assured him.

Jax and Griggs walked in with Lawrence.

"Hey, D, these two have some questions for you," Lawrence said.

They glanced through the women standing in front of mirrors, adjusting their costumes.

Sirese, or Deva, as they were told her name was, sat at the end of the long dressing room.

Jax took Sirese to be her stage name.

She waved them over.

"You were the two who found Sadie?" Sirese asked.

"We are. We have a couple of questions for you." Jax said.

"I already told Metro everything I know," she said.

"Okay, but we wanted to ask some specifics," Griggs said.

"Like?"

"This guy who'd been coming around. Did you tell Metro about him?" Jax asked.

"They didn't ask about him."

"Okay, we're asking," Griggs said.

A few of the dancers stared at Griggs. She turned and stared back.

"Don't mind them. They're just checking you out. Not often that we get someone that looks like you in here."

"What does that mean?" Griggs replied.

"Not many Black girls like to dance, which is too bad. Some guests come in looking for that."

Griggs frowned.

"So, tell us about this guy," Jax said.

"I told you. He's a white guy. He came in here looking for

Sadie one night. Lawrence didn't like his attitude, and they got into it. He was out of work for a few weeks."

"You're talking about that dinosaur out front?" Griggs asked.

"Yep, the very same," Deva said, "Lawrence is a strong dude, but this guy, he took him to church. He had a black eye and a bit of damage to his ribs. Lawrence is the Cooler. He deals with the big problems."

"So, why'd Lawrence and this guy get into it?" Griggs asked.

"He was getting loud with Sadie. Jimmy, the manager, doesn't mind me having a girlfriend. He tried to get Sadie on stage. Gave her a tryout and everything. That woman can move her hips in bed, but you get her on stage, and she's a dead fish."

"Anyone else coming looking for her?"

"One guy did. He was kind of quiet. Only came in once. He said he needed to talk to her. He gave Lawrence a bill and talked to Sadie for a minute. They left. I asked her about it, and she said it was nothing."

"When you say a bill, you mean a hundred dollars?" Jax asked.

"Yeah, sorry," Deva said, "it's industry speak."

"You seen the other guy in here since?" Jax asked.

"The last time I saw him was when he entered her apartment. He carried a suitcase. That was a couple of days before you showed up."

Deva froze and stared at both of them.

"Holy shit. Sadie was in that suitcase, wasn't she?"

"I don't have an answer for that," Griggs said.

"How do you remember that?" Jax asked.

"It was a good night. I made a lot and got home at five." Deva said.

She stood up, unfastened her bra, refastened and adjusted her bottoms, glanced up, and winked at Jax.

One of the dancers stepped through them and held up her two fingers.

"I have to get on stage. My song is coming up in two minutes. If there's anything else, you can wait until I'm done with my set," she said.

Jax smiled, and Griggs nudged him.

Deva walked out of the dressing room as Motley Crüe came on.

"Original," Griggs muttered.

They walked out of the dressing room, and Jax stared at the stage as Deva acted out on stage as 'Sirese' and wrapped her legs around the pole and slid down.

"Pick your tongue up off the floor," Griggs suggested.

Jax turned and glared at her, "We're done here," Jax said.

They walked to the door, and Lawrence stopped them.

"Everything okay?" he asked.

"Yeah, it's fine. She said there was a guy who came in that put you out of work?" Jax asked.

Lawrence stared at the floor.

"I tell you, this guy was trained in some shit. I've taken Aikido and Jiu-Jitsu since I could walk. The shit this guy did, I've never seen. I've never been struck so hard by someone. I don't know where he pulled the energy, but I was out of work."

"What did he look like?" Griggs asked.

"He's about your height, but he had that wiry muscle. When I tried to get a hold of him to toss him out, he did this kick that knocked me on my ass. I've never been knocked down."

"Face, eyes... the usual?" Jax asked.

"Dark eyes, white guy. He carried himself well. I think he's probably ex-military."

"What about the other guy that came in to talk to Sadie?" Griggs asked.

"They argued for a minute, then hurried out."

"Argued about what?"

"Drowning," he said.

Jax and Griggs stared at one another.

"Could it be 'droning' or a drone?" Jax asked.

"Yeah, that was it."

"Thank you," Jax said and handed him a hundred-dollar bill.

"What's this for?" Lawrence asked.

"In case someone asks. We weren't here."

"Sure thing," Lawrence said.

They walked out as Motley Crüe finished. Jax stared back as Deva stepped off the stage.

"Come on. We have to get going."

"Let's get some lunch," Griggs said.

"I need to go to my hotel first," Jax said.

"What for?"

"A hunch," Jax replied.

CHAPTER TWENTY

JAX AND GRIGGS stepped off the elevator and walked toward his room.

The maid came running towards them.

"There was a man in your room," she said.

"What, man?" Jax asked.

"He was a bald, white man. He was in there for a few minutes. I wanted to call security, but he scared me. He's the type my husband says could break you."

"Did he ask any questions?" Griggs asked.

The woman stared at her.

"She's with me. It's okay," Jax said.

"He asked how long you've been in the room. If you'd have anyone in the room with you."

"What did you say?" Jax asked.

"That you'd only been in the room a couple of days and that no one but you had been in the room."

"Thank you..."

"Alicia," the maid replied.

She hurried back to her cart at the other end of the hallway.

"So, someone is on to us?" Griggs said.

"I think they have been for a while, but we haven't seen them."

Jax walked to Alicia and handed her a fifty.

She stared at it.

"Thank you," he said.

Her face broke into a big grin.

"Oh," Alicia said, "thank you so much, Mr. Reed."

"I hope they haven't been to your house," Jax said to Griggs.

Griggs frowned, and they ran to her car and drove to the western side of the Las Vegas Valley.

The door was closed to her house, and they walked in.

There was no one inside.

"Well, they're following me and not going after you," Jax said.

"Yes, I guess that's a good thing," Griggs said.

"From what I've heard about this guy, I'm not sure I could win a fight."

"Yeah, I don't think so either," Griggs said. "What do we do now?"

"I think we should talk to Webb," he said.

"I think that's a good idea. This all leads to him. That person Lawrence talked about sounds like Webb." Griggs said.

"I agree," Jax said.

CHAPTER TWENTY-ONE

JOHNATHAN MILBURN STARED out the front windows of his cabin at the aircraft on the strip of the tarmac.

He'd flown it from Nevada to his little cabin the day it was stolen. It sat in the small hangar he designed for it since, but now that it was dark enough, that would change.

The mountains around him were cold, and a bit of snow covered the tarmac before he cleaned it.

He sipped his coffee, walked to the back room of the cabin, opened a large door, and flicked a light switch. The room grew bright. The command console he'd used to hijack the aircraft sat in the corner and came to life when the lights came on.

A small A/C unit was turned on to keep all electronics cool.

Milburn stepped to the controls of the command console; it lit up with his touch. He'd checked the relay between the aircraft and his console numerous times since it landed outside the cabin. There had been a minor glitch as he crossed into the Dakotas, and he wanted to ensure it wouldn't happen again.

The monitor in front of him showed the black tarmac underneath the aircraft. He throttled up, tilting the engines so the aircraft would rise vertically from its perch on the tarmac.

A red light blinked on the console, acknowledging the connection as the aircraft rose above the pine trees.

If he'd been outside, a low hum would have come from the aircraft as it ascended. Instead, he saw only a red light aglow on his console, and the camera from the plane turned on and showed a pile of snow, pine trees, and the small cabin.

He initiated the flight controls and adjusted the engines' angle again, switching them from vertical to horizontal.

As he'd been called his whole life, John or Johnny banked the aircraft towards the small town below the cabin, where he was known as Randall Turner.

It zipped across the tree line and followed the freeway for a while before he brought it to cruising altitude.

No one would see or hear the aircraft at that time of night. There were no lights on either side; he'd disabled them after the drone touched down. It was nearly invisible to the radar. Those who would swear they saw something would be considered crackpots or alien hunters, but they knew they saw a black streak moving across the sky.

Johnny flew it towards the bright lights of the tower and airport he saw on the camera attached to the aircraft's nose. He pulled back on the flight stick and flew it higher. The airport had a busy schedule, and he wanted to ensure the drone wouldn't be picked up by radar.

A few days ago, it had been a year since he'd flown the aircraft, but it was like riding a bicycle.

He rolled right and stared at the lights of the big 777 in front of him. He quickly banked to the left, and the pilots would swear they saw something but, needing their flight status, wouldn't report it.

He flew it past the aircraft coming into Reagan and dipped low as the White House appeared on the horizon. The night sky was clear, and the glow of the lights of the building excited him.

He turned away from the White House, coming up and over the Mall and heading towards the open ocean.

The blue waves had turned black in the night, and he skimmed the surface of them, pulled back, and the aircraft screamed into the sky.

John turned the aircraft around, following the route he'd follow in a couple of weeks. It wasn't a practice run that would come later. He was using it to make himself familiar with the terrain.

He dipped low, going around Reagan and up into the mountains.

The aircraft turned, and John realigned the engines to vertical.

The drone lowered slowly to the tarmac below where the flight began.

John parked it and turned off his console. The lights, A/C unit, and other instruments were turned off.

The aircraft sat silently outside.

He walked into the kitchen, pulled a Poptart from a box in the cupboard, slid it into the toaster, and poured a glass of milk. He waited for the Poptart, pulled it when it rose, went to the window, and gazed out at the aircraft on the small plot of tarmac.

The milk tasted good going down, and combined with the strawberry of the Poptart, it hurt his teeth, but he enjoyed it.

The snow around the small piece of tarmac steamed, and he set his food down, slipped his boots on, and walked out the door.

He got in the small buggy, attached the cable to the front of the aircraft, and towed it into the hangar.

Two racks of bombs, a set of Hellfire missiles, and links of bullets rest against one wall of the hangar.

John thought of marking them up the way he'd done in previous conflicts but felt he better not.

He towed the drone into the hangar, closed the doors, and parked the buggy.

Smoke rolled out the chimney, returned to the house, grabbed his milk and Poptart, which had gone cold, and turned on the TV.

CHAPTER TWENTY-TWO

PRESIDENT THOMPSON STARED out the window of the Oval Office at the snow falling across the White House grounds.

He'd taken in as many of those moments as possible in the past couple of weeks.

The time he had left was limited, and he wondered what he'd do next.

His wife wanted him to spend time with his grandkids, but his mind was set on doing other things.

He could retire to some place to paint, sit on his ass, and do nothing like some former presidents, or he could influence the future. That's what he wanted to do.

The meeting he'd have with Miles Frank, the Speaker of the House, would help him define his post-Presidency, he knew that, but he still didn't like the man.

The President-Elect had come in, sweeping most of his party from government. He was amazed that Frank could keep the house, even if it were by the slimmest of margins.

He hoped Elaine Franklin would be up to the task, but in a couple of conversations they'd shared, she'd come across as naive, frightening him. He'd seen trouble behind the desk in his eight years and knew the world was horrible.

The first four years had been relatively peaceful. Other things happened, and he had to work on the economy, which had crashed. Unemployment numbers were high, and he hadn't found a way to stimulate anything, which cost his party the White House and Senate.

He watched the lights beyond the grounds, staring at the signs for the inauguration.

The following week would be the hardest of his presidency. He knew that. He'd hated his home from the moment he stepped foot in it, but now that it was ending, his thoughts ran the gamut from tiredness to exhaustion and then peace.

Whatever lay in front of him, he was ready, though apprehensive.

He hoped the people had chosen someone that could handle the office, but hope was all it was. His fears were more profound, and they ran counter to his hopes.

CHAPTER TWENTY-THREE

JAX PULLED the car through the gate, again having to follow another vehicle into the community.

He drove right towards Webb's house.

The lights upstairs were on, then went out as Jax and Griggs stepped out of their car.

It was only six o'clock, a bit early for sleep, Jax thought; then he saw the car in the driveway.

He didn't know whose it was, but he and Griggs stared at it as he rang the doorbell.

No one came to the door for a few minutes, so Griggs pushed the bell again.

Webb came to the door wearing a black robe and frowned when he saw who'd been ringing the bell.

"I'm a bit busy," Webb said.

"It looks that way," Griggs said, "but we have a few questions, then we'll leave you alone."

"Come back in the morning," Webb said.

"We have to do this now. It can't wait." Jax said.

Webb sighed and closed the door.

"Webb, open the fucking door," Jax said.

Webb returned with a woman who had hurriedly dressed.

Jax recognized her as one of the flight crew members but hadn't caught her name.

Her hair was messed up, and her makeup smeared. Her uniform was partially done up, and her boots weren't tied. Jax and Griggs smiled at her as she hurried to her car.

"I guess we caught you at a bad time?" Jax asked.

Webb mumbled under his breath, something Jax didn't catch.

They walked into the house, led by Webb. They sat on the couch and stared out the window.

"Thanks for coming over. Could I get you a drink or refreshments? Maybe you could get the fuck out of my house?"

"David, we need to talk," Jax said.

"Reed, I wish I could help you, but I don't have answers to your questions," Webb said.

"Wrong answer," Jax said.

"We've been to the club. We know you and Dickson were working together to steal the drone." Griggs said.

Webb stopped and stared at both of them.

He felt his throat tighten and glanced across the water, unaware that Drake sat in the house across from them.

"How did you figure it out?" Webb asked and sat down in a chair.

"The bouncer told us about the fight. Then we put it all together. Dickson needed the money, and you offered her a job. Moseley told you no."

"That dude with his new baby could have used that money. But he got all self-righteous. They started talking about turning me in. When he died, I thought it was over, but Sadie didn't call."

"You also didn't anticipate another player," Griggs said.

"What other player?" Webb said.

"Who the hell do you think killed Sadie?"

"I've been thinking about that, and I have an idea, but I've never met the person. This was all set up through someone else."

"Who?" Jax asked.

"Someone contacted me. I was up for review, and they discovered I'd been sleeping with my subordinates. The person said they could make it go away. I didn't want to lose my job."

Jax's face turned red, "Mother fucker. It sucks to lose a job that you love, huh? One that keeps your family together?" Jax said.

"What the hell are you going on about?" Webb asked.

"I know you're the one that got me kicked out. I'll do whatever I can to ensure you go down." Jax said.

Webb laughed.

"You're such a fucking *hero*. They wanted you for this, you know. I knew you wouldn't do it and would go to the higher-ups. Getting rid of you made this all possible. How are Sarah and her soon-to-be new husband, anyway?" Webb asked.

Jax pulled his gun and leveled it at Webb's face.

* * *

Drake admired the scene before him, wondering what Gods could have favored him in such a way.

He'd spent the day playing with the gas nozzle on the house while Webb and his friend had been upstairs, busy with each other.

He pressed a button on a remote in his hands that he'd attached to the gas nozzle.

Gas slowly seeped into the house.

His rifle by his side resting upon his perch, his sidearm next to it, he watched the event play out before him on the video screens.

The video feed played, though he'd disabled the sound that morning when Webb had left. He sat and watched the people talking back and forth in their perceived safety.

He took his shot, and Webb's head erupted in a shower of red and grey.

* * *

Jax stared at the blood and body on the floor.

There was a glint of glass on the other side of the lake, and he dropped to the ground.

"Sniper," he called out.

He crawled across to Webb, checking his pulse, but nothing was left of the man's head.

Webb was dead.

There was no coming back from half of your head missing.

He lay on the ground, looking for Griggs. She lay on the floor. Her head pressed to the floor.

"Griggs, you okay?" he asked.

"Yeah, I'm okay. That round came from the house across the water." She said.

Another shot flew through the window, and Jax crawled towards Griggs.

"We have to get out," he said.

"He's from an elevated position," she argued, "we'd be torn apart."

"We have to move," Jax said.

He crawled towards the back of the couch, using it as a shield as another round ripped through the floor.

Griggs was on his six, and they rushed towards the door.

She grabbed his leg and pulled on it.

"What?" Jax asked.

"I smell gas," she said.

Jax sniffed the air.

* * *

Jax fired through the window. He knew it wouldn't hit anything, but he needed a type of diversion.

He and Griggs made it to the front door as another round struck the house.

Jax ran out of the house, with Griggs running behind him. He followed the road until it met with where he knew the shot came from.

He reached the other house as Webb's house exploded behind him. He glanced around for Griggs. She lay on her stomach in the water. He grabbed her and dragged her to the shoreline.

She was breathing and coughed.

"You okay," he asked.

"Yeah, I'm good," Griggs replied.

"I'll call 911," Jax said.

"Don't. I'm sure these other people already have." Griggs said.

He glanced around, and people stood on their decks with phones in their hands.

He helped her up, and they stumbled to the curb as the sounds of emergency vehicles filled the air.

"What are you going to say to my dad...I mean, Decker?" she asked.

Blood ran into Jax's eyes, and he wiped it with the backside of his hand.

"I don't know. I don't know who could have shut down the

investigation into him. That's pretty high up the food chain." Jax said.

"Whoever paid him is a lot higher than my pay grade," Griggs said.

An EMT came over to them.

"You two okay," the EMT asked. She was a blonde woman with short hair and studied both of them.

Jax nodded.

"You have a wound on your scalp. Come with me," she said.

She led them towards an ambulance, checked Jax's vitals, and cleaned his wound. She then checked out Griggs, who only had a couple of scratches.

"Jackson Reed, I thought you'd be here," Abrams said.

Jax glanced up.

"Detective," Jax said.

"You two okay?" he asked.

"Yeah, I think we're all right," Griggs replied.

"He may have a slight concussion from the blast, her too, but other than that, they're okay," the EMT said.

"I need you to sit in my car while we go through this," Abrams said.

The flicker of red flames on Webb's house danced behind Abrams. Jax thought of the burned-out shell where Jared Moseley had died.

"Is there anything you'd like to tell me about this?" Abrams asked.

"Not really," Jax said.

Griggs turned away.

Abrams walked away, and Jax pulled out his phone and called Decker.

"Sir, we've hit a roadblock," Jax said.

"What kind of roadblock?" Decker asked.

Jax glanced at Griggs, her face smudged with dirt, her wet hair glistening in the streetlights.

He walked away from where Metro could hear him and related the story to them being checked out by the EMT.

There was silence on the other end of the phone.

"Sir," Jax asked, "are you there?"

"Yeah, I just don't know how to deal with this," Decker replied.

"Is Vanessa okay?" Decker finally asked.

"She has a couple of scratches, and our heads are ringing, but she's okay," Jax said.

"I want you to report. I want you to fly back asap. I will talk to Vanessa's CO and get her out here. I will feel safer with her closer."

"I think you may have some problems with that," Jax said.

"Let me worry about those things," Decker said.

"The locals are going to have a fit with us leaving."

"I know, but this is a federal investigation. I will send agents from Vegas out there. I want both of you on a plane as soon as possible."

"Yes, sir," Jax said and stared as Abrams walked towards them.

"I need an explanation of what happened. The Fire Marshall asked people to get away from the house. They think it was a gas leak."

Jax stared at his hands. His wedding ring was covered in soot, and Webb's blood littered his face.

Jax nodded at Abrams.

The man walked away.

"What now?" Griggs said.

Jax glanced at the Suburban they'd driven in. The roof was caved in from debris, and the windows were shattered.

"We'll have to call for a ride," Jax said.

"What about Abrams?" Griggs asked.

"He'll have to wait until the Fire Marshall gives the all-clear. That's when we'll leave."

It took ten minutes before the all-clear was given, and Jax and Griggs watched as Abrams disappeared around the other side of the house.

Griggs pulled out her phone, called for a ride, and hurried out the gate towards their escape.

They went straight to Jax's hotel.

He grabbed all his gear, and they took another car to the airport.

CHAPTER TWENTY-FOUR

DRAKE GATHERED his rifle and other things before leaving the house.

He'd watched as the blast blew Jax and Griggs clear of the house.

It happened just as he stepped outside the house.

Jax would have run right into him if it hadn't happened then.

He stowed his gear in a bag.

While the EMT was cleaning up Jax's face, Drake was scaling a fence and crossing the street where a car was waiting for him.

He picked up his phone and dialed.

"It's done, and I have something that will distract the FBI and put that agent out of commission for a while," Drake said.

"Good, he was getting too close." The voice said.

"What do you want me to do now?" Drake asked.

"Everything has a ribbon on it out there. You can come in. I'm sure I can find something for you here. If you get him out of the way, everything will be ready."

"Send the plane. I'll be leaving."

"It's already on the tarmac," the voice said.

He took the car to the airport, dropped it off after wiping it down, and took a shuttle to the Executive Terminal.

The plane was sitting on the tarmac, as the man on the phone said.

He walked inside the plane, sat down, and had a shot of whiskey.

CHAPTER TWENTY-FIVE

WHILE DRAKE'S plane taxied down the runway, Jax and Griggs stood next to one another at the airport check-in.

They hurried through the TSA.

Jax's phone rang, and he stared at it.

"Who is it?" Griggs asked.

"Abrams," Jax replied.

"The man is like a hound on a trail," Griggs said.

"Yep, and I'm the raccoon," Jax said.

He put it away, and they walked to their gate and waited.

The flight boarded, and they took their seats.

They had no idea what was going on with the investigation in Las Vegas or why Abrams had called them.

But Webb's body had been found. Abrams wondered why half the man's skull was missing.

It was a question he'd have to ask Jackson Reed when he saw him.

CHAPTER TWENTY-SIX

JOHNNY SAT at the counter of the diner, eating his lunch.

It was the first time he'd been out of the house in a week, and he needed to get supplies. He also wanted something other than ramen noodles and canned soup, which led him to the diner.

"The darn thing roared over my farm. It was the damndest thing I ever saw. Black as midnight and quiet as a ghost," he heard from a table and tried not to laugh.

"What are you laughing at, Randall," the man asked Johnny.

It took him a minute to realize the man was talking to him.

"Just listening to you talk about this thing. Are you sure it wasn't an alien? Have your cows been mutilated?"

The man glared at him, "You can joke all you want, but it hovered in the air for a minute, then took off."

"You haven't been down from your mountain in a while. The whole county is talking about this thing. They said it looks military or something. Black as a raven and glides around like a ghost."

"You saw it?" the man asked.

"Nope," Johnny said.

"What are you doing on that mountain of yours?" another man asked.

"Just waiting for spring to arrive. Got a lot of planting to do."

There was a lot of agreement on that topic as it moved around the diner.

"You know," another man said, "they say that mountain is haunted. My daddy said there's supposed to be an Indian burial ground up there. I have never seen it, but I heard tell about it."

"Did he say that before or after they put him away?" the waitress asked.

"You say what you want, but that thing flying around is a bad omen. Stuff like that leads to other things." The man said.

"Lights in the sky, little green men. Those kinds of things?" Johnny asked.

"You can joke all you want, Randall, but that thing flying around means something," the man said.

"You better watch out, "Johnny said, "it may getcha."

He stood up, paid his bill, and walked out to his truck.

The snow started when he'd come down the mountain. Then it came down harder once he reached the road's end.

He brushed the snow off his truck, checked the chains he'd put on his tires, and pulled out of the parking lot.

It was a long drive up to the cabin, and when he reached the gate, he pressed the button, and it opened.

He pulled through and watched it close behind him as he drove to the cabin.

When he reached it, he got out, carried his few groceries into the house, and put them away.

Afterward, he ran the snowblower over the patch of tarmac.

The drone was in the garage, and he loaded it with all the armaments he'd need.

The guns under the nose were the most difficult to load, as the small chambers in the front of the aircraft were inside, where a cockpit would be. He was barely able to secure them. The bombs and missiles were attached securely, and he pulled them out of the garage.

When he'd finished, the sun was barely below the horizon. He went inside, opened his room, and fired up the drone.

It rose above the trees with no problems.

Johnny watched on his screen as the treetops disappeared from view and the lights of the town illuminated the horizon.

He banked left and followed the road to the man from the diner's house.

The drone hovered in the air. Johnny watched the man and his family eating dinner.

He turned right and flew towards DC.

He made his practice run. It was the first he'd done in a few days and the only one he'd done with the drone fully loaded.

He'd become completely comfortable with the drone on his flights and understood how it would handle any condition.

The trial run finished, he turned the aircraft around and flew back to town.

He stopped at the man's farm again and stirred up the cattle.

Johnny pushed the throttle as hard as it would go and stared as a warning popped on his screen.

Bomb partially detached.

Flashed on his screen.

He flew it back, landed, and ran out to the drone.

The front part of the bomb had come off the railing and hung by its backside.

He hadn't armed them, but a bomb falling in the middle of a field, even unarmed, would cause a lot of noise.

Johnny stared at them, brought the rack out, unloaded the bomb from the pylon, and checked the connections. The aircraft was secure, but the quick throttle-up had caused it to come loose.

I need to keep a better eye on that.

CHAPTER TWENTY-SEVEN

THEIR PLANE TOUCHED DOWN, and Jax stared at a nearby TV as breaking news appeared on the screen.

It was a video of a man in a house.

His gun was raised, and what looked like a powder flash came off the gun as the other man's head exploded.

Griggs stared at the screen.

"Shit," she said, "you're being set up," she said.

"Yeah, I think we both are." He said.

They hurried through security and out to the street.

Then text messages and calls started on their phones.

"Jax, it's my dad. What do I tell him?" she asked.

"I already told him the truth. What else can we tell him?" he asked.

She answered the phone and stared at him. She put it on speaker.

"Vanessa, where is Reed?"

"We took separate rides back from the airport. He's probably on his way home." She smoothly replied, glancing up at Jax.

"Good, we're at his place waiting for him. Did you see the video?" he asked.

"Yes, I did. But that's not how it happened." Griggs protested.

"That doesn't matter. I need both of you to come in." He said.

"We're being set up." She argued.

"The press is having a field day already. Since the video dropped, it's crazy in here." He said.

"When did it drop, and from where?" she asked.

"Someone put it up on YouTube and tagged a few news agencies. It's gone viral since then." He said.

"I need you to come in. If you talk to Jackson, have him do the same. Vanessa, please be careful. Love you," he said.

"I will. Love you," she said.

The call ended, and Jax and Griggs stared at each other.

"Do you have somewhere you can go for a while?" she asked.

"Not really," he replied.

"Okay. I'll go in and find out what the hell is going on. You should get yourself a burner phone." She advised.

"Already on it," he replied.

He pulled the sim card from his phone and snapped it.

Griggs turned her phone off and put it in her bag.

"I'll find out what's going on. Call me when you're able." She said.

"I will," Jax assured her.

The car dropped him off at a rundown hotel outside of DC. He hurried into the office of the hotel and booked a room.

It was small, not like the one he'd had in Vegas. He wasn't sure if the room had been updated since the eighties.

He walked out of the room and across the street to a convenience store.

Jax purchased a phone and a few minutes.

He got back to his room and called Sarah.

"Hello," she answered.

"It's me," he said.

"Jackson? What the hell is going on?" she asked.

"I can't talk long. I want you to know I didn't do what that video says."

"It's pretty damning," she said.

"I know, but I didn't do it. I don't know what's happening, but someone wanted me off this case. They killed a man to do it."

"Okay," she said and hung up.

"FUCK!" Jax yelled, then thought about the rooms around him.

There weren't many cars in the parking lot, and it never crossed his mind that this place was rented by the month, not just the night.

The person in the room next to him stared at the wall and scratched at his skin. They set down their pipe and slid it under the bed.

Jax lay down on the bed and waited for whatever would happen next. It didn't take long before he fell asleep.

CHAPTER TWENTY-EIGHT

THE RIDE SHARE dropped Griggs off at her apartment. She took two steps towards the front door when officers moved in.

"Vanessa Griggs, you need to come with us," a man said.

"What's this about?" she asked.

"Vanessa, let's go," Decker stepped past the other officers.

"Hi, Daddy," she said.

Decker frowned at her.

"Search her and put her in my car," he ordered.

She stared at him.

They found her firearm and handed it to Decker.

"Where is he, Vanessa?" he asked.

"We took separate cars. I told you that on the phone."

"Fine," he said, and they put her in the back seat of Decker's car.

The car drove through the morning traffic of DC, making detours until they found themselves stuck in it anyway.

"Tell me what happened?" Decker said.

"You've seen the video and don't believe me."

"Vanessa, I'm your dad too. Give me a break," he said.

"Okay, but this is what happened."

She relayed the exact thing that Jax had told him the night before.

"The video says something different." He said.

"I don't know anything about the video. The house looked clean. But from what I saw, the camera was in the corner of the room."

"Okay, let us go from that. The camera shows the bullet striking Webb in the head. Then he's dead."

"Right, but Jax never fired his gun. When you find Webb's body, you'll understand that there's no way the bullet fired from Jax's gun did the damage to Webb's skull. It was a bigger round than Jax's sidearm. The person was in the house across the water. They were from an elevated position. They could have shot both of us; luckily, that didn't happen. I think they must have wanted Jax and me out of the way. We did a lot of interviews, and all the evidence led to Webb, though...."

"Though what?" Decker asked.

"A few witnesses said there was another man involved. He was probably the shooter. He looked like the military type, from what everyone told us."

"So, this other person, who did he work for?" Decker asked.

"I have no idea. We didn't get that far. We were talking to Webb about it when his head exploded."

They pulled up to the FBI building, and Decker pulled his car into the underground parking after showing his badge.

The guard's stare shifted to Vanessa, who had been silent in the backseat.

"Prisoner?" the guard asked.

"Something like that," Decker replied.

He drove to his parking spot, and they got out.

"Vanessa, I know you're trying to protect him, but we need to talk to him too. Hearing it from you makes me feel better, but those above me will want to hear it from him." Decker said.

He led her to the elevator, swiped his badge, and the doors opened.

The elevator rose with them in it, and once it stopped, they stepped out.

The agents glanced from Griggs to Decker.

"Sir, they're waiting for you," the agent said.

Decker led her towards a large meeting room. It was in the middle of the floor, separated from the other cubicles and offices.

Decker frowned as they approached the room.

Griggs looked inside the room, and her heart skipped a beat.

CHAPTER TWENTY-NINE

"NOW, take it easy. They only want answers. Be honest, and it will be over. We'll go home and see your mom." Decker said.

He opened the door, and DNI Williams sat at the head of the desk.

"Please, take a seat," he said.

"Sir, I wasn't aware you were sitting in on this?" Decker said.

"I'm not sitting. I'm leading," Williams said.

Griggs stared at her father, then at the other two people around the table.

"I am FBI Director Johnson," a man to the right of Williams said.

"And I am CIA Director Phillips," a woman to the left of Williams said.

Griggs stared at both of them.

"Why are you all here?" Griggs asked.

"We'll be asking the questions, and you will answer them," Williams said.

"You can leave, Decker," Director Johnson said.

"Sir?" Decker asked.

"Thank you for bringing her in. We'll handle it from here," Williams said.

Decker mouthed. 'I'm sorry,' and left the room.

The glass around them frosted, and there was a moment where the whole room buzzed as listening countermeasures engaged.

Griggs glanced at the glass, shook her head, and stuck her finger in her ear to try and clear the buzzing noise.

"We have enabled countermeasures to eliminate recording devices," Johnson said.

"Tell us what happened in Las Vegas," Williams said.

Griggs stared from him to the other two.

Griggs related the events of the past few days to the best of her recollection.

"Why didn't you stay at the scene as Detective Abrams suggested?" Williams asked.

"I know how it might look. I know Jax's history with Webb."

The group stared at one another, opened a file folder, then closed it.

"So you know about the rumors about Jackson Reed and David Webb?" Johnson asked.

"Jax told me the circumstances of his departure from the Air Force. He didn't hold back. He was convinced Webb was the reason."

"But you have no evidence of this, do you?" Phillips asked.

"No, we don't. I would have recorded the conversation if I'd known I'd be covered in Webb's brains moments later."

"So you saw the event then?" Williams asked.

"I've said this already. We were talking to him and then...."

"Then what?" Williams asked.

"Webb said something to antagonize Jax, who pulled his gun, then the bullet ripped through Webb's head."

"So Reed did pull his gun as the video shows?" Johnson asked.

"Yes, but it was because Webb said something to piss him off. Jax was going to put the gun away when the bullet blew Webb's head open."

The group stared at her.

She knew they didn't believe her or felt they didn't.

"So, this drone, what did you find out about the crash?" Johnson asked.

Griggs smiled at him, then glanced to DNI Williams, who looked frozen in time.

"It didn't crash. It was stolen." Griggs said.

Williams glanced away from her.

"Are you saying someone stole a top-secret military drone?" Johnson asked.

"Yes, but I thought you all knew that. DNI Williams did. He's the one who put Jax on this case."

"What are you talking about?" Phillips asked.

"When the case came down, someone decided that Jax should be the lead. He was on leave with his daughter when he got the call."

Williams stared at her, his face turning red.

The other two turned to face Williams.

"Aaron, what is she talking about?" Phillips asked.

"When the case came before my desk, I felt Reed was the best person for the job. I knew he was on leave, but he knows the base, knows its people. Putting him on the case was a no-brainer."

"And you called the AG to have an agent assigned specifically to a case?" Johnson asked.

"I did," Williams said.

"Wait," Phillips said, "what's going on with the drone?"

"We've been putting pieces together. Webb gave us some

information that will help, but there are other things we were investigating."

"So the drone is gone?"

"Yes, we have no idea where it is," Griggs replied.

Phillips turned and stared at Williams.

"Why would you keep this from us?" she asked.

Griggs stared at the woman.

She knew her, as did most in the Air Force. She'd been a pilot in the first Gulf War, shot down, and made her way to safety. Then she'd been shot down in the first days of Afghanistan. That time she did not make it to safety. She was able to escape, turned in her wings, and moved to Air Force Intelligence, where she rose quickly through the ranks. Her determination led her to get the CIA Director's chair.

Griggs watched her confirmation hearings and greatly admired the woman.

"It was a need-to-know basis. The President didn't want it out. He felt it would tarnish his legacy."

"So, you're telling me we have no idea where this drone is?" Johnson asked.

Griggs had watched his confirmation hearings as well but found them boring. He'd been a politician before being appointed. He had almost no history as a lawman or agent, but the party in power pushed for him anyway.

Griggs didn't care for him much, but she still wanted to be an FBI agent, and she'd have to choose her words carefully.

"No, we don't," Griggs said.

"So, your investigation led to Webb, who said someone contacted him about making some extra money. They told him what needed to happen, but he never met the person?" Phillips asked.

"Yes, but he thought it was someone high up on the food chain."

"What made him think that?" Phillips asked.

Griggs cleared her throat and wiped her hands on her pants.

"He'd had a couple of disciplinary filings from female airmen. It was whoever made those go away," Griggs said.

Phillips stared at her. The woman's face was scarlet, with the rage building up in her.

"So he attempted to assault female airmen, and what, someone took care of it?" Phillips asked.

"That's the gist we got from Webb," Griggs replied.

"Who would have that kind of power?" Johnson asked.

"There are so many names above him. It could take a while to figure out who the person was," Phillips said.

"Do you know where Agent Reed is?" Williams asked.

"As I told Agent Decker, we took different cars from the airport. I'm not sure where he is."

"Let me see your phone?" Williams asked.

"Sir?" Griggs asked.

"I want to have it run. It will tell us where you've been."

"Sadly, the blast destroyed my phone. I landed on it when the house blew up." Griggs said.

A flat-out lie. Griggs's phone rested in her pocket.

"Fine, do you have Reed's number?"

"Yes, I do," she replied.

"Could we have it please?" Williams asked.

"I'm sure you already have it," Griggs replied.

"Okay, we're going to let you go, but if he gets a hold of you in any way, please let us know," Phillips said.

Griggs stood up, adjusted her shirt, and walked to the door.

She walked into the hallway as the room erupted. Griggs knew what was happening in the room, but she wanted no part.

"Vanessa, what happened?" Decker asked.

"I'm to report to them if Jax calls."

"That's it? They're not going to lock you up?"

"I think I'm the bait. They want to see if he'll contact me."

"I'll take you home," Decker said.

"I'll get a ride," she replied.

He followed her down the main elevator to the front of the building.

She opened her phone and called for a car.

It arrived a few minutes later. She got in, and the car drove off.

Decker watched her disappear into the late morning DC traffic.

CHAPTER THIRTY

JAX STARED out the window and wondered what was going on with Griggs.

He picked up the phone and her number.

"Hello," she said.

"It's me," Jax replied.

"You shouldn't call me. I sat in a meeting with the DNI, Director of the FBI, and CIA. I'll call you later."

Jax ran through everything he'd learned up to Webb's skull decorating the living room.

The test pilot, Johnny Milburn, the other person everyone had mentioned, whom he was near certain had been the shooter. He got out a notepad he'd found on the desk in his room.

He thought about it, and his stomach rumbled.

His wallet sat on the nightstand. He set the pad down and opened it. There were a few hundred dollars in it, which he felt would get him through the next couple of days.

Jax walked out of the room, locking the door behind him.

The door to the room next to his opened. A skinny white

guy stared at him. The man's face looked like his skin had been pulled tight around his skull.

Junky.

"Hey, buddy," Jax said.

The guy flinched and backed away.

"I want to give you something," Jax said.

"If it's anything like that screaming I heard in there, I'll pass," the man said.

"Sorry if I scared you. What do you say we be friends? You tell me if anyone comes near my room, I give you this," Jax said, producing a twenty from his pocket.

The man stared at it.

"We have a deal?" Jax asked.

"Sure thing," the guy said, "just don't do that screaming again."

"Right, sorry about that. I saw something in the room." Jax said.

"Yeah, these rooms do that. I thought I saw something last night, but it was a nightmare."

Jax handed him the twenty and hurried towards the stairs.

He'd seen a McDonald's when the car had dropped him off, and he was starving.

Jax nodded at the man when he reached the bottom. The man snapped to attention and fled into his room.

Jax laughed and walked to the McDonald's.

The restaurant was quiet. He was the only one in the dining room, though a man sat in the children's play area with his two kids, staring off into space.

A TV was on in the corner, streaming the day's news, and Jax glanced up after ordering his food.

His face was the topic of the day.

The video replayed over and over but cut out the part where the back of Webb's head exploded.

He walked to the back of the dining room, sat down, and waited for his food. It came a few moments after he'd sat down.

Jax glanced up at the kid, maybe sixteen, who'd brought his food.

He devoured his breakfast. He'd always liked the pancakes at McDonald's, but he wasn't sure if he'd tasted them this time. His coffee sat next to him as he watched the man in the children's area. The man's two kids, a boy and a girl who were possibly twins, ran around the room while he tried to wrangle them. It was not going well for the man.

Jax turned away and peered through the window.

Snow had started, and while the hotel was close, he hadn't brought his coat. It sat on the bed with his other clothes.

He froze when a cop car pulled into a slot.

Jax hurried into the bathroom as the cop pushed on the door. As the cop ordered his food, Jax came out and fled through a side door. Jax glanced back and saw his picture on the screen one last time.

The kid who'd delivered his food saw him, turned, and stared at the picture on the screen.

"That guy was just in here," the kid said to the cop.

"What guy?" the cop asked.

"That one," the kid pointed to the TV screen.

CHAPTER THIRTY-ONE

JAX TURNED to the right and ran towards the motel as the cop pursued him out of the McDonald's. The sirens burst to life, and Jax ran to his room, grabbed a few things, and stared out the window as the cop's car flew past the motel.

Jax opened the door, and the skinny man next door stared him down from across the hall.

"That for you?" the man asked.

"Maybe," Jax replied.

"Well, if they come back, I'll tell them I didn't see ya," the man said.

Jax knew better. He'd bribed the man with a twenty. The cops would do the same to get the information out of him.

He took off running, and the siren was approaching quickly. Jax ran to the back of the parking lot and winced as the fence came into view. A big open field stood beyond it, but the siren grew louder. Jax scaled it and landed on the other side, his feet sinking into the mud.

Tall grass grew in the field, and Jax hid in the snow and dead grass as the cop car pulled into the lot.

He watched for a minute as the cop got out and hurried into

the motel's office. The man came out a few minutes later with the person who'd checked him in earlier. Jax turned and ran, his feet sloshed in the muddy field and dead grass. At times, the mud swallowed his feet up to his lower shins, and he'd had to grab onto them to yank them free.

Jax glanced down at his shoes. They were his work shoes. He knew the shine they'd once had would never return, and he wished he'd worn other shoes.

He pulled his jacket tight around his shoulders and hurried to the other side of the field, reaching one of the more run-down areas of the city.

A couple of men walked out of their house and stared at him.

"Hey, that for you?" one of the men asked, pointing to the emergency lights at the motel.

"Maybe," Jax said.

"What did you do?" the other man asked.

"Long story. Is there a Metro station near here?" Jax asked.

"Sure, man. Go down this street, turn this way," he waved his hand to the right, "take a left, and there's a station."

"Thanks," Jax said.

"It's cool. We've all had the law after us," the man said.

Jax took off running, his feet sliding around in his shoes. He knew he'd have blisters with how wet his feet were but kept running.

He made the left and stared as a Metro line descended into the earth's bowels.

Jax stared at the few people standing around and pulled the hood over his head. He hurried down the escalators into the station below.

Most of the stations were well lit; the current one he stood in was not one of them.

Jax's bag was over his shoulder. It was not much beyond an

overnight bag. He'd stuffed a few things in the bag but had left the rollaway in the room. He bought his ticket from a kiosk and passed through the gate.

Electronic boards warned of delays coming for the inauguration.

Jax had heard they shut down service during inaugurals for safety reasons. You can't have the trains running under The Mall with the possibility of an explosion.

He got to the station below. The train was nearly full, but Jax knew it would take him in the direction he needed. Jax held onto the hand grips as the train moved along.

When it reached its destination, he disembarked and followed the crowd up the escalators.

The Mall itself was full of people, which made him feel better. He could blend into the crowd and disappear. At least, that was his hope.

Some people wore t-shirts proclaiming their party allegiance, while others wore shirts of Elaine Franklin. There were others with pictures of President Thompson and Vice-President, which made no sense to Jax. If you lost, you lost. Why carry the torch?

He followed the group past a cop, who studied him as Jax walked by.

Jax was on The Mall with a bag slung over his shoulder, his hood over his head, he hadn't shaved since the day before, and his eyes darted back and forth in the crowd.

The crowds of people converged on the Washington Monument, and Jax moved with one group as it meandered towards the White House. He stayed with this group as it moved down Pennsylvania Avenue towards the scaffolding set up for the inauguration.

Jax glanced up at the scaffolding and ducked his head, hurrying away as security moved swiftly about the site.

He pulled his phone out again and called Griggs.

"Where are you?" she asked.

"On The Mall," Jax replied.

"Why on earth would you do that? The security is crazy tight."

"Yeah, but there are tons of tourists. I'm blending in well."

"We need to talk," she said.

"Sure, where?" Jax asked.

"The Cascade Cafe at the National Gallery," Griggs replied.

"Sure, I'll wander around for a while, dodging cops." He said.

"Jax, come on," Griggs said, "I'm near there, anyway."

"Okay, but if you're not here in fifteen minutes," Jax said, "I'm walking."

The call ended, and Jax stuffed the phone in his pocket.

As flurries started, he walked across the Mall, and the wind picked up. He pulled his jacket close, but its fleece lining was no match for the bitter cold air coming off the Potomac.

By the time he'd reached the Gallery, his hands were red, his face was chapped, and his hands were raw from where he'd kept rubbing them.

The snow had moved from flurries to a full-blown blizzard in the time it took him to reach the Cafe.

Griggs sat at a table in the corner. Two cups of coffee sat in front of her.

Jax walked up behind her, grabbed one of the cups, and sat down.

"Hey," she said, then saw it was him.

He sat down, pulled his hood off, and glanced around.

"Don't worry. It's just me. I didn't bring anyone with me."

"What were you doing near The Mall?" Jax asked.

"I'd just left the Hoover," she replied.

"Did you check for tails?" he asked.

"Yes," Griggs said, "I took two trains back and forth to lose my tail."

"So, what happened at the meeting?" Jax asked and sipped at his coffee, and although it could use some sugar, he wrapped his hands around it to warm himself.

Griggs relayed everything that happened at her meeting.

Jax sat quietly until she finished.

"So, Williams didn't even tell the member of the Security Council?" Jax asked.

"Sounds that way," Griggs replied.

"I think this other pilot, Johnny Milburn needs to be found," Jax said.

"I agree, but where do we start?" Griggs asked.

"Maybe we need to talk to Williams? He's the one who put me on this case. He must have a reason for doing that."

"What did they say about Webb when you told them the truth?" Jax asked.

Griggs averted her gaze from her coffee to the pictures around her.

"They didn't believe you, did they?" Jax asked.

"I don't think so," she replied.

"What did your mom say when you went home?" Jax asked.

"Haven't been home yet," Griggs replied.

Jax opened his bag and pulled out a giant pink flamingo.

"I need you to get this to Lizbeth," he said.

Griggs stared at the pink thing. Its eyes took up half of its face and made her skin crawl.

"'It's kind of creepy looking," she said.

"I don't think so. She'll like it, trust me," Jax said.

He glanced around the room as a security guard walked in.

"I have to go. I need to find a place to crash," he said.

Griggs stared at him.

"What happened to the motel?"

He relayed the story about the cop.

"Well, that didn't take long," she said.

"I'm sure the FBI is all over the motel," Jax said.

Griggs nodded and sipped her coffee.

It had turned cool in the time they'd been talking.

"Is there anyone you can stay within DC?" she asked.

"There are a couple of old Air Force buddies. They work in the White House, so I'm not sure they'd agree to it, but that's all I have."

"Try them. If that doesn't work, we'll figure something out."

Jax glanced at the security guard, who stared at him and spoke into his wrist. Jax stood up.

"I've been made," he said.

Griggs handed him some money.

"I can't take that," Jax said.

"You need some different clothes. You look like you're homeless." She said.

He nodded, stuffed the money in his pocket, and then hurried to the door.

The security guard ran towards him, but Griggs stood up and blocked his way.

Jax hurried onto the plaza, towards some shops on the outskirts of the Mall.

He entered a store and stared at the boots on the wall.

His feet had become sore from the shoes he'd been wearing. The blisters on his feet, where they'd slid, chafed, and rubbed against his sock and shoe. He nearly screamed when he sat down and took them off.

"Can I help you, sir?" one of the salespeople asked.

"Yes, I need some shoes. These are not working in this weather." Jax said.

The man stared at Jax's feet. He'd slipped his socks off, and blood came from one of the blisters and soaked his sock.

"Do you have money for shoes?" the man asked.

In his early twenties, a stripe of purple ran through his blond hair.

Jax stood up. There was a mirror in front of him that he hadn't noticed. His hair was matted from the snow, his beard was messy, and the redness around his eyes worsened.

He pulled the money Griggs gave him and showed it to the salesperson.

"Yes, I can. I also need pants and shirts," Jax said.

"What size?" the man asked.

"Extra-large shirts and 36 by 34 pants, size eleven boots," Jax said.

The salesperson walked away, and Jax rubbed at his feet, carefully avoiding the bit of torn flesh on his feet where it had been bleeding.

He glanced up at himself in the mirror.

"A fine mess we've gotten into," he said to his reflection.

The salesperson returned with everything he'd asked for.

"Where is the changing room?" he asked.

He showed him a set of doors in the back of the store.

Jax hobbled on his foot, carried the items to the changing room, and locked the door.

The changing room was small, and Jax sat on the bench inside.

After trying everything on, he carried what fit up to the counter.

Jax grabbed a beanie and a pair of socks off the rack, adding them to the pile.

The salesperson at the register rang it all up. Jax paid and smiled at him, "Is there a place I can change into these?"

"They're yours. Use the changing room you used before." She said.

"Is there a pharmacy or something around here?" Jax asked.

"There's a CVS up the street to the right," they said.

Jax changed into his new clothes and waved as he left, tossing the old ones into a trash bin.

His foot still hurt, but he walked in the direction the salesperson directed him. He stopped in front of a Patagonia store and purchased a coat. The snow came down heavily, and Jax felt the wind striking him as he hurried towards the CVS on the corner.

Security in the mall was tight, which he expected.

He hurried into a restroom after purchasing a razor and something for his foot in the CVS. He shaved off his beard and mustache, straightened his hair to look better, and walked out.

He hurried toward The Mall and noticed more people with Elaine Franklin shirts, but there were still the others from the losing party. An agitated group drew Capitol police and allowed Jax to lose any tails he'd attained.

He pulled out his phone and dialed a number he hadn't wanted to call.

"Fred, it's Jackson," he said into the phone.

"Jax, you shouldn't be calling me," the man said.

"I know, but I need a place to stay," Jax said.

"You can't stay with me. Try one of the shelters. You'll have better luck there, and you'll be invisible."

"Where are the shelters?" Jax asked.

"There's the 801. If you get there early, you can get a bed. It's only for those who identify as male, and you can get a shower and a meal. I helped with that one."

"Oh, that's right, I forgot you were doing that," Jax said.

"Go to that one," Fred said.

"I was set up," Jax said.

"Jax, I can't talk to you. If they trace my phone, I'll lose my job. Go to the shelter. They'll take care of you there. Most people go there when they don't have another option. It's going to get cold tonight. Please stay warm." Fred said and ended the call.

Jax glanced up at the falling snow and headed towards the shelter.

He'd passed by it and hadn't noticed it but got in line.

The person at the door asked for his ID, he showed them, and they let him in.

CHAPTER THIRTY-TWO

DECKER STEPPED out of the car and walked toward the National Gallery of Art.

Griggs sat in a chair with an FBI agent standing next to her.

"What's she doing here?" he asked.

"She was seen talking to the suspect," one of the security guards said.

Decker stared at her.

"Who called in the sighting?" he asked.

"Security," the agent replied.

"You take his statement?" Decker asked.

"Yes, sir," the agent replied.

Decker only started at Griggs.

"What are we doing with her, Sir?" the agent asked.

"I'll talk to her," Decker said.

"She refused to give us anything. When this man approached, she said she was here to look at art. He was haggard-looking. The guard said they talked for a few minutes before he realized who the man was."

"Really? I guess I'll have to interview her about this," Decker said.

The agent walked away, and Decker sat in the chair Jax had occupied earlier.

"So, talk," he said.

"Not much to say," Griggs replied.

"I thought I told you to stay away from this?"

"I've been involved with this since it started. I will finish it. We're still chasing things here."

"Here?" Decker asked.

"We left Vegas and ended up here because it went cold when Webb died. We have a few leads, but that's it. We're still on the case."

"No, you're not. After you left, DNI and the others pulled me aside. You are off the case until this situation with Reed is solved. I don't know what you said to those people, but they were pissed. When I walked in, DNI Williams looked like he was going to have a stroke."

"Yes, I'm sure he did," Griggs said.

"Vanessa, where has Jax gone?"

"I have no idea," she replied.

"We found a motel he was staying at in the worst part of the city. A cop saw him and gave chase, but Jax vanished on him. We have his bag and a few of his things."

The agent returned and stared at Griggs.

"The guard said she gave him something before he took off. She also ran interference so he could get away."

"Damn it, Vanessa," Decker said.

"You know her?" the agent asked.

"He's my dad," Griggs said.

The agent studied Griggs with her dark skin, then Decker with his white skin.

"Right," the agent said.

"She's not my biological daughter, but my daughter," Decker said.

The agent hurried away.

"I'm expecting a call from the Director after this. I think you should go home and stay there."

"It sounds like you're grounding me?" Griggs asked.

"Call it whatever you want. But you're not only being taken off the case, but you're also being placed on leave," Decker said.

"Under whose authority?"

"There were calls made to your CO, and it was requested that you be put on leave. So you're on leave until all of this is figured out."

She stood up and walked to the door.

"Vanessa, I'm sorry," he said.

"Yeah, I know," she said.

The agent stepped forward.

"What are we doing with her?"

"Take her home," Decker said.

The agent walked over, leading Griggs by the arm out the door. She pulled away, and Decker sat at the table.

His phone rang, and he stared at it.

"Yes, Director," Decker answered.

"In my office," Director Johnson said.

"Yes, Sir," Decker replied.

He walked out of the National Gallery across The Mall to the Hoover building, showed his badge, and took the elevator to the top floor.

The Director's secretary smiled at him.

"Go in, Agent Decker," she said.

Decker took a seat in front of the man's desk.

"DNI wants you suspended," Johnson said.

"On what grounds?"

"Your agent is AWOL, your daughter is in the middle of this case, and then there's the tape. He talked to the AG, who called me. We believe pulling you would be detrimental to the safety of this nation. We don't know what's going on with that drone; amazingly, it hasn't made it into the press. I don't know what's happening with DNI, but he's lying to Director Phillips, which unnerved me. Your priority is Jackson Reed. Your daughter is at home?" Johnson asked.

"I sent her there with another agent," Decker said.

"Good, let's get this solved. You're excused," Johnson said.

CHAPTER THIRTY-THREE

AFTER GRIGGS ARRIVED HOME, she stared at the flamingo Jax gave her, and along with the address, she knew where she'd be going.

The agent who'd dropped her off sat outside in his car.

He'd told her he was supposed to watch her, make sure she didn't go anywhere.

Griggs, alone in the house, stepped out the back and crossed into the neighbor's yard. She called for a car and had it take her to the address.

She rang the bell and waited. A man with a beard opened the door.

"Can I help you?" he asked.

"I'm looking for Sarah Reed," Griggs said.

"What is this about?" he asked.

"I work with Jax. He told me to bring this for Elizabeth," Griggs said. She pulled the flamingo from her bag.

The man smiled and led her inside.

"Hold on," he said, "I'll get Sarah."

Griggs glanced around the entranceway. Little knick-knacks

laid on every shelf, and there wasn't a spot that wasn't taken by some small ceramic, doll, or animal.

A dark-haired woman came in from a pocket door in the back of the room.

"I'm Sarah," she said.

"I'm Griggs. I work with Jackson," she said.

"Ah, what can I do for you?" Sarah asked.

"He asked me to give this to Elizabeth. He's currently unable to do so," Griggs said and handed the flamingo over.

Sarah stared at it, and a girl of about eleven ran up to her.

"You saw my dad?" the girl asked.

"I did. He told me to bring this to you," Griggs said.

"Where is he?" Elizabeth asked.

"He's not able to bring it over, but he wanted to ensure you got it."

"Thank you," Elizabeth said as she hugged the flamingo tightly.

She ran to another part of the house, leaving Griggs and Sarah in the foyer.

"So, how is he?" Sarah asked.

"'Jax is stressed with the video and other things," Griggs said.

"Other things?" Sarah asked.

"It's taking some adjusting for him."

"Well, it's been a couple of years, and I couldn't wait any longer," Sarah said.

"I'm here to give her the flamingo. Jax is good at his job and cares about you and Elizabeth."

"Funny, he never said any of these things when we were together. How did you get so close in such a short period?"

Griggs felt funny standing in the foyer and glanced into the other room.

"Oh, yes," Sarah said, "let's sit down. You're probably tired."

"You have no idea," Griggs replied.

She glanced around the room. It was all in a floral print. Flowers of one type or another decorated the shelves in either ceramic form or shadow box.

"We've been through some things. I'm sure you saw the video, but you don't know the truth behind it. That video was doctored. Jax didn't kill that man."

Sarah stared at her, then looked to the other side of the room.

Griggs turned around and saw the man who'd opened the door.

"This is Tom," Sarah said.

"We met, but we were not introduced," Griggs said.

Tom looked from one to the other, then retreated down the hallway.

"You know he still wears his ring?" Griggs asked.

Sarah stared at the ring on her finger. It was completely different from the one on Jax's finger.

Griggs smiled.

"I heard you're getting married. Congratulations," Griggs said.

"Yes, it will be sometime in the fall. Tom needs to get past the inauguration. It's a busy time for him." Sarah said.

"What does Tom do?" Griggs asked.

"He's going to be the Chief of Staff for Elaine Franklin," Sarah said.

"Oh, wow, that's great," Griggs replied.

"We're taking Elizabeth to the inauguration."

"Nice," Griggs replied.

"Yes, Tom has been with Elaine for a long time."

Griggs glanced around.

"Well, I think I better go." She said.

"Can you do something for me?" Sarah asked.

"Sure," Griggs replied.

"Tell him that I worry about him," Sarah said.

"You were with him for a long time?"

"Yes, right out of the Academy. He was a good pilot, then he was forced out, and everything changed."

"Why was he forced out?" Griggs asked.

"It was bad intelligence. He was doing a run over Afghanistan and dropped bombs on a wedding. There happened to be a photographer there. The picture went viral."

Griggs remembered the photo. It was published in TIME.

"If it weren't for Aaron Williams, I don't know if Jax would have recovered."

Griggs stared at her for a minute.

"You're talking about DNI Aaron Williams?" Griggs asked.

"Yes, Jax and Aaron flew together when Jax was just coming up. Williams felt bad about this intel, and he made sure Jax landed on his feet, which ended up being in the FBI."

"They have a deep history then?"

"Oh, yeah," Sarah said, "until Aaron went to intelligence, they were best friends."

"Why did Williams go to intelligence?"

"He was injured and couldn't fly anymore. So he piloted a desk," Sarah said.

"Did they have any contact after Williams went to intelligence?"

"They kept their lives separate. Aaron was on a different tract than Jax. They fell apart, but I know Aaron felt bad about Jax losing his wings."

"Did that failure cost Jax his wings or something else?"

"It was the publicity the picture received. The Air Force couldn't fire someone higher, so Jax got it."

Griggs stood up and walked to the door.

"You know he loves that little girl more than anything?"

"I know," Sarah replied.

Griggs walked out the door, staring up at the darkening sky.

Snow fell, and she thought about Jax and where he could be in the city.

She hoped he was safe and warm.

CHAPTER THIRTY-FOUR

DETECTIVE NATHAN ABRAMS walked into the ME's office and sat down.

The call had come at five that morning, and he'd stared at the clock. His wife rolled over and glared at him.

"Come on, Baby," he said.

She rolled over, and he sighed. He got up, put a clean suit on, and stopped to check on his kids, who snored in the rooms around him and his wife's room.

He returned to his wife.

"I won't be gone that long. I promise we'll go out to Town Square like you wanted to," he said.

"Okay, but I want to get lunch while we're out."

"Fine, I'll let Marcus pick, though. It's his turn." He said and bent down and kissed her.

He hurried out of the house, stopped at his favorite coffee place, and picked up an extra coffee for the ME.

The sun was cresting Sunrise Mountain, and Abrams pulled his sunshade down as he turned left into the ME's office.

The bench he sat on was an old wood one, and he thought

about how many people had been on that bench waiting to see loved ones for the last time.

"Nathan, come in here," Dr. Barkov called from the room she'd talked to Jax and Griggs in.

He handed her the extra coffee, and she smiled.

"Oh, thank you so much," she said and set it down on the table next to the burned body of David Webb.

"So, why'd you bring me here so early?" he asked.

"There are a few reasons," she pulled back the sheet from Webb's body, and the smell nearly sent Abrams over the top.

"Don't you dare puke in here, Nate," she demanded.

He swallowed hard and walked back to the body.

"So, what do you have?" he asked.

"I assume you've seen the video?" she asked.

"It's kind of hard to miss. It's been on replay everywhere. The press is having a field day with it."

"Right, well, when I watched it was before I'd examined the body and something felt off about it. When I got the body, I found out what it was."

He stared from her to the body on the table.

She held a metal stick as if she were doing a class. Which he assumed she was, and he was the student.

The stick moved to Webb's head.

"You see this entrance wound?"

"Kind of hard not to," he replied.

She slipped on some gloves and handed him the box.

He stared at it.

"He's not going to bite you, Nate," she said.

He pulled the gloves out.

"Help me turn him over," she said.

They turned him over, and she pointed to the back of Webb's skull.

"Holy shit," he said.

"You see what I'm seeing?"

"Yes, there is no way Agent Reed's 9 mm could have caused that type of damage." He said.

The entirety of the back of Webb's head was missing.

"You're saying the video is doctored?"

"Not just that," she said, "this round was powerful, possibly a rifle. Something high caliber and designed for damage."

"You're thinking a sniper round?"

"I went and talked to one of Metro's snipers. He told me that whatever struck Mr. Webb here," she pointed to the front of his head, "was high velocity and struck hard enough that there wouldn't be anything left for an exam. Then you throw in the fire, and we have almost no forensic evidence. The shell was designed to break apart on impact and blow out the back." She said.

"Thank you. I have a couple of calls to make," he said and hurried from the room.

"I'm sure you do," she said as he left.

Abrams pulled out his phone and dialed the FBI field office in Las Vegas.

"This is Detective Abrams with Metro. I need to speak to whoever is Jackson Reed's boss." He said.

He sat on the phone for a few minutes as he walked out of the building into a cool desert drizzle.

He sat in his car as the rain pattered the roof and windshield.

"Detective, this is Agent Decker. I understand you needed to speak to me about Agent Reed?"

"We did our autopsy on Webb. There is no way Reed's 9 mm fired the shot that killed him. That video is a fake."

"How do you know it's a fake?"

"If you'd seen the remnants of Webb's head, you'd understand."

"Can you send me the ME's report?" Decker asked.

"Yes, sir," Abrams said.

"Thank you, Detective Abrams," Decker said.

"Sir, is Griggs still in Las Vegas?"

"No, she flew out with Reed. Why?"

"This got me thinking. What kind of a person would frame an FBI agent?"

"Right, I can see that reasoning. I will make sure she has security around her," Decker said.

"I think she may need it," Abrams said and ended the call.

CHAPTER THIRTY-FIVE

DRAKE PEERED out his window at the sun dancing on the Potomac.

He turned on the TV and sat down.

The chyron on the news caught his attention.

'President-Elect Elaine Franklin met with incoming dignitaries this morning.'

A shot of Franklin outside her Maryland residence followed, with numerous Secret Service agents flanking her on all sides as she was ushered into a waiting car.

He picked up the phone and dialed the number.

It rang twice.

"Who is she meeting with?" he asked.

"Don't worry about it. Everything is still a go. It will be fine." The voice said.

"Right. This better pay off."

The call ended, and Drake turned off the TV.

He'd already dressed and got ready, but the sunlight glinting off the Potomac caught his attention. He watched as it rippled against its frozen banks and thought about what would come.

He started his run at the Lincoln, moved down The Mall, and across the bridge to the Jefferson Memorial.

The place always gave him comfort when he felt none. He glanced up at the writing on the dome. The statue of Thomas Jefferson appeared to stare down at him.

He crossed through the dome, past the gift shop, to a bench overlooking the river beyond.

A man walked up and sat down next to him.

"You know, this will change a lot of things if we pull it off," Drake said.

"I know, but this woman will stop at nothing to disassemble what we've created over the last eight years. It must be done." The man said.

"I will speak to him soon. His last report said everything was working fine, and he'd already done a loaded flight with no glitches." Drake said.

"I will talk to him soon as well," the man pulled a sandwich out of a bag and ate it.

He left the bag on the ground next to the bench.

Drake picked it up and carried it with him as he continued his jog across the bridge to The Mall.

He had one more stop before heading home.

There were several armed guards in front of the White House. Some of them looked like Special Ops. He wasn't sure if it was their haircuts or how they held their rifles. He speculated why the President would put Spec-Ops teams around the White House.

Drake walked past, the brown bag still in his hand. A guard watched him, but Drake continued.

He stared at the gates, the security around the gates, and moved down the road towards his residence but found himself instead staring up at the scaffolding around the Capitol.

It rose from the stone steps, wrapped around pillars, and

onto the balcony where Elaine Franklin would give her inaugural address.

The workers ignored him as he stared.

"Hey buddy, keep walking," a voice called out.

He turned, and a Capitol police officer glared at him.

Drake waved and continued on home.

CHAPTER THIRTY-SIX

GRIGGS GLANCED AT HER PHONE.

"Dad, what's going on?" she asked.

"I know you're pissed, but it looks like that video was doctored," he said.

"No shit, what made you realize that?"

"A Detective Abrams called. He said he thinks you should get a security team."

"Why?"

"He said, 'what kind of people would frame an FBI agent?',' " Decker said.

"Yeah, that is a good question. Jax and I were working on something when this video happened, but this whole thing adds another wrinkle. Are you having Jax reinstated, and me as well?"

"Yours is up to your CO, but I'm sure that will happen. After talking to him and thinking about it, I would prefer you fly out there and get the ME's report personally," Decker said.

"Why? You think someone will try to intercept it?"

"I think that we should be careful. We don't know where that drone is and have no clues."

"Well, Jax and I do, but we must look into this first," Griggs said.

"I already called your CO. You're on the next flight out."

"What did my CO say?"

"You'll have to talk to him when you get back, but Vanessa, please be careful," Decker said.

"I will, and thanks, Dad," she said.

She hurried upstairs, and her mom, who'd been in the kitchen listening to the one-sided conversation, followed her up the stairs.

"Vanessa, what's going on?" she asked.

"I have to fly back to Vegas," Griggs replied.

"Go back? I thought you were suspended?"

"It's complicated. Dad will tell you what's happening, but I have a flight to catch."

Griggs grabbed a bag, then stared at the room. It had been hers from the time she was little, but there were no clothes that fit.

Her mom continued to watch her.

Carol Decker was in her early sixties. Her once dark hair had turned gray and hung down on her face.

The lines along the woman's eyes scrunched up as she watched her daughter hurry around the bedroom.

"Dad told me I have to pick something up."

"Why can't they email it or something?"

Griggs got quiet.

"He's worried about this, isn't he," Carol Decker asked.

Griggs nodded.

"I'm flying out and going back. I'll talk to my CO when I get out there."

Her mom grabbed her by the shoulders and looked into her eyes.

"I know things haven't always been great, especially after

everything with your dad, but please be careful. You're all I have to remind me of him." Her mom said.

Griggs smiled. Her brown eyes shone in the dim light of her room.

"Don't go doing that. I'll be back either in the morning or late tonight." Griggs promised.

"Vanessa, you've had a hard time being your dad's kid. I know you got teased about how he died. Your teachers told me, but you remind me so much of your dad. He was so determined. I look at your brown eyes and see him staring back at me."

Griggs wiped at her eyes.

"Mom, what's gotten into you?"

"Nothing, I just haven't seen you in a while, and it was nice you being home." Her mom said.

Griggs hurried out the door as a car that she'd called for pulled up.

The car drove her to National, and she hurried to the gate.

When she reached it, she glanced at the clock and found that she was thirty minutes early.

She called Jax.

"I thought you said we shouldn't talk?" he said.

"I did, but I'm flying back to Vegas," she said.

"The Air Force calling you back?"

"No, my dad got a call from Abrams this morning. Said there was something wrong with the autopsy. I'm flying out to pick up the report."

"Why doesn't he just email it?"

"Abrams didn't want to. He's worried something bigger is going on, at least that's what I inferred from my talk with my dad."

Jax got quiet.

"This may get me reinstated, right?" Jax asked.

"That's what my dad thinks. Abrams believes the video was doctored."

"No shit," Jax said.

"Where are you?"

"I'm safe," he replied.

"Good, stay that way," she said.

The call ended, and Griggs stuffed her phone into her pocket.

CHAPTER THIRTY-SEVEN

JAX LOOKED at his phone and then to the ceiling overhead.

The lights of the dormitory rooms at the 801 had come on twenty minutes ago, just in time for his phone to ring.

A few people glanced in his direction, but he didn't acknowledge them, only turned away.

"Hey, buddy," a man to his left said, "aren't you the guy who blew that other one's head off?"

"Nah, it wasn't me. You have me confused with someone else," Jax replied.

Having taken a shower the night before, Jax grabbed his gear and hurried out the doors into the blowing snow.

He stared up and down the street at the people leaving the shelter, but none of them looked his way. He didn't want to look back, worrying the man who'd recognized him would be there.

Snow blanketed the streets, and the people with cars parked along it would have a hell of a time digging themselves out.

Jax ducked into the Metro and glanced around at the impressive police presence, none of which looked in his direction. He was well dressed. The clothes he'd purchased the day before looked better than those he'd tossed in the trash.

The Metro was full again, and he moved into a group of tourists.

He got off at the Castle and hurried up the stairs.

More snow blew across The Mall, but that didn't stop the multitude of people moving along The Mall.

He stared at the same guards in front of the White House that Drake had seen but was too late to see him two hours later. Not that he would have made the connection to recognizing the man.

Jax watched the guards and hurried down The Mall towards the Lincoln, crossing the street and moving away from where he had less chance of being seen.

He walked around the neighborhood, thinking, and found himself near his apartment.

A black car sat across the street, and a van was farther down. *Inconspicuous was not their strong suit.*

Jax went around the back of the apartment building and, once inside, hurried up a set of stairs.

No one was watching that side of the building, at least not that he could see.

He unlocked the front door and walked into his living room.

Books lay strewn about. The gaming console he'd bought for Elizabeth was broken. Stuffed animals lay gutted in Elizabeth's room with their internal fluff strewn about the room. His anger rose to a swell that would splash down at any moment.

The toys not destroyed sat in a line along the wall, their eyes surveying the damage to their toy brethren.

He turned and walked out, having to breathe to calm himself. He'd have to replace the damaged toys, some of which came home from the hospital with her.

He walked into his room and entered his closet. He pressed the wall on the back of the closet, and a panel opened. Jax found it when he'd moved in and wondered what the previous tenant used it for. He made no mention of it to the landlord.

A small safe lay within the panel; Jax had put that there. He opened it, removed a gun from its interior, grabbed the shoulder holster next to it, and slid the firearm into the holster.

He closed the hole as the front door opened.

Jax stepped lightly to peer around the corner.

A man, his face covered with a black ski mask, stood in the living room.

Jax stepped out.

"FBI, freeze," Jax called.

The man jerked at seeing Jax and ran out the front door into the hallway.

Jax, in pursuit, ran after him.

Moving as fast as he could, Jax ran down the stairs as the exterior door slammed. He reached for the door when something struck him from behind.

Jax collapsed to the ground.

The man in the ski mask stared at him, then ran out the door.

CHAPTER THIRTY-EIGHT

ELAINE FRANKLIN AND HER VICE-PRESIDENT, Daniel Goldman, sat across from each other and ate their lunch. It had become a tradition since they'd won the election.

"You know, Daniel, I think we have a lot of work ahead of us," she said.

He smiled and glanced at their surroundings.

They sat in the dining room of her house. Bill, and any others who'd been home when Daniel arrived, were shooed out of the house while they discussed the coming inauguration.

"I think that's an accurate assessment," he said.

"So, tell me about the people you're bringing in?" she asked.

"They're all being vetted by the Secret Service and NSA. I don't believe they enjoy their intimate details dissected like this, but it is what it is."

"I understand that feeling. I went to see the President yesterday. That man doesn't like me much, does he?" she asked.

I understand where he's coming from. You buried his Vice-President in the EC and the popular. You made his two terms look like a farce.

"If the shoe fits?"

"Yes, but I still didn't care for a few of the ads. They were ruthless."

"I liked how you buried the Vice-President's selection to replace him in the debate. Well done."

He took a drink from his coffee cup and smiled.

"Elaine, you called me here. What are we doing? Reminiscing?"

"I wanted to discuss a few things with you. You said you wanted in on all of the fine details. That's what I'm doing. We may have to deal with developments in China in the first week, and I want you to be prepared."

"Like what?"

"It appears there is a breaking off, or at least attempted breaking off, from the mainland."

"An uprising in China?"

"I received the briefing this morning. I'm sure you received it as well?"

"I did, but I haven't gone through all the material. There was quite a bit this morning."

"Yes, but the noise coming from overseas is loud."

"How did we hear about this?"

"It's in the briefing, but the location is in Xinjiang. If you remember, most of the population are Uyghur, and the government persecuted them."

"I remember the pictures and stories that came out. Are they armed?"

"We haven't heard about any of that, but when we were in Congress, there were reports of the Pakistani government bringing weapons."

"I remember, but wouldn't a move like that by the Pakistanis cause a greater conflict with China?"

"It would, but only if there is proof. The Chinese won't attack someone over a rumor. But I will say the rumors about how they're trying to quell this uprising are what disturbs me."

"What is the rumor?"

"Let's say we don't want it coming over here. It could cause another outbreak," she replied.

"I see. Have you talked to the President about this?"

"I have a meeting with him later today. I'm not looking forward to it."

"I assume DNI Williams will be there?"

"That is what I believe but have not been informed one way or another."

Daniel got up and walked to the window at the cadre of Secret Service members beyond the windows.

"What is it?" she asked.

"Look, Elaine, I know you were the star for the party, and maybe you felt pushed into this, but I am here to help," Daniel said.

Daniel Goldman had been a Senator and a pilot in the Marines. He walked with a limp from an accident. The Osprey he'd been flying was hit by small arms fire and limped back to the carrier. He lost seven soldiers.

Luckily, they'd fished him out of the Gulf. When he set the aircraft down, the rotors he'd thought had circled up were still horizontal and clipped the ship. He'd injured his back and spent months in rehab at Walter Reed. He ran for office after getting out. He sat on the Senate Intelligence Committee and had been minority whip. If Elaine Franklin hadn't selected him, he would be Senate Majority Leader in the new term. It was something he'd worked hard for.

When the offer came from Elaine Franklin, he jumped at it.

A heartbeat away from the chair was more appealing than negotiating with the other side.

"Thank you for your honesty, Daniel. I think we'll do well together."

"So do I, Madame President, so do I," he said.

CHAPTER THIRTY-NINE

JAX GLANCED up at the sky and stared around himself. A man and woman stood over him. The man wore a black coat and pants, while the woman wore a thin jacket with slacks.

"Hey buddy, you okay?" the man said.

Jax moved to get up, and his head spun.

"No, lay back. You have a nasty bump on your head. We called for an ambulance." The man said.

"I can't. I have to go," Jax said.

He grabbed the man by the shoulder and pulled himself up. The man tried to push him back down.

Sirens filled the air, and Jax knew there was no way he was going to get in an ambulance.

He took off running as tires screeched behind him.

Checking his head, it came away red and wet.

Great, I don't have time for this.

He ran into the Metro station and got on the train, using the handholds to keep himself up. There weren't as many people on the train as earlier. He walked up the stairs, crossed The Mall, and entered the Hoover.

The agent at the desk stopped him.

"Sir, you can't be in here," the woman said.

Jax, who'd kept the hood of his coat around his face, pulled it back.

The agent stepped back and drew her gun.

"I need you on the floor," she said.

Jax knelt, and his head spun again.

He woke up to the feeling of stitches being administered to his head.

"So, can't stay out of trouble," Decker asked.

Jax stared through a hazy vision at Decker.

"I guess we both have trouble with things like this," Jax groaned.

Decker sat on a chair across from him as a nurse stitched him up.

"So, who did you piss off?" Decker asked.

Jax laughed.

"I was in my apartment, and this guy comes in. I tell him to stop. He runs down the stairs and out the door. Or at least I thought he did. He faked it and hit me over the head."

"And you thought you'd run out... and do what?"

"I knew I wouldn't find him. I was out for at least ten minutes."

The nurse stopped what she was doing.

"You were out for ten minutes?" the nurse asked.

"Yes, is that bad?" Jax asked.

"You should probably get this looked at by someone else. You probably have a concussion." The nurse said.

"But I got the call from Griggs this morning, and she told me what was going on. Has the news apologized?" Jax asked.

"Well, some of them have. Another one says it's a vast conspiracy against President Thompson." Decker said.

"Figures," Jax said.

The nurse laughed and left the room.

"So, where do we go from here?"

"You're reinstated. We have someone working on the video, or at least that's what I was told." Decker said.

Jax breathed a sigh of relief, but his head pounded like a jackhammer.

CHAPTER FORTY

GRIGGS DROVE towards the front gate of Nellis Air Force Base. The line was short, and she was glad; since her flight arrived, she'd driven frantically on I-15 to reach the base.

Her flight was routine with no problems, but she faced intense scrutiny at the TSA since she was flying alone and had no baggage. As she walked through the magnetometer, it beeped. She was pulled out of line for a special screening.

She showed the TSA agent her ID, but it didn't matter, and it wasn't the first time.

Upon reaching her gate with a few minutes to spare, she hurriedly purchased a book for the flight after barely looking at the cover.

The book has been good and kept her mind off other things. Griggs received a call about Jax and his run-in with whoever had hit him over the head when she landed.

Her frantic driving along I-15 resulted from nerves and concern over Jax and whether she'd been followed to Las Vegas.

Arriving at her office, she rapped on the door of her CO's office.

A friendly "Come in" came from the other side of the door.

She walked in, and her CO stood staring out the back window.

Clinton Summers stood at almost six and a half feet tall and had played football at the Air Force Academy. She knew this because she'd once gone to a party where he'd told everyone about his past exploits on the field. This came after a few shots of Jägermeister, which Griggs did not take part in.

"So, Griggs, I understand you would like to work for the FBI," her CO asked.

'Yes, sir, that is what I plan on doing. I wanted to get my feet wet with military service, and my dad was in the Air Force, so it felt like a good fit.

"Yes, your dad was a great pilot. I looked up your father's history when you were sent to me after school. I knew I'd heard the name Griggs but wasn't sure of the context. I won't mention what happened to him, but if this is what you want, I will do everything possible to make it happen. It would be for your benefit to keep this goal to yourself. Some of your fellow airmen have an issue with success outside the ranks... They're in it for life."

"Yes, sir," Griggs replied.

"So this job, you're working with Agent Reed; what do you make of him?"

"He's a good man who got the short end. I know the news media is having a field day with the video that came out."

"To hell with the news media," her CO said, "they will find a new bone to pick for the next news cycle. I want to know your assessment of Jackson Reed?"

"He's skillful in his role as an agent, and he does good work."

"I know, Jax. I know what happened at Creech and want him to do good. I know he's had a few rough cases in the past, but I hope whatever you're getting from Detective Abrams helps your case and clears him."

"I believe it will, Sir," Griggs replied.

"We need good people like him handling things."

"I will tell him you said so if I see him again."

"If you haven't been talking to him on the side during all of this, then you're not the capable investigator I took you for. I'm sure you and he have spoken. I sometimes come off as a hard ass, but I like to care for those I've seen screwed over, and Jax is one of those."

Griggs thought about the phone call upon landing and the hit Jax took. She couldn't say so, at least not until she was cleared too, but with her CO's tone, she suspected he already knew about Jax.

She smiled.

"Dismissed, Griggs," Summers said.

Griggs turned and walked out.

She left the base, stopping at Metro downtown to pick up the report from Abrams.

Griggs walked up to the desk and asked for Abrams. They gave her a visitor's badge and motioned to the elevator.

"He'll be waiting for you on the third floor, Ma'am," the desk officer said.

Griggs rode the elevator to the third floor; the doors opened, and Abrams stood in front of her.

"We need to talk," he said.

He led her to a small desk in the corner of the office. He grabbed her a chair, and she stared at the manila folder in his hands.

"What is in here will exonerate Agent Reed. I don't know what you are chasing, but I didn't want to send it through email. A physical copy is more reliable and less likely to be seen if someone is monitoring machines. Let's begin."

Griggs stared at both of them. She'd read ballistics reports before, but the strangeness of the one in front of her threw her for a loop.

Noticing her discomfort, Abrams smiled.

"You are seeing what we're seeing?" he asked.

"Maybe," she replied.

"There is no way Agent Reed's weapon did the damage to Webb's head. It's impossible. Dr. Barkov talked to a few of our snipers. They told her that it was possibly a sniper round. Something fired at high velocity with puncturing abilities. As for the video, we had our guy go over it. There are glitches in it. He said it's pretty clean, but there are glitches in it. Have you had any of your team run the video?" Abrams asked.

"We're in the process of doing that right now," she replied.

"We've done a bit on it, especially after the report came in. I've enclosed their analysis in the folder as well."

"Thank you," Griggs said.

"I'm doing my job, according to the FBI. As for the damage to the house, there was a gas leak and residue from a device."

"So you're thinking a bomb as well as gas?"

"He needed something to trigger the gas, though...."

Griggs stared at him as he paused, "Though what?"

"It could have been an incendiary round, but I'll let the FBI look at that. We looked at the house where we believe the shot could have come from. The house was clean, immaculately clean. No prints anywhere. Whoever was in that house knew to clean up after themselves. We did find some powder residue on some curtains in an upstairs bedroom. That is where he probably fired from."

"Wow, you're thorough as hell," Griggs said.

"It's a big city, and something like this draws press, as you've noticed from the video. But what is crazy is this: I talked to a friend of Sadie Dickson. They said Webb had been to see her with another man. The other man scared the hell out of the bouncer in the club she worked at."

"We were working that angle when the video was released."

"I see. Well, he doesn't seem too friendly. He may also be the shooter. That's what I think anyway." Abrams said.

"So all of this is in the folder?" Griggs asked.

"Yes, we couldn't get a ballistics match on the type of round as it broke apart when it struck Mr. Webb. But from the video, I'm not sure we could have had that anyway. The damage was extreme, and if there were any fragments, they might have burned up in the fire."

Abrams stood up and handed her the folder. Griggs stuffed it in her bag and zipped it up.

"Is there a copy of this?" she asked.

"Yes, it's on the hard drive at my house. I worked on it late last night, then into the morning after I met with the ME."

"Thank you so much, Detective," Griggs said and stuck out her hand.

"You're welcome," he replied.

She rode the elevator to the first floor, pulled out her phone, and called Jax.

"How are you?"

"I'm okay. The stitches itch, but I'm good. What have you found in Las Vegas?"

"I'll tell you when I get back." She said.

CHAPTER FORTY-ONE

DECKER GLANCED out the window at the street below. It was the first time he'd looked out in a while.

All the people out there are oblivious to the problems around them. Not knowing that somewhere a person with a drone had plans, Decker had no idea what they could be. He'd left that up to Reed, but the man made a mistake. Where had the error been?

He lifted his phone out of its cradle and called his daughter.

"Dad, what's going on?" she asked.

"I know you're going to bring back that file, but was there anything the two of you were running down that may have caused this? What was the last thing you were looking at?" he asked.

"Are you on a work phone?" she asked.

"Yeah, why?" he asked.

"When I get back, we'll get dinner, and then we can talk about it. Just remember what Jax told you," she said and hung up.

He thought back to what Jax had told him as he walked to the elevator.

"Early lunch?" another agent asked.

"Yes, I didn't eat much breakfast," he said.

The doors to the elevator opened, and he rode it down to street level.

He'd have to think about what she said and what Jax had told him on that last call.

There was a small cafe frequented by business and FBI types. He walked in and sat in the back.

He needed the space from the early lunch crowd to parse things out.

The biggest was who would set them up and why.

The last question was the more accessible part. They'd gotten too close. The first was more difficult.

Decker ordered a BLT with fries while writing things down on a napkin. He covered it when the server returned.

She glanced at his hands, covering the napkin.

"You all are sure fidgety today," the server said.

"What do you mean?" he asked.

"Some FBI types in here today. You're hiding things like you are with that napkin. I don't usually say anything, but a few of you are doing it. Something I should know about."

"No, just a case I'm working." He said.

"You have nice hands." She commented.

Decker stared up at her.

He flashed his ring, and she smiled.

"Honey, that doesn't matter to some people as much as you think. But I respect a man who respects his wife," she walked away, and Decker smiled.

He couldn't remember the last time someone hit on him.

Of course, he'd keep it to himself. He couldn't tell Carol, his wife. She'd get upset.

The other person they were looking at, what was his name?

He pulled out the notebook he'd been jotting down details they'd given him and found it.

Johnny Milburn, he'd have to look the person up. They said he died in an accident, but as Reed and his daughter had, Decker wondered if Mr. Milburn hadn't died.

He finished his meal and paid the bill. The server smiled at him again, and he walked into the falling snow.

Decker took a left, hailed a cab, and got home.

He opened the door, and Carol stared at him.

"What are you doing home so early?" she asked.

"Had something I needed to do." He said.

He picked up his cell phone, walked out on the back porch, and redialed his daughter.

"Are you somewhere we can talk?" she asked.

"Yes, I'm home but outside." He said.

"Okay. So here is what I discovered from the autopsy and Abrams." She began.

She told him all they'd talked about, including the residue they'd found at the other house.

"So, there was an assassin?" Decker asked.

"It seems that way. Abrams was adamant about the video being doctored. We need to get our team on it." She told him.

"Our team?" he asked.

"Okay, your team. If we can clear Reed, we can bring him back on this." She said

"You sound like you're already with the FBI. You're doing good work, Vanessa." He said.

"Thanks, but you sound like there's something else on your mind. What is it?" she asked.

"This Johnny Milburn; what do we know about him?" Decker asked.

"Only that he was a test pilot for this drone program. Oh,

and he was also close with Webb, which may be our connection."

"You think Webb used him for this or the other way around?"

"There's a connection to them with this and Jax, but I'm not sure if they connected before or after. There is someone higher up on this."

"Okay, do you know where Reed is?" Decker asked.

"Nope," she replied.

"Vanessa, you need to be careful. If they're willing to kill Webb, they'll come after whoever is working this case. You need to be cautious." He said.

"I will, Dad," she replied and hung up.

CHAPTER FORTY-TWO

GRIGGS STARED at the phone after disconnecting it and returned it to her purse. She skimmed through reports and put them away again. She knew she'd read them on the flight and thought it was better to do that.

It had been nice to see her mom, but being home felt good.

No one had been there, not that she'd keep anything about the case in the house after the last break-in.

She walked into her room, stuffed some clothes into a bag, and her phone buzzed.

"Hey, what's going on?" Jax asked.

"I just got back," she said.

"What did our friend in Las Vegas have for us?"

"What I have should prove your innocence. Do you know why the FBI didn't analyze the video?" she asked.

"I don't think they had a reason too. Like the rest of the world, they believed what they were shown."

"I think Decker will get an FBI crew on it. The ballistics aren't there. I don't think they will find much in the shell that blew out his head."

"Neither do I," Jax said.

"Oh, did I tell you I dropped the flamingo off?" she said.

"How did that go?" he asked.

"Elizabeth was thrilled to get her flamingo. She asked about you, and Sarah talked to me about a few things."

"Like?" he asked.

"She said that you and Williams worked together."

"We did. He was my CO for a while. Then I lost my wings," he said.

"Look, I just got home, and I'm tired. I'll make sure to have Decker check all of this out." She told him.

"I appreciate it."

The call ended. Griggs set the alarm in the house, something she'd forgotten to do, and walked out to her car.

She drove back to the airport, got on the plane, and stared out the window for a few hours of the flight.

When it landed, she drove to her parents.

CHAPTER FORTY-THREE

DECKER RETURNED to his office and walked down the hall to another agent's office.

"Hey Derek, I need you to review that video," Decker asked.

Derek Barber glanced up through his long hair. He worked on the technical side of the FBI. He analyzed terrorist videos and internet stuff and sometimes did favors for agents and their home computers.

He is who they all came to when they needed help with something electronic.

"You're talking about that video of Reed?" Derek asked.

"Yes, when could you run it?" Decker asked.

"I've been working on it. The Director came down here earlier. He asked me to evaluate things in the video."

"And?" Decker asked.

"A lot is going on in here. Someone did some shit to it."

Barber brought up the video on his computer monitor. There were overlays of different things on the video, and it moved when he touched one of them.

"What did you do?" Decker asked.

"Someone has gone over this with a creative tool. They've

made it look like the gun went off and that it fired a bullet. But there's more." He said.

He grabbed his mouse, turned the camera angle around, and made the room in the video look like it was from a different angle.

"How did you do that?" Decker asked.

"Don't worry about it. That's not the important part; this is." He said.

He ran the cursor over one of the overlays, moved it, and smiled.

"That's the bullet hitting him, isn't it?" Decker asked.

"It is, and that means that Reed didn't shoot him, but someone else did, and it was a huge round. Probably from a high-caliber rifle. If you look in the reflection, you can see a white light." Dereck said.

He zoomed in on it.

"Okay, what is that?" Decker asked.

"It's a muzzle flash. I thought it was lightning, but I looked at the weather in Vegas over the last couple of weeks. There was rain but no lightning. This is from a house or building across from this."

"So this clears Reed?" Decker asked.

"It does, but someone needs to sit down and ask him a few questions when he comes in. I don't know what the case he's working on is, but this is top-of-the-line stuff. It's a Hollywood level of good. I worked there doing special effects and coloring for a few years before being recruited by the FBI. This is that type of stuff. If I hadn't done that before this, I never would've seen it, but whoever he's chasing has a lot of money behind them." Derek said.

Decker knew the real story of why Derek was recruited; he'd been using his talents to make spoof videos for people on the internet. One of them was directed at the President. He was given a choice, join or go to prison.

"Thank you, Derek," Decker said.

"No problem, but this is some top-level design shit. Make sure you let him know that."

"I will," Decker said.

He walked out of the room and to his desk. He dialed the Director's number.

"Decker, what can I do for you?" the Director asked.

"I guess you had Derek run the video through some program. Well, it appears the video was faked, or at least part of it was."

"So would you like me to send a letter to the press asking them to stop running the video?" Director Johnson asked.

"A cease and desist order would be great."

"Okay, you need to bring Reed in or have someone bring him in."

"I will," Decker said.

"Decker, good job on this," Johnson said.

"It was all Reed and Griggs on this. They just kept me informed on what was going on. She is on her way back to DC," Decker said.

"Good, get ahold of her and have her bring Reed in," Johnson said.

"Yes, sir, Director," Decker said.

He ended the phone call and dialed his daughter. It went to voicemail.

CHAPTER FORTY-FOUR

JAX'S PHONE BUZZED.

"I have good news," Griggs said.

"What's that?" he asked.

"The video has been proven fake, and the Director wants you to come in. He's sending cease and desist letters to the media."

"Well, hell, I'm happy about that. Now I can get back to work. This hiding out shit sucks." Jax said.

"I'm at my parent's. Would you like me to pick you up?" she asked.

"Yes, I'm near The Mall. I'll meet you at the parking lot by the Jefferson." He said.

"Fine, I'll be there soon." She said, ending the call.

He stared at his phone and ran through the last couple of days in his head. He was on the run from all agencies. He'd walked more in the previous days than he had in a long time.

The walk made him think about his life and what had happened, but he knew he had to move forward.

Twenty minutes later, he was in the car with Griggs on their way to the Hoover building.

She stopped at security, and the guard stared into the car.

"Glad to have you back, Jax," the guard said.

"Thank you," Jax said.

They parked in the garage, and Jax got out. A group of agents formed around him.

"What's this all about?" he asked.

"I don't know," Griggs said.

They hurried him into the building.

Griggs followed as fast she could.

They entered the elevator, and Reed studied the small space.

The doors opened, and he stepped out.

A cheer rose from the room.

The FBI Director stood in front of him and put out his hand.

"Sorry about all this," the Director said, "I would like to speak to you privately."

Jax nodded and followed him to the same room Griggs had sat in with the Directors.

"Please take a seat." The Director said.

Jax took the same seat Griggs had been in.

The door closed, the window frosted, and Director Johnson stared at him.

"Jax," FBI Director said, "Do you know I've read your file a few times? You were a good pilot, and it appears you got screwed by bad intel. It seems to be a common occurrence with you. When the video came out, I wanted it to be wrong. Other than that one hiccup, your military career was exemplary. You were at the top of your class in flight school. Shot down a few planes in Bosnia and what happened in Iraq, but this whole thing is different. You're after someone, but they don't want you to find them. Do you have any idea who this person could be?"

Jax sat in his chair and looked up at the Director.

"Sir, we've been working on this case for over a week. I'm not sure what's happening, but valuable assets are involved."

"What do you mean by that?" he asked.

"There is someone high up that is involved."

"Do you have any idea who this person could be?"

"No, I don't, but I will let you know after we dig deeper."

"I know you want to keep going, but I've been told to pull you off this case. After Webb died, rumblings from above. I was ordered to remove you from this case."

"Is that what you're doing now?" Jax asked.

"After what happened, I am putting you on leave for a few weeks. I will not tell you to stay away from this case; you are still an agent. I am not asking for your badge or firearm, but I want you to be careful. I believe something big is going on as well; otherwise, I wouldn't have been ordered to take you off this case."

"So I'm on leave, but you won't have a problem with me working this case while I'm on leave?" Jax asked.

"I don't know what you're talking about, Agent Reed. I will tell you happy hunting," Director Johnson said.

Jax stood up and walked to the door.

"Jackson, take care of yourself. My orders came from high up, I don't know the exact person, but someone wants you off this case. Watch your six, Agent Reed."

"I will. Thank you, Sir," Jax said.

He walked out of the conference room, and Griggs was waiting for him.

"What's going on?" she asked.

"We need to talk," he said.

They hurried through the office as Decker watched them.

Once on the street, Jax turned right and went into the same cafe Decker had eaten at for his early lunch. It was now quitting time, the wind blew down the canyons of offices, and they sat in the back of the cafe.

Jax ordered a beer, and Griggs stared at him.

"So, spill it," she said.

"I am on leave," he said.

"They put you on leave, for what reason?" she asked.

"They're probably waiting until this settles down. They don't want anything to interfere with the outgoing President's record or the inauguration. I am still going to work on the case. It sounded like the Director was ordering me to do it."

"Really?"

"The orders to bench me came from high up. He didn't know the exact source, but I can take my guesses."

"So we go back to work?" she asked.

"Yes," he replied as the server came over. They ordered some food, and Jax drank his beer in two swallows.

A TV was on at the bar, and his eyes diverted to it.

The story was about the video and how the authorities now believe it was modified to throw them off the trail.

Jax smiled and picked up his phone.

"I'm going to call Sarah," he said.

"Okay," she replied.

He went out the door, and a few people were hovering in the entryway.

"Sarah, it's me," he said.

"I just saw the news." She replied.

"Yeah, I'm reinstated but on leave."

"So Elizabeth can come over?" she asked.

"No, not now. I have a few things to work on." He said.

"But you're on leave. Are you going to work the case anyway?" she asked.

"I am on leave, but things have changed," Jax said.

"Okay, can you come over and see her? She'd love to see you. She saw the video. It upset her."

"How did that happen?"

"One of her friends at school showed her. I had to get her from school." Sarah said.

"Okay, I'll come over tomorrow. I promise," he said.

"Have you been home?" she asked.

"Yes, why?" he replied.

"I sent the papers to your lawyer," she said.

"I'll go through them and send them off."

He ended the call and walked back into the cafe.

Griggs smiled, but Jax sat down and stared at the steak in front of him.

"Went that well?"

"She sent the papers. I haven't talked to my lawyer since I got back, but I'm sure he's been trying to get ahold of me," he said.

"Okay, well, where do we go next?" Griggs asked.

"I think we need to find out about Johnny Milburn," he said.

"You think that's where this is going?" she asked.

"I just know that's our only clue." He admitted.

"Okay," Griggs agreed.

CHAPTER FORTY-FIVE

DRAKE STARED at the phone for the last twenty minutes waiting for the call. It finally came, and he didn't want to answer it.

"Yeah, this is Drake," he said.

"What the fuck is going on? I thought you set him up to be knocked out of this?" the voice said.

He didn't know who the voice was. It was male and older, but as to who it belonged to, he had no idea.

"Yes, I didn't think they'd figure out the video so quickly."

"Bullshit, I heard that Metro in Las Vegas solved the damn thing and told Griggs to have a better agency take a look at it. How fucked up do you have to be for a police department to figure it out?"

Drake pulled the phone away from his face and glared at it.

No one had talked to him like that in a long time, and he didn't care much for it.

"Okay, it was fuck up. There are still roadblocks in the way. We still have time. The final dance isn't until next week." Drake said.

"Yes, but I don't want them getting close." The voice said.

"I will stop them if I have to put one of them in the morgue. It won't interfere with the final dance."

"It better not, or I will send everything in my power after you." The voice said.

Not knowing who the voice was didn't give him much power, but knowing what the person on the other end had orchestrated, Drake felt something he wasn't used to. Fear.

"As I said, if it comes down to it, I'll do something to make them stop looking."

"You better. This is the perfect setup." The voice said.

Drake learned shit fell through, intel was wrong, and sometimes the men around you were all you had to rely on. When he stopped feeling supported, he moved to another team, one more elite. After that, there was no turning back. When he left that team, he disappeared, much to the chagrin of the military.

They were unhappy losing the most significant asset on the battlefield. The man on the other end didn't know these things. He only knew that Drake was the best, and he needed the best.

"I'll take care of what needs to be taken," Drake said and ended the call.

He knew the person on the other end wouldn't be happy with him ending the call abruptly. Still, he needed to clear his head rather than drop everything to hunt the man down.

Drake stared at the TV. The video had been removed from the news websites but was still on the internet. Things like that never leave the internet.

That darker part is where people like Drake are hired.

He shut off the TV.

The lights from the Capitol building illuminated the falling snow, and Drake wondered how the aircraft would handle the change in weather. He'd have to get ahold of the pilot. That would have to happen in the next couple of days, but first, he left his apartment, drove downtown, and stared at the Hoover building as he drove by.

He saw Jax and Griggs making their way through the falling snow.

He knew it might come down to eliminating one of them, but which was the question?

It was a decision for another day.

Drake turned and drove across the bridge. He had a stop to do. It would take him a few hours to get there, but the pilot needed to be talked to.

He didn't look forward to dealing with the man calling himself Randall. He felt the man was unstable. Do as many missions over enemy territory as he had, get shot down, survive on the land for a couple of weeks, and make it back. It changes you.

Maybe that's why they had stationed the man at Groom?

Drake mulled over all these things and shifted into lower gear once he reached the mountains. These were towns in parts of West Virginia where coal used to be king, though jobs in that industry were now few and far between.

The towns had started to shrink as people left for better jobs. Ones where they'd be able to breathe and not come home looking like a nineteenth-century photograph.

Drake knew that part of West Virginia, as it was his own house that Randall was in.

He found that that part of the state was the best place to be in. Most people supported the current President, and others shunned those that didn't.

Drake knew this.

Growing up in that area, Reagan was king, and anyone who talked badly about him would be dealt with.

Drake pulled into the driveway of the house and stepped out.

"Hey, you shouldn't be here," a voice said behind him.

"I know, but I was told to check on all of this. The man wanted to ensure this thing could fly in bad weather." Drake said.

Johnny Milburn stepped from behind the garage; a shotgun rested against his shoulder.

Drake motioned him to lower it.

"You could have called," Johnny said.

"You know, I thought about that. You know we can't have much contact with each other, but I have something for you," Drake said.

He pulled out the bag he'd been given at the Jefferson and handed it to Randall.

"So, Johnny, what are the problems with this thing?" Drake asked.

Johnny stared at him.

"I'll take you inside and show you. The snow shouldn't cause any problems. I was ready to take it up. I, too, wanted to see how it would handle in the colder weather."

Johnny led him inside and back towards the door with the control console.

"You never did tell me how you got ahold of one of these?" Johnny asked.

Drake ignored his question and glanced around the room.

He closed the door behind him. The fans for the control console turned on, and the room grew colder because of it.

Johnny turned it all on, and the camera from the drone popped up. It showed Drake's vehicle and the little cabin.

The drone rose out of the West Virginia Mountains and took off south.

"Are there any issues with ice on the wings?" Drake asked.

Johnny tapped a piece on his console, and the readout was green.

"No, it doesn't appear to be," Johnny answered.

"The weather may turn bad in the next few days. I wanted to make sure that everything worked."

Thirty minutes later, Johnny banked the drone to the right. It flew over the top of the Capitol building. He took it higher and set the control to hover.

"Have you run through everything?" Drake asked.

"A couple of times. I took the armaments off after the last run."

"What for? Was there a problem?" Drake asked.

"No, just wanted to secure in case someone came up to visit."

"Who would come up here?" Drake asked.

"I went into town to get supplies, and there were a few questions. The waitress at the diner hit on me." Johnny said.

Drake stared at Johnny, then at the screen in front of them.

"You can't bring anyone up here. You know that, right?" Drake said.

"Yes, I know that. It would endanger everything."

"As long as we're clear on that," Drake said.

"So, I saw the news," Johnny said.

Drake stared at the screen as the drone flew over a few trees and returned to the cabin.

He'd gotten stuck watching the flight and forgot to speak.

"Sorry, what about the news?" Drake asked.

"Saw the Vegas news about Webb," Johnny said.

"Oh, that," Drake said.

"Yes, did you have a hand in it?" Johnny asked.

"This operation has many working parts. Some of them break and are unnecessary for the remainder of the operation."

"I see. Will I be one of those parts?" Johnny asked.

The drone landed outside the cabin, and Johnny parked it.

"We all have things to do. There are still a lot of things to do." Drake said.

"Now that you've seen it fly in the weather, are you satisfied?" Johnny asked.

"Yes, if the weather turns, it should handle the weather fine," Drake said.

He pushed the button on the wall to open the door.

Johnny shut down the drone and the console.

Drake stopped and stared at the living room.

He'd spent many nights in that room as a child. The TV on the mantle wasn't there as a kid. He'd only seen a TV in town growing up.

He turned towards the rest of the house and stared down the hallway towards where his room had been. The one he'd shared with his four brothers. He knew the bunk beds were gone. He'd moved them out himself when setting the house up.

There was no stick near the front door, no chair in the basement for when they'd been wrong.

The blue chair had been his mother's idea growing up. She said it would make her boys strong.

His father went along with it.

Drake's earliest memory was of being in that chair, the lights out, things crawling in his hair. The scuttling of bugs, the squeak of rats, and sitting there, scared of everything.

His mother was right. It made her boys strong, but it also made Drake resent her. He wasn't afraid of anything after sitting in the dark for hours at a time. When you no longer feared your toes being bitten by rats or spiders in your hair, moving through the bushes in some far-off land was easy.

It's why he did well in the Teams. It was why he worked better alone.

He didn't like having to check up on Johnny, but he knew he'd needed to. At least to give him some cash.

"You okay?" Johnny asked.

"Fine. This will be the last time we see each other. There is the remainder of your payment in that bag." Drake said.

Johnny smiled and watched Drake hurry through the door.

Drake stared at the drone parked on the tarmac beyond his vehicle.

Its black surface glistened in the falling snow.

After walking around the house, Drake got in his car and drove down the mountain.

It would take him a while to get back to DC.

CHAPTER FORTY-SIX

THE PERSON behind the voice stared out at the DC skyline.

Everything was falling into place, and though Jackson Reed and Sarah Griggs were on the hunt for the next tier, he knew it would not happen.

He knew that after next week, he'd be sitting in the chair.

There was another meeting with the President tomorrow, then with Elaine Franklin before the inauguration.

There were five days until the inauguration, and he would guide them back while the loss would shatter the country. It was his goal to continue the current administration's plan.

The old man didn't know it; hell, the old man barely knew anything. It had been him that told The President what to do. Sure there were others, but he pulled the strings more than they did.

The President couldn't do a damn thing without him, but he had other further-reaching plans for the country.

He watched the skyline and the snow drifting past his window and wondered if the aircraft was out there.

It would be a terrible day, but he wouldn't be there. He'd be safely secured somewhere else during the event.

He turned off the lights and walked out of his office.

He'd already called for his car. He knew it was waiting for him.

It shuttled him home, and he walked in the door.

His wife was already in bed.

The pictures on the mantle were of his kids. He would give them a better life. Make sure they were secure in the country of their birth, while others were not allowed in.

His thoughts went to the next few days. He sat in his office, worked on his speech a few more times, and around three in the morning, he climbed into bed.

CHAPTER FORTY-SEVEN

AS THE VOICE climbed into bed, DNI Aaron Williams sat at his desk.

It would be another long night. He had to figure out how to deal with the blowback from the FBI and CIA, not to mention the President.

The man had called him earlier in the evening, yelling at him about the debacle.

How had it gotten so bad?

Aaron Williams got up from his desk, called his car, and took the elevator to the garage.

His car sat waiting for him.

"Home," he said to his driver.

He'd thought long about staying in the building and sleeping in the room next to his office. He'd spent many hours as DNI over the last two and half years doing that.

He hated the trips to the White House. He found the President as incompetent as some of his detractors and was glad the old man couldn't run for a third term. It would have put Aaron Williams in an early grave if he had.

The car moved along the road, and he watched the lights of

the building disappear as they reached the outskirts and the vehicle turned towards his house.

It sat down a long dead-end street and was one of the only three houses. He'd helped design some of the house's features and watched it come together.

It would be a place for him to take meetings of all sorts. There was a secure room for him to take those calls, a basement with a shelter, and the guards out front.

The car turned into the gate and drove through.

Williams stepped out and went into the house.

The walls were covered with pictures of his wife and kids.

He checked on his son, ensuring the seventeen-year-old was asleep. He kissed his head and walked down the hall to his daughter's room.

She was a couple of years younger than her brother, and her walls were adorned with boy band posters and artwork she'd done in school.

He kissed her head and walked up the stairs to the main bedroom.

His wife rolled over and stared at him.

"I thought you were going to be early?" she asked.

"Things came up," he said.

He took off his clothes and walked into the bathroom.

The bathroom door opened, and she continued to stare at him.

"Shiela, it's been a long day. I have to be back in a couple of hours. Can we not fight?" he asked.

"I'm just worried about you. You seem more stressed than usual."

He turned on the water and smiled at her.

"I'm okay, just exhausted." He reassured her.

"So, does this have anything to do with Jackson Reed?" she asked.

"You know I can't talk about things." He said.

"I know, but I also know you feel responsible for how Jax was pushed out of the Air Force. It was your intel that led him to bomb that wedding."

"Shiela, I would love to have a conversation about Jackson, but can we do it in the morning? It's late, and I have to meet with Elaine Franklin and her Vice-President tomorrow."

"So it is about Jackson?" she asked.

He ignored her and stepped into the shower.

She walked out of the bathroom, and he noticed she wore a thin nightie.

Fucked that one up, didn't we?

He put his hands on the wall beside the spout and leaned into the water.

It ran down his back and legs.

As he stood there, a thought occurred to him. He finished his shower, pulled out his notebook that he'd left in his pants, and wrote it down.

He knew the meeting with the President-Elect would be long, and he'd need as much caffeine as possible to get through it, but he wrote down his entire thought.

It might help him get through the next five days.

Shiela lay in bed. She'd changed into pajama bottoms and a top.

He watched her sleep for a moment and lay down. He was out in five minutes.

CHAPTER FORTY-EIGHT

JAX WOKE up and stared at the ceiling.

His sleep was fitful, and he'd need an extra dose of caffeine today.

The shower woke him up slightly, and he ensured all his work clothes were clean. The bag he'd left at the motel had been returned to him. The FBI no longer needed it.

Jax ate and hurried through the rest of his routine.

He wondered what would happen next in the case. He was glad to be cleared of all charges by the FBI and Metro homicide.

The Post had published an article about the ordeal, and he'd thought of looking up the reporter.

First, he had to call Griggs.

The Air Force had reinstated her and assigned her to the FBI for the time being.

"I was wondering when you would call?" she asked.

"I'll be over soon. I had something I wanted to run down," Jax said.

The hallway was empty, and he hurried to the garage.

He pulled onto the road, picked up coffee for him and

Griggs, his second of the morning, and stopped at Decker's house to pick her up.

Jax pulled into the driveway and stopped.

He stared up at the house and waited.

Ten minutes passed, and he got out of the car and walked to the front door.

Decker's wife opened the door and smiled at him.

"I know who you are. You've been all over the news." She said.

"Yes, Ma'am," he replied.

"She's on her way down. She overslept. I heard her talking to you this morning. She wasn't even awake when your call rang through." She told him.

Jax smiled, though in his head was a bit upset about it.

"Hey, Jax," she said.

Her mom stared at her.

She wore a pantsuit and pulled her hair into a bun.

"I thought you were with the Air Force?" her mom asked.

"I am," she replied.

"Then you should dress like it. Your father will not be happy with this. You're on loan to the FBI, whatever that means. Vanessa, if you want the job, play your part in getting it."

Jax stared at her. He didn't know how to respond to the chastising.

He sipped his coffee and walked into the living room.

Griggs fled up the stairs.

She returned ten minutes later in her work uniform.

It worked better than her other outfit, and Jax knew it would draw less attention from other agents than the one she'd been wearing.

"That's better," her mother said.

Jax handed her the coffee, and they walked out the door.

Her mother stood in the doorway until they got in the car.

"I swear that woman is insufferable sometimes," Griggs said.

"You know she's trying to help, right?" Jax said.

"I guess, but why did she have to do that in front of you?"

"Would you prefer she does it in front of another agent? She's trying to save you from screwing up."

"What do you mean?" she asked.

Jax pulled out of the driveway, stared at Griggs, and shook his head.

"If you can't realize that your mom is trying to save you from doing something stupid, then I don't know what to tell you." He said.

She stared out the window at the falling snow and glanced at Jax.

The car was quiet for ten minutes. He felt she was going to say something during each minute, only to find that she couldn't or wouldn't.

He hoped it had nothing to do with either of those. He wanted her to learn from her mistakes, as he had.

CHAPTER FORTY-NINE

WILLIAMS SAT AT HIS DESK, and Elaine Franklin sat across from him.

"So, this article in The Post today, do you know anything about it?" she asked.

She'd arrived ten minutes ago. Williams poured her some coffee, her third of the day, and exchanged pleasantries about the upcoming inauguration.

Then the question came.

"I read it, but I don't know much about what it says." Williams lied.

Elaine Franklin felt the lie but ignored it.

"I've been looking into this affair since the video came out. An aircraft went down in the Nevada Testing Range, and this Agent Reed was sent there on your orders. How does the Director of National Intelligence have such pull with the FBI?"

"It has nothing to do with pull. I've known Jax for years. When the alert came through, I felt he would be the best Agent to handle it. The AG felt the same way. I don't know where this reporter is getting his information."

"Why was Jackson Reed sent to handle this investigation?" Elaine Franklin asked.

"As was written in the article, Jax worked at Creech. He knows the CO and the facility's layout and has good contacts in the Las Vegas area. I felt that he was perfect for the job, and as I said, AG Smilah felt the same way."

"I read the article about Agent Reed, but you seem to have a personal investment in this?"

"Jackson Reed is among the most gifted pilots I've ever seen. He did things we didn't know about. His engagements in Iraq and Afghanistan were exemplary. Then he had a problem."

"Yes, I understand that was from bad intel," it was a statement rather than a question.

"It was. That question is valid if you're asking if I feel responsible for how Jax left the service. I knew Jax for a long time before I moved to intelligence. Jackson Reed is a good pilot and man, and I will stand up to anyone who says otherwise."

"When there are intelligence failures, you seem to be all over it."

"What does that mean?" Williams asked.

"This OSI is working with him," Elaine Franklin said, "her father was a pilot in Iraq. He was shot down, captured, and killed by Al Qaeda in Iraq. That failure was on you as well, wasn't it?"

"No, that was not me. I had no hand in sending him up. He was in rotation, and I didn't handle that intel."

"Why was Reed made the fall guy for the wedding? The higher-ups approved it, and nothing happened to them or you. You sit in this room while he and others in his position lost their jobs, some of their marriages."

Williams smiled, "We risked the lives of many on-the-ground sources to get that intel. We used our Afghani sources, and they burned us. They had a vendetta against the man in the video. They told us where the target, a tribal head, would be. In that area, it isn't easy to verify. We were told he was having a party. We were not given the details of the party. When the drone launched, we had verification on the ground that a party was taking place. By the time the drone was cleared to release its payload, our ground forces had put to abort, but it was too late.

"If we had used someone else as a fall guy, we would have lost our sources. If you ask why Jax is at the FBI, I feel he needed a break. His wife left him soon after he joined, and I understand they are going through divorce proceedings."

"Yes, he is. That is the reason for my inquiry. Tom asked me to mention it."

"I see. You felt it necessary to come here and discuss this little thing with me?"

She frowned and leaned towards his desk, "I take care of my people. If there is something you're hiding from me, I will find out what it is. I will take your job from you and ensure your retirement is hell. I didn't pursue this job as much as the press would have you believe, but I will do it to the best of my abilities. And if you get in the way of that, I will bury you."

Williams stared at her. He'd heard she could be fierce, but being on the receiving end of her words put a bit of fear in him.

She leaned back in her chair and sipped at her coffee. Her face was relaxed, and she set her coffee down.

"Is there anything else, Madame President-Elect?"

"No, I have to be going. I have a meeting with the President in a few hours. I must make sure he understands my stance as well."

"He won't take things as well as I have," Williams replied.

"We'll see," she stood up and opened the door. Her security team stood beyond the door.

"We're leaving," she said.

Williams watched the woman who'd extended a personal threat to him walk out the door.

Well, shit.

He picked up the phone and dialed the number he'd been given.

"It's me," he said.

CHAPTER FIFTY

JAX DROVE into the parking garage.

They talked to a guard at the front desk and were given visitor badges. They stood waiting for an escort.

The person walked them down the halls to an office.

The escort walked in, stopping in a small office with a secretary. She smiled at Jax, who nodded.

He'd known her for years, but it was not a friendly visit.

They were buzzed into the next room, walked in, and sat down.

Aaron Williams smiled at Jax.

"I was wondering how long it would take you to get down here," Williams said.

"Aaron, it's good to see you," Jax said.

"What do I owe this visit?"

Griggs glanced across at Jax.

"Why did you put me on this case?" Jax responded.

Williams frowned and stared at the closed door behind them "'Jax, there are a few reasons for that. Most of all, I wanted to see what you could uncover."

Jax leaned forward.

"Why?"

"I know you're enjoying being an Agent. I've read about your first couple of cases. You did well on them, and although I'm sure they were trying, you caught the person. That's good, but I thought you'd want to get back out there. Maybe find something out about why it went so badly. I heard about Sarah, and I'm sorry."

Williams glanced at the ring on Jax's finger.

Jax spun the ring with his thumb.

"Who told you?"

"Does it matter? In this town, everyone knows everything. Tom is a good man. He's done a lot of work for Elaine Franklin."

"What did you mean, you wanted to see what he could uncover?" Griggs asked.

"When this case landed on my desk, I thought of all the people I could have the DOJ send out there. I knew the field office in Las Vegas would do a good job, but I wasn't sure they would have the connection I felt the case needed. None of them knew Creech. None of them knew Webb. You had a vendetta against him, and I wanted to see if you could put it aside."

"So you set me up to fail, but I didn't, and now you're gloating about it?" Jax asked, a puzzled look on his face.

"There are other factors in play. I knew someone could uncover more about this. I was surprised by your trip to Groom. I hadn't thought you'd go there. Receiving your call was nice."

Jax waited for him to say something else. When he didn't, Jax glanced at the wall.

Williams's awards from the Air Force, his medals for the intelligence service, and others lay in a collage on the wall with pictures of Presidents and dignitaries.

"You're still an Air Force guy?" Jax asked.

The question struck Williams, and he thought about it before answering, "I always will be. I may have this office and thousands of people to order around, but I am still an Air Force guy. You don't spend that much time in Saudi Arabia, Italy, or Afghanistan and not have it affect you, but it made me who I am. It got me to this chair. An Air Force man I'll always be."

"So, what? You did it out of the worry that someone from the field office would screw it up?" Griggs asked.

"Not screw it up, but not work as hard as the case needed. When you went to Groom, how did Black feel about you being there?"

"He didn't give me a hug if that's what you're asking."

"Right. Black, and you go way back. How he got out, there is a mystery even to me. He was there before I got to this chair, but he knows what he's doing.

"What can you tell us about Johnny Milburn?" Jax asked.

Aaron Williams was DNI for a multitude of reasons. One was that he was rarely rattled.

He sat back and stared from Jax to Griggs. His eyes narrowed as he watched the two of them.

"Why do you want to know about a dead pilot?"

"We're not sure he's dead," Griggs said.

"His family would disagree with that assessment. He has a marker in Arlington."

"I'm sure he does. But he was one of only three pilots who flew these drones."

"Jax, do you remember your last flight on the big birds?" Williams asked.

Jax hadn't thought of the last time he flew something other than drones. He stared across the table, wondering where the discussion was heading.

"I do. It was a caravan. We'd received intel that Saddam was on the caravan. This was just after a series of strikes by Bush number two. He sent in a couple of birds. Mine was one of them. We were supposed to knock it out with one strike. The war would have been over, or at least that was the hope."

"So, what happened?"

"The intel was wrong, and I lost my wings because of it."

"There is more than that going on with this. The intel was wrong because of situations we couldn't control. Much like the reason you left the Air Force. But the factors we see are not the ones we should be holding onto. Yes, I was head of intel in those days of the war. I moved from that office afterward. But there were other factors. Things that influenced those decisions. Do you remember what they were?"

Jax stared at the floor for a minute, then glanced up. His eyes met Williams'.

"I'll be a son of a bitch," Jax said.

"Is it there? You got it?" Williams asked.

"So this whole time, that's what's been going on?" Jax asked. Williams nodded.

"What about other things?" Jax asked.

Williams didn't say anything, "You know, it's been great talking to the both of you, but I have a meeting with the President in an hour."

Jax stood up and saluted Williams, who returned it.

They walked to the door. Griggs turned around and stared from Jax to Williams.

"I guess this is goodbye?" she said.

"Yes, but I'm sure I'll see both of you again," Williams said.

They walked out the door and into the hallway. The exact escort they'd had upon arriving led them to an elevator.

He rode down with them to the main entrance.

They returned to the car, and Jax kept his eyes on the road the whole time.

"Okay, now tell me what the hell happened in there?" Griggs asked.

"I will tell you what I can," Jax said.

The car moved out the front gates of the Pentagon and into Virginia.

"Jax, where are we going?" Griggs asked.

"I have to check something."

"What is so important about flying through traffic in this snow? We could slide off the road or into another car!"

He ignored her. He drove to the middle of Washington, parked at the Smithsonian Castle, and rode up the elevator to the main floor.

Jax paid the entrance fee for both of them and led Griggs to the Air and Space Museum.

"Why are we here?" Griggs asked.

The place was packed with people. They milled around the entire site. He led her out the door and onto The Mall.

She stared at him as if he'd gone mad.

"What the hell are you doing? You paid for us to get in, leading us into the falling snow."

"We have a tail. I've been trying to shake it since we left the Pentagon."

"So that's why you were trying to kill us?"

"I didn't try hard enough. Let's get across The Mall. I want to look at the setup they have for the inauguration."

"It's just a bunch of scaffolding."

"Yes, but Sarah and Tom are going to the inauguration with Elizabeth."

"We still have a tail, don't we?"

"Yes," Jax said, "And I can't shake it."

Jax stared up at the Capitol building. A lone man stood by the steps. He watched them approach and spoke into a radio near his collar.

"What can I do for the two of you?" he asked.

"We've been walking through The Mall, and these two men

are following us. They were there when we walked into the Air and Space Museum and are still back. We think they're following us," Jax said.

Jax turned around and pointed out two men in plain clothes.

The men stopped and stared as Jax pointed them out to the Capitol police officer.

They turned around and casually walked away.

"See," Jax said.

The Capitol police officer radioed for another unit.

"No problem," the officer said, "I'll take care of it."

Jax thanked him, and they walked towards the exit where Senators and Congresspeople came out after work.

"What are we doing, and what did Aaron Williams say to you?"

Jax stared across from them at a restaurant, "You hungry? I'm hungry," Jax said.

"Sure, I could eat," she replied.

They got a table in the back so Jax could watch the door.

"I think the Capitol police got the tail off of us," he said.

"I think so too," Griggs said, "now tell me what the hell is going on."

"Your dad flew, right? He was shot down in Iraq, and I know the rest well."

"We've had this discussion. Yes, and the whole world saw his death."

"You know, it's a funny thing about pilots. We're so used to the aircraft doing so much work; we forget what we can do when we push it."

"What are you going on about now?"

"I haven't looked into it, but your dad was on a different rotation than I was. I flew regular aircraft before I flew drones. I had my wings taken away in that caravan incident. Maybe he was there when I was."

Jax glanced at the door again, then continued, "So, I never met the man. I heard what happened to him, and we all did. But I was flying drones not too long after that. We had the same command structure. Whoever was above me was above him as well. That's what I'm saying."

The server arrived and smiled, "What could I get for the two of you?"

"Some wings and a pitcher of beer," Jax replied.

The server walked away, and Griggs smiled, "Right. I would assume so."

Jax leaned back as the server returned with the pitcher of beer and tray of wings, along with two glasses.

"Aaron told me he was with intel, but someone was above him. This person approved missions. He would know about a drone pilot losing his life and maybe not dying."

Griggs leaned in as Jax poured them two glasses of beer.

"Okay. Yes, the person who ran the intel office would know that. They would've been high enough to know these contacts within the intelligence or the dark fields. They'd know what places could potentially help a person get out of the service incognito." Griggs said.

"Do you know who the head of those groups was when flying missions over Iraq and flying drones in Afghanistan?"

"I'm dying for you to tell me," Griggs said.

"I will, but first, we have to go further. What person from the Air Force left the service and moved up so quickly that people wondered if they were buying votes?" Jax asked.

"There was a scandal about it, but he was cleared," Griggs replied.

"There was, and the scandal didn't hurt him one bit. It gave him more drive to work harder. He attempted a run in the last election but was struck down by the President and Vice President. They led the party, so the Vice President from the previous administration was the candidate. Not our guy," Jax said.

"Yes, and he got creamed by Elaine Jackson."

"That's right, but I bet our guy thinks he would've won if he'd been the chosen candidate," Jax said.

"You think the Speaker of the House set this all up?" Griggs asked.

"I think it's a possibility," Jax said.

"Why would he do all of this?"

"When I lost my wings, he took a hit in the press. I was a good pilot, and many people stood up for me. They put me on drones because they didn't want to lose me."

"Is that what you know?"

"I've been told by numerous people that was what happened within the command structure, even by Colonel Black," Jax said. He let it hang in the air for a minute.

"Colonel Black from Groom Lake?"

"Yes," Jax replied.

"So, why would Miles Frank, the Speaker of the House, want to steal a drone?"

"If the President or Vice President cannot carry out their duties, the Speaker of the House becomes President."

"Oh shit," Griggs said.

"Miles Frank doesn't know what we think is going on. We need to keep it that way." Jax said.

"Yes, he would probably be pissed you were put on this case."

"I know he would. We've had words between us since. They were always in hallways, just the two of us. He would not be excited about me taking this case."

"Well, I think we need to find the company that helped get Johnny Milburn out?"

"Right, but if this is true, we can't tell anyone about this. I'm not sure your dad would believe me."

Griggs sipped her beer and glanced across the table.

"So, Miles Frank, the Speaker of the House, is behind this?"

"Let's see what the evidence shows," Jax said, "He would've known about Milburn. He knew Webb had his issues. He would've been able to toss them out as he was headed out the door, and he is a hair's breadth away from the White House."

"So, how do we find this company?" Griggs asked.

"We can call people he knows. They would know something, even if it is partial. People in intel know those kinds of things."

CHAPTER FIFTY-ONE

MILES FRANK, the Speaker of the House, watched the snow fall among the people beyond his window.

"Sir, she's here," his secretary said.

He walked to the door, brushed off a few crumbs from his lunch, and smiled as Elaine Franklin walked into the room. Tom, her soon-to-be Chief of Staff and Sarah Reed's fiancé, stood on her left side.

"It is wonderful to see you again," he said. It was a lie; every moment he'd spent with her had angered him further.

She sat down on the couch in the middle of the room. Miles sat down across from her.

"I know how you feel about all of this, Miles. I would have enjoyed our debates more than the ones I had with the Vice President."

"Yes, they would have at least been more interesting."

"But I'm not here to speak of things lost. I was visiting with Aaron Williams. We talked about the drone that was lost."

"Oh, that," Miles said, "I heard they found their parts scattered through the desert."

She smiled and glanced at Tom.

"Tom has clearance. He discussed it on the way over from the Pentagon."

"If this is about a drone that crashed, why are you here?"

"Look, I know the President wants to go out without getting mud on himself. We all know he's gotten enough on himself in the past eight years. But if you sit there and lie to me, I will leak what I know to the press."

The Speaker stared at her.

"I don't know what you're talking about." He said.

"The drone didn't crash. It was hijacked, stolen, whatever term you prefer to use. But let me tell you, I know the truth," she said.

"Okay, so why are you telling me this?"

How could she have found out?

Miles smiled at her.

"You know, Miles, I remember when you got to Washington. You were green and didn't know what the hell you were doing. Now you're Speaker. How did you move up so quickly?" she asked.

"Elaine, I know we've been enemies on the floor and in the press sometimes, but I want to work with you. I want to make sure your first term is wonderful."

She smiled and stared at the open curtains and the light from the Washington Monument in the distance.

"That story about Washington and the cherry tree? It may be great, but it's still a lie. It never happened."

Miles didn't notice that he flinched, but Elaine Franklin did.

"No, we're not. I must ensure my security team is ready if there is nothing else. I'm heading to get some lunch."

She glanced at the crumbs on the floor and smiled.

"Of course you are," she said.

She and Tom walked out the door and into the hallway.

A press contingent stood outside, wanting pictures.

Her security team led her down the hallway to an elevator. There weren't many people who could use that particular elevator, but she was one of them.

Elaine Franklin and Tom stepped into the elevator, her security team closed around her, and the elevator descended to a private garage beneath the Capitol complex. It was primarily used for those in the higher echelons of the United States government, and while she wasn't there yet, she was able to use it.

* * *

Drake's phone rang, and he stared at the number.

He'd walked The Mall and stood outside the Capitol building.

The motorcade of the soon-to-be President left the Capitol building.

"I take it the meeting didn't go well?" Drake asked.

"That worthless bitch. She talked to me in a way no one ever has. I wish the inauguration were tomorrow," the voice said.

"I do have some news for you. If you'd like to hear it." Drake asked.

"Yes, I'm in the office. We both know who each other is. It's past time for us to meet in person," The voice asked.

"I agree. Enough of the cloak and dagger bullshit," Drake replied.

"We need to meet. You still have the card that was given to you?"

"Of course," Drake replied.

"Come to my office. That card will get you through security."

He watched the motorcade leave the building and make its way along the road.

Drake walked across the street, up the steps, and into the office building where the Speaker kept his office. He showed his pass and went through the metal detectors.

The guard stared at it and handed it back.

"Thank you, sir," the guard said.

Drake took the pass and hurried to the elevator.

He was sure who the voice was. When the task was given, it confirmed most of what he knew.

He would have to be gentle with him.

There's no use stirring the pot when the man is already upset.

He reached the office and stared at the placard on the wall, Miles Frank, Speaker of the House.

The door opened, and a young woman with a short skirt walked out.

Another woman held the door for him, "I'm here to see the Speaker,"

"Yes, he said someone was coming." The woman said.

The door opened, and Drake stared at the man who'd paid him a king's ransom to do what he'd been doing. Miles Frank was older than he expected.

He knew the story of the Speaker, as did most who worked in his craft.

When he got the message on the boards he frequented for work, he wondered at first who would be the person asking for such things, then another note showed up, this one from Johnny. He'd known Johnny for other reasons. It all came together afterward.

"Good to finally meet you," Miles Frank greeted him.

He waved Drake into the room, and Drake sat in the exact spot Elaine Franklin had been in only thirty minutes prior.

Miles stared at the man he knew only as the person on the

other end of the phone. He was taller than he thought he'd be and firmer looking.

There was a distance to his look. As if he couldn't look someone in the eyes.

It was a terrifying feeling, and Miles didn't care for it.

"So, this Jax Reed? He's back on the case?" Miles asked.

"That is what the situation appears to be," Drake confirmed.

The Speaker glanced out the window as snow fell, and the lights along the streets left an effervescent glow on the city below.

Drake frowned.

He wasn't used to being ignored, and he stood up.

"No, sorry, I was thinking of something." The Speaker said.

"You know Reed, don't you?" Drake asked.

"I don't want to get into specifics, but I knew him when he was a pilot. He was good, then something happened, and it affected us." He said.

"I see. So you think he will come at you full boar if he discovers you're behind all this?" Drake asked.

"He was a smart pilot. He was good at what he did. From what I understand, he's been the same at the FBI."

Drake sat down and stared at the man he knew was only a breath away from the Presidency. If they both had their way, he'd be living at 1600 Pennsylvania Avenue in the next few days."

"So, you want something done?" Drake asked.

"If he gets closer, then maybe, but it's this damn woman that's pissing me off."

Drake stood back up to protest.

"No, I know the timelines and everything that is coming. We have everything planned. People will fall after what we do, but it won't be me." Miles said.

Drake took his seat.

He was growing tired of the man ranting to him.

"If that is all you have for me, I will be leaving. I need to set up a few things." Drake said.

"Yes, sorry for the rant, but I won't survive this woman if this fails. I'll kill her in a fit of rage."

Drake stood up and walked to the door.

"Sir, remember we are on the same team," Drake said.

"Yes, yes, I'm aware. But please, take care of things when they need it."

Drake nodded and walked out the door.

The secretary in the other room stared at him.

"What was your name again?" she asked.

Drake ignored her and walked into the hallway.

He followed it until he came to the elevator.

The snow fell heavily, and the clouds overhead blocked out most of the light.

The moon wasn't visible, though Drake didn't think about that.

His mind was on what he would have to do next. He had ideas but worried stepping up the game would make this more of a problem, so he would hold off for a while.

He walked through the snow, across the bridge to where he'd parked his car.

It was growing late, but he knew he'd be able to get his car.

The roads were already slick, and a couple of cars slid as they moved across the bridge.

Drake pulled onto the road and headed home.

He had an early day tomorrow, so he showered, changed, and slipped into bed.

CHAPTER FIFTY-TWO

JAX BOOTED UP HIS LAPTOP, and his home screen came up. He needed to find out how a person in the military would be able to disappear.

He picked up his phone and dialed Aaron Williams.

"I didn't think I'd hear from you for a while," Williams said.

"I wasn't sure I'd have to talk to you. We're not where we need to be if you're asking."

"No, I'm just curious. What can I do for you, Jackson?"

"Where would a person go if they wanted to disappear?"

The other end grew quiet.

"You know you called my home phone, right?"

"I'm the one who called you, remember?"

"So, give me a second, and I'll transfer this to a secure line."

"Okay," Jax replied.

He waited on the line as it beeped then Williams came back on.

"So, yes, there are companies that do that, but they are expensive. Who are you looking for?" Williams asked.

"I'll tell you later, but can you give me a company?"

"I can, but Jax, this could disrupt many people. These

companies take pride in their work to erase people. If you look into this, you might rattle some cages that those in government would prefer stayed still."

"I understand," Jax replied.

"If you want to talk to someone about this stuff, especially if it's about who I think it is, you need to discuss it with Black."

"Sir?"

"How many people at Groom do you think to disappear? People who work there know all of our secrets. They've seen them. Colonel Black is the one you need to talk to."

"Can you arrange that?"

"I can make something available. And Jax, leave her at home. She doesn't have clearance."

"I wouldn't think of bringing her."

"Good, I will have something available for you. Give me ten minutes."

"Yes, Sir," Jax said and ended the call.

A clock sat on the far wall, and he'd wanted to call Elizabeth, but the hour was late, and he was sure she was in bed.

His phone buzzed with a number he didn't recognize.

"This is Agent Reed," Jax answered.

"Agent Reed, we have a car waiting for you downstairs." The person said.

"Okay, thank you," Jax said.

He ended the call.

That was fast.

He walked to the door, ensured everything was locked up, and headed downstairs.

A long black car sat in front of his apartment.

A man stood next to it and ushered him inside.

He got in and stared at the person across from him.

"Hello, Agent Reed," Elaine Franklin said.

Jax wasn't sure how to respond and glanced to her right. Tom sat there.

"Tom says you've been very busy in Las Vegas?"

"I had been, but then the video came out, and things changed."

"Yes, but you've been reinstated, as has Vanessa Griggs. I want to discuss your investigation with you." She said.

Jax frowned.

"I can't do that."

"I assure you I have clearance, and so does Tom," she said.

The car pulled away from the curb, and Jax's mind kept going back to the scenario he had in his head. If he didn't stop what he believed to be happening, the woman across from him, the man next to her, and many others, including maybe his daughter, would be dead. The burden weighed on his shoulders as the car moved along the Washington DC streets.

"I see your mind working. I know your record. I know quite a bit about you." She said.

"From Tom?" he asked, and Tom shuffled in his seat.

"Some, but after recent events, I've looked into other things. I saw your flight status and that you were a good pilot. I feel for you. It was a bad thing that happened. I want to fix it." She said.

"Ma'am?" Jax asked.

"This whole thing you're working on with Miss Griggs," she said and smiled, "is there anything you can tell me?"

"Not much to say. We were investigating a downed drone." She frowned.

"Now, I will say this, you're not a very good liar. I am aware of the circumstances with the drone. I know it was not merely downed but taken. I read between the lines of the Post article."

Jax stared from her to Tom.

"Don't look at me. She runs the show." Tom said.

"We're following leads, or we were until the video. I was

waiting for a call so I could fly back to Nevada, but I may not be able to."

"Why is that?" she asked.

"The place isn't on regular flights."

"I see; I don't have control over things like that yet. Can this wait until after the inauguration?"

"No, it can't." He said.

Jax's phone rang. He stared at it.

"Go ahead," she said.

He answered it.

"There's an aircraft waiting for you at Hyde Field. Do you have a way to get there?" Williams asked.

"Yes, I do," Jax replied as Elaine Franklin and Tom stared at him.

"Good luck, Jax," Williams said and ended the call.

"Can you take me to Hyde Field?"

"I think we can manage that." She said.

Tom picked up the phone to talk to the Secret Service agent in the front seat.

"Hyde Field," Tom said, and the car made a left.

The car rolled through the gate, and Jax got out.

"I hope you find what you need," she said.

Jax nodded and walked towards a small aircraft.

A security guard with no badging led Jax to the aircraft. It bore no tail markings or logos of any kind.

"Get in the aircraft, Sir," the guard said.

Jax hurried up the stairs, and the pilot stood next to the cockpit door.

"Where are we going?" he asked.

"Groom Lake," Jax replied.

The pilot stared at him.

"I will have to make a call," the pilot said. He didn't wear a name tag or identify as anything other than the aircraft's pilot.

Jax walked into the cabin as the pilot reached for the phone.

Jax listened for a moment as the man spoke.

"Yes, sir," the pilot said, "we'll arrive in six hours."

Jax stretched out on the seats and fell asleep.

The plane's landing bounced him from his sleep, and he toppled to the floor. There were no lights on beyond the wings of the aircraft. Once the plane rolled to stop, five trucks, with their lights, hurried out of the plane. The pilot came out and stared at him.

"I suppose they're here for you?" he asked.

"Yes," Jax said as the pilot opened the aircraft's door.

Jax walked down the ramp into the early morning desert air. It was still a few hours from dawn; a crisp line of red glowed from beyond the eastern mountains.

Black climbed out of a jeep and crossed the tarmac to Jax.

"So, you commandeered an NSA aircraft?" Black asked.

"It helps to have friends in high places."

"I guess, but let's not talk out here," he said, leading Jax to the jeep he'd climbed out of.

Jax sat down in the jeep, and Black smiled.

"I understand that you're looking for a way to disappear?"

"Not for myself, but I know there are companies that do that kind of thing. It's a black ops type of thing. I know when someone has gone dark, they look for ways to get out."

"So there is this company that a few people I know have used. And no, I'm not giving you their names."

"What the company?"

"It's called Executive Actions. The guy who runs it was in the teams, and I'm talking Delta and deeper. He knows his shit, and he is not someone to fuck with. They have an office in Las Vegas, but I'm sure they also have one in the DC area. If you want answers, that is the place to find them."

"Thanks, Colonel," Jax said and stepped out of the jeep.

"Hey, when I get a call that said there's an NSA plane coming, I don't know who to expect. I hope you find what you're looking for," Black said.

"Thank you. I hope so, too," Jax replied and walked towards the aircraft.

"Oh, by the way," Black yelled over the sound of the aircraft's engines, "did you hear about the other drone?"

Jax stopped in his tracks, "What about the drone?"

"The Navy is looking into it. They're moving the thing to Virginia," Black said.

"That does change a few things," Jax said.

Black stared at him.

"Never mind. Thank you, Colonel," Jax said and hurried into the aircraft.

The jeeps drove off, and the plane moved down the runway as the jeeps fled into the night.

They were in the air for ten minutes when Jax picked up one of the phones along the wall.

"Hello," Griggs said.

"Hey, so I have a lead on that thing." He said.

"Jackson, do you know what time it is?" she asked.

"Six am in DC."

"Yeah, but—"

"I'll be there in a few hours. Be ready." He said.

Jax ended the call and looked up Executive Actions on his phone. They had a DC office with the other lobbyists on K Street.

He set his phone down and fell asleep.

CHAPTER FIFTY-THREE

JOHNNY MILBURN GOT in his truck and drove down the hill.

He was tired of oatmeal and a hot breakfast that tasted like something other than low-quality cement.

Two trucks were in the diner's parking lot, and he got and walked inside.

The waitress smiled at him.

"Just one?" she asked.

He nodded, and she pointed to an empty seat at the end of the bar. There were only a few people, but he liked sitting at the end of the bar. It gave him a good view of the door and the waitress.

"You know, Randall, I'm not sure you're coming in here for breakfast anymore," she said, calling him by the only name anyone in the town knew him by.

She poured his coffee, winked, and smiled.

"It's a funny thing you say that," he said.

The chair next to him moved, and he glanced at its occupant.

Drake was perusing the menu.

"What's good this morning?" Drake asked.

"Coffee is fresh. Hotcakes are good too." The waitress replied.

"That sounds great. I'll have the hotcakes with coffee and a side of bacon." Drake said.

She walked away, smiling at Johnny.

"I see what you're talking about," Drake said.

Johnny sipped his coffee and glanced at the door, "Why are you here?"

"Don't worry," Drake said, "it's just me. There have been some developments."

The waitress returned, set Johnny's plate down, and smiled.

"Damn, that does look good," Drake said.

His food came a moment later, and he ate slowly. Johnny did the same.

Johnny's hand twitched a couple of times, and Drake stared at it.

"You good?" Drake asked.

"Yeah, I'm good," Johnny replied, his hand shaking a few more times.

"Does that happen all of the time?"

"No, just when I'm nervous."

"Well, you don't have anything to be nervous about."

They ate in silence for the next twenty minutes. The waitress returned and handed Johnny his bill and a slip of paper with her number on it. Johnny paid his bill, folded the paper, tucked it in his jacket, and walked out to his truck.

Drake paid his bill, smiled at the waitress, who rolled her eyes, and walked outside.

Johnny stood next to his truck, waiting.

"So, what's this all about?" Johnny asked.

"Let's talk when we get to the cabin," Drake said.

They drove their vehicles up the hill, stopping at the gate and then driving through after it closed behind them.

Johnny parked and got out.

He waited for Drake.

They sat down in the living room, and Drake went over everything he'd witnessed the last few days in the press and with Griggs and Jax.

"So, what are you going to do?"

"Not a hundred percent certain yet, but I have ideas. It depends on what those two discover."

"I'm on a timeline. I have things to get ready for. I have flights to perform before the final day, but I must wait until it's completely dark."

"Why?"

"I've heard a couple of farmers talking about seeing things. I know it's the drone, so I haven't taken it up in a few days."

"Why would they see it?"

'The first night I took it up, I took it low. I needed to assess the aircraft and how it would fly over the tops of trees at low altitudes. I got too close and was seen."

Drake's face turned red, and he glared at Johnny.

"Do you know how much money we're going to get at the end of this?" Drake asked.

"Yes, but I still needed to test the aircraft."

"How do you know they saw it?"

"I went to breakfast a few days later. A few people were discussing it. They asked if I'd seen anything on the mountain. I told them no."

"Okay, but be careful," Drake said.

He walked out the front door and stopped.

"Sorry," Johnny said.

"It's okay. But be careful. I know being out in the desert

with all the chemicals fucked you up, but you have to be more cautious than that."

Drake closed the door. An enormous lock was on the barn where the drone was kept. He walked around the property, checking a few things, then glanced inside at Johnny, who sat on the couch staring at the TV.

Drake got in his vehicle and drove back to DC.

* * *

Drake's phone rang as he drove down the mountain. Only a handful of people knew the number. He thought about not answering.

"Hello," Drake answered.

"Hey, it's Blake," the voice said.

"I told you only to call this in an emergency."

"I know. That's why I'm calling. That FBI agent was at Groom again."

"What does that have to do with me?"

"He was asking questions about your company."

"What did you tell him?"

"I didn't. Colonel Black did."

Drake pulled the phone away and screamed until his voice hurt.

"What did the mother fucker say?"

"He gave the name of your company."

"Well, fuck me," Drake said.

"Anyway, I thought you should know," Blake said and ended the call.

Drake stared at the road in front of him.

CHAPTER FIFTY-FOUR

JAX SAT IN THE CAR, and Griggs handed him a coffee when she got in.

He glanced at it.

"I figured you had a long night. The least I could do is supply coffee."

Jax sipped at it and smiled.

"This is much better than the stuff I had on the plane."

"Where is this office?" Griggs asked as Jax pulled out of the driveway.

"On 'K' Street," Jax replied.

"Of course it is."

"I called their number last night and left a vague message. We'll run with that." Jax said.

"Okay," Griggs replied.

"Just let me lead," Jax said.

She nodded, and they drove towards DC and turned left on K Street. They found parking across Farragut Square Park and crossed the street to the address. Snow lined the roads, and Jax felt the weariness of all the flying back and forth creep in.

The lobby was plain, and a board listed the building's occupants.

Jax found the one for Executive Actions.

"Third floor," Jax said.

The elevator was a gold and silver, a glass-enclosed thing that looked as if it were going to eat them.

Jax glared at the glass warily and stepped inside with Griggs.

Both watched the doors close, and the ground floor fell away.

"This is what it feels like to get too close," Jax said.

"Why do you say that?" Griggs asked warily.

"This feels off. We're snooping about Milburn, and we get the name of the company he used to go to the ground and disappear. It feels too wrapped in a bow."

"You think it's a setup?"

"I don't know," Jax replied.

"But you think Milburn is still alive?"

"Yes, absolutely," Jax said. The doors opened, and Jax and Griggs stepped into a large lobby covered with leather sofas and chairs.

"Welcome to Executive Actions," a woman said from behind a large cherrywood desk.

Jax walked over to her and smiled.

"I left a message last night. I didn't receive a return call but thought I'd come in." Jax said.

"We don't do walk-ins. This isn't a salon," The woman said.

"I heard about this place from a man named Webb," Jax said.

Griggs walked up and grabbed Jax's hand.

"We've had a bit of bad luck recently. There is this person who died. Maybe you saw it on the news, but she was our friend. The circumstances of her death are not of the ordinary type. We think whoever killed her is coming after us next." Griggs said.

"Well, the boss isn't in right now," the woman said, and the elevator rang.

A man of just over six feet entered. He wore a dark suit with a matching tie and a white pocket square. His bald head shone under the lights.

"It's okay, Christina. I will see them in my office." The man said.

"I guess we've been helped," Jax said.

They followed the man down a hallway.

"Don't mind her. She's new and young. She doesn't know how life is."

Jax smiled, though the man made his hands sweat.

"You said in your call that you're looking for, how do you say, to be absent for a while?"

"Something like that," Jax replied.

"Well, that's not what we do here. We help people with their lives and help them get situated." The man said.

"What was your name?" Jax asked.

"Oliver Warren," the man replied.

"We heard from a former client that you do exactly what we're talking about?"

"Who is this former client?"

"David Webb," Jax said.

The man stared at him.

"I don't know what you're talking about," Warren said.

"Well, I guess we're at a loss here. David said you could help us." Griggs said.

Jax glanced around the room. Pictures of the man in front of them standing next to dignitaries and former Presidents lined the wall.

"Thank you for your help, Mr. Warren. I will let David know you couldn't help us." Jax said.

He pulled Griggs out of the room, and they headed for the elevator.

When they reached the elevator, Jax turned and stared at Christina. Her phone buzzed when they got to the elevator.

Jax leaned over to Griggs.

"I think we stirred something up," Jax said.

"Yes, I think this will get things rolling," Griggs said.

When they got in the car, Griggs glanced over at Jax.

"I thought you were going to mention Milburn?"

"I think that would've brought too much attention."

"But why Webb?"

"Did you feel weird being in that room with him?"

"I guess. He sure knows a lot of people."

"Yes, did you see the arms on that guy? That suit looked like it was painted on. He's ex-military. You think he'll be in the system?"

"Not under Oliver Warren," Jax said, "we'll have to find him some other way," Jax said.

"I'll check out the company. It felt shady as hell. I glanced into the other offices as we walked past them. There was no one in them. Just empty rooms."

Jax pulled out of the garage and turned left toward Lafayette Square.

CHAPTER FIFTY-FIVE

DRAKE STOOD at the window looking down as Jax and Griggs's car moved towards Lafayette Square.

He picked up the phone and dialed one number.

"We have a problem," he said.

"What is it now?" the voice asked.

"Griggs and Reed were just here. They told me Webb told them about my company."

"But Webb is dead?"

"But I also got a call from a friend. He said Colonel Black told them about my company. So they were lying to cover up what they knew. They're getting too close."

"How did they get on to you so quickly?"

"I don't know, but Black's information didn't help."

"How would they know to talk to Black again?"

"I don't know," Drake said.

"I may have an idea. This doesn't move our timeline. That's in stone. But it can cause a disruption. I have an idea on how to handle this."

"I feel like I'm in the open right now."

"You're not going to run. Are you?"

"Not now," Drake said, "it's too close. I think he wanted to drop another name, not Webb's."

"Which name?"

"Johnny Milburn," Drake said.

"Well, fuck, that's not good."

Drake gazed out at the park below as an airplane crossed the sky overhead, wishing he were on it.

"You figure out what needs to be done, and I'll make sure it happens."

"All right. If Reed is snooping around, it may not take them long to figure things out."

Drake ended the call and sat at his desk.

CHAPTER FIFTY-SIX

THE SPEAKER of the House tucked his phone into his pocket and walked across the room.

"What's going on? Have they canceled the meeting?" his chief of staff, Tom Warner, asked.

"No, that's still on. It's time we got to the car." The Speaker said.

Secret Service stood outside his office, leading him to an elevator that took them to the parking garage underneath the Capitol complex.

A black SUV was one of three in a procession, and it pulled out of the underground, turned right, and drove towards the White House.

It was a last-minute meeting, but Miles Frank was sure he knew the topic.

The car rolled through the gates of the White House and stopped at the entrance.

Miles Frank stepped out and smiled when he looked at the white building.

Secret Service led him through the hallways towards the Oval Office.

President Thompson's secretary buzzed them through, and Speaker Frank stepped into the room.

The carvings on the walls, the seal on the floor, and the gold curtains. He hated the gold curtains, but President Thompson loved them.

"Mr. President," Miles Frank said.

The President was approaching his mid-seventies, and the last eight years had not been kind to him.

Most Presidents aged twice as fast as usual while occupying the residence; President Thompson looked like he aged three times that.

He looked withered and frail. His stature had been one of command, but after eight years, the man looked skinny and small.

His hands looked as if the bones protruded from them, and Speaker Frank wondered if the rumors he'd heard were true.

"How are you this morning, Sir?" Frank asked.

"I'm doing as okay as my body will allow. I wish I could run for another term, but I'm also not sure I could survive another term in this dirty old house."

"The demands of the job are heavy. It takes a lot of strength to get through them. You've done a great job the past eight years."

"Thank you, Miles," the President replied.

"Tell me, what's this all about?"

The President looked from the floor to the Speaker.

"I've heard rumblings about you wanting to run in the next election. I want to back you on that. This woman she's horrible and doesn't deserve eight years. The things she said during the debates about the Vice President and me were horrible. She's a terrible person. I want to make her a one-term president."

"I can help you with that, Sir. What would you like me to do?" Miles asked.

The President smiled.

"I don't want her to get anything through. She's too afraid to abandon the filibuster in the Senate. I want everything to halt while she's in office. I don't care what happens, but she gets nothing through. If you do that, you'll get my endorsement."

"I greatly appreciate that, Sir. Should the need arise, I've been working on finding someone within our party to replace me as Speaker. I'm still narrowing choices, but I have it down to five people."

"Wonderful, let's plan for that. I want to see you sitting in this chair in four years."

"Thank you," Miles replied.

"That's all I have for you today. That woman is coming over later. I have to play nice, but it will be difficult."

"I understand. I had a meeting with her as well. She's a brilliant woman. She will try and dismantle everything we've built. I will make sure she doesn't. Your legacy is important to me." Miles said.

"Thank you," President Thompson said.

Miles stood up and walked to the door. He glanced back at President Thompson as he sat behind the Resolute Desk.

CHAPTER FIFTY-SEVEN

ELAINE FRANKLIN HAD BEEN a gymnast in college, and though she was older, it showed how her shoulders filled out her suit.

She stared as Miles Frank walked out of the Oval Office.

"Madame President-Elect, he's ready for you," President Thompson's secretary said.

Elaine smiled, and she and Tom walked into the office.

The gold curtains would be gone in a matter of weeks. She'd already given explicit instructions on the things she wanted to be removed from the Oval. The painting of Andrew Jackson over the fireplace would be replaced with one of Thomas Jefferson.

She felt better with Thomas Jefferson watching over her. She studied all she could think about him in college, and though there were things about the man she didn't like, his thoughts on government were not part of them.

The President stood up from behind his desk and tried to embrace her. She stepped back.

"No offense, Mr. President, but I'd rather not get into that habit." She said.

The President smiled. It was the same smile he'd used on TV numerous times. It was the condescending look he gave nearly everything and everyone.

"You've been briefed on everything going on this week?" he asked.

"I have. This whole China thing is crazy. I'd like to see some resolution to it." She said.

Thompson nodded.

"I would as well. I only have a little over a week in this chair, but I'd like to get somewhere with the Chinese."

"I'm glad to hear it. We should coordinate something."

Then, as he smirked, she realized the wrong words had come out of her mouth.

"Look, Mrs. Franklin, the world knows we don't like each other. I'd rather have my Vice President take over for me. At least then, I'd know things were going in the correct direction. So please don't act like I'm going to show deference because you're taking over this job. I'm still President for a few more days, and if I can get this thing done by then, I will."

The President-Elect smiled, glanced at Tom, then around the room.

"Did you know that the President hasn't always had this office? It was added when Truman rebuilt the White House during the nineteen fifties. He was tired of using the old office, and when the place needed to be rebuilt, he found a way to have this room put into the construction plans. It was modified in the early two-thousands because of terror threats."

Elaine paused to study Thompson before continuing.

"I understand you will be here for a while longer, but when the Oval Office was built, things that were not needed were tossed away. I want to think of your administration that way. It will be tossed on the heap of what your administration has done to our great nation."

The President stared at her. No one had ever spoken to him in such a way. It left a sour taste in his mouth.

"You want to start this way, fine. But when you leave this office in four years, remember what you said just now. It will come back to haunt you."

"I'll remember your Vice President lost, which has nothing to do with debates or anything you mentioned. It has to do with his connection to this administration." Elaine stood up.

"I wasn't done with this meeting," he said.

"I'm done listening to your drivel, Mr. President, or should I call you Mr. Thompson?" she said and walked out the door.

The outer room was full of people waiting to see the President, and they stared at her.

She felt her skin prickle with warmth, and she wanted to scream. Tom followed close behind her.

When they got in the car, he turned to look at her.

"That wasn't very nice," Tom said.

"I don't care. That man thought he could talk to me the way he's talked to every other woman in his life. I won't have it. I will put him in his place. This country needs to get out of its shell game, and they have. In another week, he'll be relegated to the history books, but his daily diatribes will go ignored except by a radical few. I'm looking forward to it, and I'm sure the American people are also."

"What if you need his help with something later?"

"There is nothing that man could help me with. We're bringing in good people that know what they're doing. This man was an infant in an adult pool. I'm surprised the son of a bitch didn't drown in the last eight years. Now the pool is being drained, and the remnants of his administration are being bled out in the gutter."

Tom smiled at her words, "That's the Elaine I know."

She smiled, "We have to get back to the house. My grandkids are coming over, and I'd like to see them for a while. They calm me, and after dealing with that pompous ass, I need the calm."

The car pulled onto Pennsylvania Avenue and turned left.

CHAPTER FIFTY-EIGHT

THE WATER on the Potomac lay in sheets of ice crashing against its shores. Jax watched the crunching ice strike the banks and glanced over at Griggs.

"You know this whole thing was a swamp when they decided to put the Capitol here?"

"I know," Griggs replied.

"I just find it funny that the swamp was once the reality of this place, and now it's a metaphor for corruption."

"What are you getting at?" Griggs asked.

"This whole thing with Webb is odd, you know. Why couldn't Miles Frank wait four more years?" Jax asked.

"You mean the next election?" Griggs asked.

"Why couldn't he do that? Just bide his time, and wait four years. There has to be something we don't know."

"You think she's planning something?"

"I don't know. Maybe it's the policies she wants to implement. She's said she wants to do away with Thompson's ideas." Jax said.

"What was she like when you talked to her?" He asked Griggs.

"What, you changing your mind about her?"

"No, she was nice, forceful, but nice. She doesn't beat around the bush about anything. She will come at you full bore."

"In the last debate, I thought she came across as a bitch." Griggs said.

"I didn't. I thought she came across as someone knowledgeable about the current administration's screw-ups. She knew what to say and how to say it, and she won the vote."

"Yes, by a large margin," Griggs added.

"It was the largest margin in our history. I like her more in person than watching her on the campaign trail. She is a no-bullshit type of person."

"Right, so she's going to be running the show. What will happen if we can stop this?" Griggs asked.

"I wish I knew when they would attack the inauguration."

"It would have to be while she's being sworn in. After that, she'll be in the beast." Griggs said.

The ice crunched against the barrier protecting The Mall, and both watched it lap at the shore. Little water was in it, but the ice made up most of what struck the banks.

"So they come down from wherever they're hiding this thing, make their way to the Capitol, and blow everyone away?"

"Think of that happening? It would terrify the nation and the world. Miles Frank would be able to do whatever he wanted."

"A strike like that would make people fearful and accepting of more presidential power," Jax said.

"He'd put out a statement about it. Telling the world of the tragedy and that the people would be brought to justice. It could send this country into a spiral it might never recover from."

"We need to find Johnny Milburn, and I think it's time we involve your dad," Jax said.

"You think so?"

"Yes," Jax replied.

They walked across The Mall to the Hoover building. They rode the elevator to the fourth floor, stepped off, and walked into Decker's office.

"To what do I owe this meeting on a Saturday?" Decker asked.

"We need to learn a few things about a couple of people," Griggs replied.

"Okay, that's easy enough. Jax, you know how to do this." Decker said.

"That's the problem, Dad," Griggs said, "one of them is supposed to be dead. The other runs a company that supplies mercenaries and helps people disappear."

Decker stared at both of them.

"You've lost your minds," he replied.

"No, we haven't," Jax said.

"What have you two gotten into?" he said, though it was directed at Griggs.

"We can't say yet, but we need to know the information about these two," Griggs said.

"Okay, go for it." He said.

They left the room and walked to Jax's desk.

"So let's start small research on the company," Jax said.

"I'll get on that if you want to work on Johnny Milburn?" Griggs said.

"Done," Jax replied.

Griggs walked away, and Jax opened up the military service database. He narrowed it down by branch, then by the station. He knew there were people assigned to Groom he wouldn't be able to search for, but he also knew there were ways around that.

There weren't many pilots assigned to Groom, and he narrowed his search until a warning appeared.

UNAUTHORIZED

He stared at the warning flashing red on his screen, got up, and walked into Decker's office.

"Hey, I started looking for our guy and got an unauthorized notice."

"Really?" Decker asked.

"Yes, I should be able to access military records, right?"

"Unless intelligence agencies have locked them down."

"Why would they do that?"

"If the person worked at a government facility or did clandestine work, their name or status would be hidden."

"That would complicate things, wouldn't it?"

"Definitely," Decker said, "let me see if I can get further than you did."

He entered the information the same way Jax had, and the same warning popped up.

"Will I have to talk to someone about this?"

"Yes, but given the popup, they probably already know we've tried to access it."

"Right, because they don't trust anyone?"

"Exactly," Decker said, "do you know anyone you could talk to about it?"

"I do, but I've already asked a lot from this person."

"Maybe another ask wouldn't hurt?"

Griggs walked into the office and stared from her father to Jax, then to the screen.

"I got something," she said.

"Show me," Jax said.

He followed her to the door.

"That little girl is her mom's pride and joy. She may only be my stepdaughter, but I never looked at her as that. Take care of my girl."

"I will, sir," Jax said and caught up to Griggs.

She turned and smiled at him.

"What was that all about?" Griggs asked.

"It was nothing," Jax replied, "what did you find?"

"I learned that this company has offices all over the world."

"Okay, no big deal," Jax said.

"But most of them are in hotspots."

"So what? They've hired guns. That's normal," Jax said.

"Maybe, but the thing is, I tried to trace where their money comes from, and it sent me to all these different places."

"So, it's been washed?" Jax asked.

"Probably," Griggs replied, "when I started at Nellis, there was this big to-do about money disappearing in the Las Vegas Valley. It vanished from banks and investments, then hit the CO of Nellis. That's when we were called in. OSI handled a lot of the heavy lifting on that case. I got to see how financial crimes worked that year. What I see here is similar, but these companies and how they wash them are different. It looks like they're buying businesses, then turning them at a loss."

"They're using the businesses or the property they are on to wash things?

"I think so. This company owns airports in these hot zones. They also own an airport in West Virginia. The Air Force used it."

"Which means clandestine activities?"

"Yes, they're probably using it for rendition. But why would the government bring people into the states when they've been using other nations?"

"I don't know," Jax said.

"So, what happened after the government stopped using it?" He asked Griggs

"It made its way to Executive Actions through another company. But that's where it ends. But this airport, or airstrip, would be a better word, it has a long runway, and they could fly the drone out of there, but I looked at recent satellite images. It's deserted. That runway would tear the drone apart if they're flying out of there."

"Okay, so they're not using that. What about other things?"

"Okay, you remembered that shootout in India a few years ago? I didn't remember it, but it made a lot of noise. So I looked into it. A few witnesses said men in military uniforms were seen leaving an airstrip thought to have been abandoned. Still, when I looked up the airstrip from satellite images, it showed a new airstrip, buildings, and jeeps scattered throughout. But there were other things in the pictures I didn't understand. Maybe you can help with that?" she asked.

Griggs brought up the images, and Jax stared at them for a few minutes, "What am I looking for?"

"This spot right here," she said, pointing to a corner of the image.

Jax stared at it.

To the naked eye, it looked like trees, but to Jax, who'd flown dozens of drone and regular aircraft missions, he knew what it was.

"It's a cover. It's made to look like a regular forest or grassland. India has places that are more tropical looking, and this does that. It scans the surrounding area and plots it onto a map."

"So, whatever they're hiding isn't good?" Griggs asked.

"I'd expect not. It could be missile batteries or just trucks."

"So, where does this tie into what we're investigating?"

"I'm not sure it does. But suppose this company is tied to these operations. In that case, they may have procured these airstrips from governments or a private contractor."

"Let's look at the policies Elaine Franklin has proposed," Griggs said.

"You think there is more to it than Frank wanting to be President?"

"I do, and if there is, we may be able to find it."

"Okay, let's look at the bills she's presented to Congress while she was a Senator."

"What do you want to do with this other stuff?"

"We keep it to ourselves unless we see something bigger. There may be a use for this, but I'm not seeing it now. Let's look into this person we met as well."

"I tried, but I keep getting restrictions," Griggs said.

"I know someone who can help us," Jax said.

"You mean Williams?" Griggs asked.

"Yes, but I want to wait until we have more information."

"You've asked a lot from him," Griggs said.

"Yes, but he's all we have," Jax said.

CHAPTER FIFTY-NINE

WILLIAMS'S PHONE BUZZED, and he picked it up.

He'd spent more time at the office lately, and his wife called him numerous times a day about the kids.

There had been threats against the inauguration, but nothing credible, and he was still organizing his schedule.

"Williams," he answered.

"Hey, there's been activity on an ID that was locked away."

"Davis, is that you?"

"Yes, sir," the man replied.

"Whose ID is it?"

"The FBI has been looking into him. His file says he's dead, but a blue alert was implemented for anyone looking into him."

Williams had started to shake, and he glanced at the wall.

"Don't worry about it. Who was the agent looking into Milburn?"

"Jackson Reed," Davis said.

"Very well. Thank you, Davis," Williams said.

The call ended, and Williams dialed a number.

"Jackson, what the hell are you doing?" Williams asked.

The other end was quiet for a moment.

"Aaron, you're exactly who I wanted to speak with," Jax said.

"Why are you looking into Johnny Milburn?"

"I'm following the crumbs. They're coming fast, and they've led me to a few things."

"Those crumbs have led you to him?"

"They have. I took the plane and asked Colonel Black a few questions. Those answers have led me to Milburn. You're calling because of the alert, aren't you?"

"Look, Jax. This guy is a ghost. When people disappear from the service like this, there's a reason behind it. You need to let this go."

"Why?" Jax asked.

"This is a big jump from the murder of Sadie Dickson."

"I know that, but I'm doing my job. This shouldn't have to be this hard," Jax said.

The line went dead, and Williams stared at the phone.

The asshole hung up on me.

* * *

Jax glanced over at Griggs, who'd watched the conversation on their end.

"That was Williams, wasn't it?" she asked.

"Of course it was," Jax replied.

Griggs stood up from her desk and moved like she was going to walk away.

"Griggs, come on?" Jax said.

She stopped and returned to her desk, "Look, I'm aware people don't want me here. I get looks when I walk in. I'm sure my father doesn't like me this close to something. I assume he wants to pull me off and send me home. But I'm not leaving."

"I think he's trying to get you moved up," Jax said.

"You think so?"

"I do. Williams told us to back off Milburn. He said there are reasons people like Milburn disappear," Jax said.

"Yes, they've done something bad."

"These people either know something that makes them valuable to outside sources or can do things others can't. When they find themselves no longer useful, they get out."

"So this drone is sent to Creech, and he's out of a job?" Griggs asked.

"Then why didn't he get the job?" Jax asked.

"Maybe he was unstable. From what Black told us, that may be a reason."

"Let's look at his evaluations," Jax suggested, bringing up another screen.

"Do you think there will be something in there?"

"There may be. When I returned to Groom, Black told me some people couldn't hack it. The isolation gets to them. Maybe it got to him, and it's in his evaluations?"

"Did he have any family?" Griggs asked

"He does. He has a sister that lives in Utah. Maybe we can talk to her. She may have a better insight into this."

"What about Williams?" Griggs asked.

"We're following the case," Jax said.

He went into Decker's office and told him they needed to fly to Utah.

"All right," Decker said, "but be careful. This might have stirred up some shit."

They walked out of the building, got a ride to the airport, and booked the first flight to Salt Lake City. The flight took longer than expected. There were delays with the aircraft and then a layover in Atlanta.

When they arrived in Salt Lake, it was nighttime and snowing.

Jax rented an SUV. He didn't want to screw around with the snow.

He programmed in the directions to a hotel in the city they'd be staying in and drove an hour and a half north to a place called Brigham City. They pulled up in front of Milburn's sister's house.

"This is it. It's late. We'll have to come back in the morning," Jax said.

"Okay. I'll find us a room with two beds." Griggs said, staring at him.

He pulled into the parking lot of a small hotel and parked the car.

Jax walked into the lobby and got their room.

He came out and stopped to stare as two trucks rolled past the hotel. Plumes of black smoke poured from their tailpipes. Gun racks shone in the rear window, and large Confederate flags hung from posts mounted next to the wheel wells.

Jax continued out and motioned for Griggs to follow.

"Got a room on the top floor," Jax said.

"You think there's a place to eat this late?" Griggs asked.

"I didn't think to ask," Jax said.

He handed her a key.

"You go on up. I'll ask the person at the desk."

An old soda machine sat in the corner of a stairwell with a snack machine. The lights on the snack machine blinked intermittently, and the soda machine hummed, though its lights were off.

Griggs reached the room and pushed on the door.

Twin beds sat in the room, and the decoration was 80s ugly. She thought she'd seen the same space in a horror movie once.

She closed the door and sat on the bed. It squeaked, and she got up and walked to the window.

The view looked out on the main road. A hospital and a large building lit up with a gold figure on top sat in the distance.

The door opened, and Jax walked in.

"So, anywhere for food?"

"There's a local pizza place that delivers," Jax said.

"Okay, let's do that," Griggs said.

Jax stared around the room.

"Homey, isn't it?" he asked.

"I feel it was used in an 80s horror movie at some point."

Jax laughed and smiled at Griggs. It was an uncomfortable laugh, made all the more painful by how she looked at him.

"Okay, let's order that pizza," he said.

"Right," Griggs replied.

"Hey, we're staying at the motel on the main road. I think it's Motel 6, and we'd like to order a couple of pizzas." Jax said.

The person on the other end said something.

"A large pepperoni and mushroom, and a large...," Jax said, staring at Griggs expectantly.

"A large pepperoni and anchovy," she said.

"Really?" Jax whispered.

She nodded.

"And a large pepperoni and anchovy," Jax said.

The other end said something.

"Yes, it's room 248. Thank you," Jax said.

The call ended.

"Should be here in thirty minutes." He said.

"Great, I'm starving," she said.

"Didn't care for the food on the plane?"

"Plane food is all the same. It's prepackaged and tastes awful. I've never had a good meal on a plane."

"Ever flown in first class?" Jax asked.

"Who can afford that?"

"I've flown that way once. It was worth the expense." He said.

Griggs turned on the TV, and they watched reruns of The Simpsons until the food arrived.

The pizza delivery person was about Jax's age; his face was pockmarked.

Jax handed the money with a good tip, and the man took it.

"Hey, thanks so much," the guy said.

Jax closed the door.

Griggs grabbed her pizza. The smell of anchovies, pepperoni, and cheese wafted up from the cardboard box, and Jax thought he would lose his stomach.

"I'm going to get some sodas," he said and hurried from the room.

He returned with two cokes, two sprites, and a Dr. Pepper. Jax opened a Dr. Pepper and set the others out for Griggs to pick from.

She sat on her bed staring at the screen, picking off the anchovies, tossing them in the air, and catching them in her mouth.

"I don't know how anyone can eat those things," Jax said.

"When I was a kid, they screwed up the pizza order, and by the time the pizza guy came back, it would take too long. So I ate it. It's been my go-to pizza since then." She said.

Jax shuddered and ate his pizza.

They stayed up and watched the TV; before they knew it, they'd fallen asleep.

CHAPTER SIXTY

JOHNNY'S PHONE RANG, rousing him out of deep sleep. He stared at the alarm next to his bed. It read 02:00.

"Hello," he answered.

"Just wanted to let you know those two are still snooping around. Those two are looking into you."

"What do you mean? Don't they think I'm dead?"

"They've been out to Groom, and Colonel Black mentioned a few things that got them riled up. I don't know where they are, but they are looking for you."

"Thanks for the heads up," Johnny said.

"What are friends for?" the caller ended the call.

Johnny sat on his couch in the cabin, the TV blared across the room, and a bag of chips sat on the table.

He'd intended to take the drone up earlier but fell asleep.

Johnny sat up, staring at the face on the TV screen. It was a replay of the President-Elect walking into the White House the previous day. He smiled, walked into the control room, and turned the lights on.

The fans and electronics came on immediately, followed by the hum of the control console.

He sat down, and the monitor showed only the cabin in front of the drone. He'd cleared the snow earlier, and there wasn't any expected for a few more days.

The drone rose above the trees and took off towards DC.

He maintained his distance from the White House and kept his altitude as high as possible. He banked right, and the light of the Washington Monument shone in the foreground with the Lincoln Memorial in the background.

He stopped, hovering hundreds of feet in the air, with nothing between him and the President-Elect. He saw her in the windows and the Secret Service detail around the grounds. The sniper team's heat signatures bloomed on the rooftop.

He hovered for a few more minutes and watched as she walked from one room to another. Another light came on downstairs, and he wondered what was happening in the house.

He knew he could take her out right then. No one would know who had done it.

Was she getting up for the day? Was she nervous about the inauguration?

Johnny had no idea why she was up, and he flew the drone back to the cabin.

What was she doing up so early?

* * *

Elaine Franklin sat at her kitchen table, thinking about what she'd miss about their house. There was the mattress, and they'd be back often, but she'd miss the old house.

She knew an upgrade was coming, but she stared at the house. She touched its walls. Ran her fingers over the countertops.

She'd had trouble sleeping since her talk with Agent Reed. She felt there was something he wasn't saying.

"Are you okay, Madame President-Elect?" a Secret Service agent asked.

"Yes, just restless," she said.

The agent sat down across from her, "Don't worry. This is my fourth Presidential detail. Everyone has trouble sleeping in the days before the inauguration. It's like just before the big game."

"Well, I only did gymnastics. Before a meet, I'd have terrible stomach issues." She said.

"I played ice hockey growing up and wasn't sure how bad my stomach would get before a game. Sometimes I'd end up throwing up before hitting the ice."

"Yeah, I was the same way. Funny how things like that shape us. The little butterflies and things like that." She said.

"Yes, Ma'am," he replied.

"Can I ask you a question?" she asked.

"Sure, I'll answer it if I can," the man replied.

"What are your thoughts about the current President?" she asked.

"I'm not allowed to answer those questions. We need to keep our political thoughts separate from our jobs. It's how we're able to work with terrible people." He said.

She smiled and stood up, "I appreciate that answer."

The agent walked down the hallway, and Elaine Franklin glanced out the kitchen window at the agents outside her house.

She was looking forward to the job, but there was something about Agent Reed that made her uncomfortable.

There was no place for it in her thoughts, so she went upstairs and climbed into bed.

She'd be up in a couple of hours. She was going over the daily brief, which had become the same as President Thompson's.

She'd need the rest for what was to come.

CHAPTER SIXTY-ONE

THE SUN ROSE over the Wasatch Mountains, and Jax rolled over and stared at Griggs. Her hair fell in black curls over her eyes and mouth.

He opened his phone and looked for a place to get coffee. He found one around the corner. Jax walked out of the room, made sure to secure it, and walked to the small coffee shop around the corner.

He returned, set her coffee on the table, and picked up his phone again. There were two messages. Both of them were from Sarah. The alarm clock on the nightstand read seven, and he stepped outside and called Sarah.

"Hey, what's going on?" he asked.

"Where are you?" she asked.

"In Utah, working," he replied.

"Elizabeth wants to spend time with you," Sarah said.

He let out a long sigh, "I can't right now. There is too much going on."

"Jax, is there anything you can tell me?"

"Sarah," Jax said, "do you remember those flights I'd take, where you didn't hear from me and thought the worst?

The phone went silent for a moment, "Of course."

The softness of her voice made him feel terrible.

"It's like that," he replied.

"When will you be back?" Sarah asked.

"Later today, I would love to have her tonight if possible. It won't be long. Only overnight, but I miss her."

"I won't hold you to it because you're working. So I won't say anything to Lizzy. She misses her dad. She loves the flamingo."

The place on her pillow was reserved for whichever toy or stuffed animal was her favorite at the time.

Jax smiled at this.

"That's great," he said.

"Hopefully, we'll see you tonight," she said and ended the call.

He walked into the room as Griggs came out of the bathroom with her hair in a towel.

"Who was that?" she asked.

"Sarah, I'd like to be done with this early," Jax said.

"She wants you to pick up Elizabeth?"

"Yeah," Jax said, "Lizbeth said she misses me."

"Are you going to tell her what's going on?"

"I don't know how I can without freaking her out."

"But at least you'll have it out there."

"Right. Well, I got coffee." He said, motioning to the cup on the table.

"Coffee in Utah?" she asked.

"Yeah, I know. It's pretty good, too."

"Where'd you get it?"

"A place around the corner," Jax said, "It's called Ground for Coffee."

She took a sip and smiled, "It is good."

"It's early. We better get moving." Jax said.

Griggs finished drying her hair, and Jax went into the bathroom to shower.

He came out, and Griggs wore a beanie on her head.

"What's that for?" Jax asked, pointing to the beanie.

"You haven't looked outside," she said.

Jax walked to the curtains, pushed them aside, and glanced out. Only thirty minutes ago, two inches of snow lay on the ground where a skiff had been.

"Great," Jax said, "well, I'm glad I rented the SUV."

"So am I," Griggs said.

Jax checked them out of their room, and they drove the short distance to the house.

It looked more extensive in the daylight than it had the night before. Jax pulled into the driveway, and they stepped out of the vehicle.

He looked up and down the street. It was the biggest house on the road. The others were much smaller and looked like they hadn't been renovated since the 80s.

"This house looks out of place," Griggs said.

"Where would someone get the money to build something like this?" Jax asked.

"I guess we'll have to find out."

Jax knocked on the door, and an older woman in a housecoat answered the door. Her hair was done up in curlers, and she stared at both of them.

Jax wore his suit, and Griggs was in her Air Force uniform with her cover on.

"What can I do for you?" she asked, glancing from one to the other.

"Are you Tammy Milburn?" Jax asked.

"I was a long time ago. I haven't gone by that name in years. The name is Walker now," she said.

"We'd like to ask you a few questions," Griggs said.

She waved them inside. The house smelled like pancakes and bacon.

Jax's stomach rumbled, and he glanced around. There were tiny dolls along a fireplace, and a platter of bacon and pancakes lay on the counter.

A few teenagers walked around the house. They were all dressed up.

"Did we interrupt something?" Jax asked.

"We're getting ready for church." She said.

"Right. It's Sunday," Jax said.

"So, what kind of questions?" Tammy Walker asked.

"Huh?" Jax replied, distracted by the smell of food.

"We were wondering if you've talked to your brother?" Griggs asked.

Tammy stopped and stared at both of them.

"Who are you two?" she asked.

"I'm Agent Reed. This is Lieutenant Vanessa Griggs with OSI. You know what that is?"

"I was an Air Force brat. I know who OSI is. Why are you asking about my brother? He's dead," she said.

"We're working on a case together, and your brother's name came up. We're just following the case." Griggs said.

"Well, if his name came up, you'd know he was dead. He's buried at Arlington."

"You don't get any mail for him by chance, do you?" Griggs asked.

"Like I said. Johnny is dead. I don't know why you're here, but I'd like you to leave." She said.

Jax glanced at an envelope on the table.

"What about insurance? Things like that?" Jax asked.

"The money from his insurance went into a college fund for these two." She motioned to the teenagers, who'd taken up a spot at the kitchen counter.

"I see. Well, if you think of anything. Feel free to call." Griggs said and passed over her card.

Tammy Walker took it and tucked it into the pocket of her house coat.

Jax stood up and smiled.

"Enjoy your day," he said, and they walked to the front door.

Tammy Walker followed them to the door and slammed it as they exited.

Jax got in the car and stared up at the house.

Griggs sat in the passenger seat.

"What did you see?" Griggs asked.

"What do you mean?" Jax replied.

"We've been working together for the last few weeks. Enjoy your day. What the hell was that?"

"I bet you anything she's calling him right now. There was a piece of paper on the table. It had Johnny's name on it."

"So?"

"He's been dead for a while. Why would Johnny's sister have papers with his name on them lying around?"

"Right. So what do we do?" Griggs asked.

"I'm going to pull around the corner. There are some bushes in that backyard. I could see them from the living room. She'll want to talk privately, so she'll come outside."

Jax pulled around the corner, got out, and walked up the hill towards the bushes in the back of the house.

Tammy came out of the house, a cigarette dangling from her lips.

Jax sat quietly and listened.

"Johnny, some FBI guy was asking about you," she said.

Tammy was quiet for a moment as she listened to the other end.

"No, they're gone. I wouldn't call you if they were sitting in my living room. But they said they were investigating something, and your name came up."

She got quiet again and listened to the other end.

Jax wished he could hear the whole conversation.

"Well, okay, okay. I'll make sure to watch for them. I have to get the girls to church." She said.

"Yeah, me too," Tammy said and disappeared into the house.

Jax waited in the bushes as the snow came down and hurried off after ten minutes.

Griggs stared at him as he got in the car.

"So, did she call him?"

"Yes, she walked into the backyard and had a conversation."

"He's alive. Now we need to find out where he is," Griggs said.

"The drones have a long radius, but I think he'd want to keep it close to DC or the mountains in Virginia or West Virginia."

"Right. Now we head back?" Griggs asked.

"Now we head back," Jax said.

They drove the hour and a half to Salt Lake International Airport and booked the next plane headed for DC. They had to take one to BWI. There weren't any to Reagan.

CHAPTER SIXTY-TWO

JOHNNY SET down the phone and sat on the couch.

He didn't know who to call, but he wanted to scream.

The TV went off, and he picked up the phone.

"Hey, we have a problem. That FBI agent flew out and talked to my sister," Johnny said.

"How do you know that?"

"She called me."

"Why would she know you're alive?" the other end asked.

"Long story, but she's the only person I trust."

"What did she tell him?"

"What could she say other than I'm dead," Johnny replied.

"Okay. I'll handle it." The man said.

Johnny turned off the TV, walked into the kitchen, and pulled a beer from the fridge. It was only ten in the morning, but it felt good going down.

* * *

The man on the other end stared out the window of his house at the trees beyond the backyard. His wife had left earlier and wouldn't be back for a while. He had work to finish up. Then Johnny called.

He called for his car and walked out the door moments later to where it rested on the curb.

He got in and stared out the window, pondering his next move.

"Where to, sir," his driver asked.

"Take me to the Speaker's house," he said.

"Yes, sir," the driver said.

He knew Miles Frank would be at church with his wife and kids or at home on a Sunday. But he had to talk to him, even if it was only for a few minutes.

Thirty minutes later, the car pulled through the gates.

Security stopped him as he got out.

"He's getting ready for church, Sir," the Secret Service agent said.

"I'll be brief," he replied.

They waved him to the front door, where another agent let him in the house.

Miles Frank stood in the kitchen and stared at him.

"Aaron? What are you doing here?" Speaker Frank asked.

"We need to talk," DNI Williams said.

"I was leaving for church. It needs to wait." Frank said.

"It's about our flyboy," Williams replied.

Miles walked into the living room. His wife sat on the couch, putting her shoes on. His kids sat in other chairs, staring at their phones.

"Take the car. I'll be along in a few minutes," he said.

"Miles, what's wrong?" his wife asked.

"Nothing, a last-minute thing I need to take care of." He said.

She peered around him at Williams standing in the kitchen.

"With the Director of National Intelligence?" his wife asked.

His kids set down their phones peered into the kitchen, and then glanced at one another. They stood up and walked to the front door.

"It's work stuff," he said.

It was a straight-out lie, and she knew it was. But she ignored it, grabbed her bag, and walked toward the kids.

The kids stared at him.

"Go with your mom. I'll be along shortly." He said.

They walked out the door to the waiting car. Miles closed the door behind them and spun on Williams.

"What the hell is going on? You're not supposed to come here," he said.

"Let's take this where there aren't so many ears," Williams said.

Speaker Frank led him towards a small office in the back of the house. The door closed, and a slight hum rose from the walls.

Frank sat down in one chair while Williams took another, "What's this all about?"

Williams relayed the information he'd received from Johnny, and the Speaker stared at him.

"Have you spoken to our other man?" Frank asked.

"It's not a good idea to involve him with this. Let them dig a little longer. We've put roadblocks up. They won't get to the end by the time you're in the Oval. Then you can squash it."

"That's true, and they've been to see you a few times."

"Jax trusts me. You can always back out of this. It's not too late," Williams said.

"Not a chance," Frank said, "that woman doesn't deserve that office."

"Okay, I'll disable the failsafe then."

Miles stood up, and they walked out of the room.

Williams walked to the front door while Speaker Frank went to the garage.

"Everything okay, Sir," Williams's security detail asked.

"Fine. I just had to clear something up." He said.

They got in the car and drove home.

* * *

Speaker Frank got out and walked into the church with his detail on both sides of him.

His wife and kids stared at him when he sat down.

"Everything is fine," he said.

His wife didn't feel like everything was fine and worried about the long hours he'd been working.

CHAPTER SIXTY-THREE

WHEN THE FLIGHT landed at BWI, Jax walked down the jetway and hurried towards the exit.

Griggs was close behind him.

"I can get a ride if you want?" she suggested.

"That would be great," he replied.

Jax waved to her as he hurried to his car.

He called Sarah when he sat in his car.

"Jax, where are you?"

"Just landed. I'll be there in half an hour."

"Great," Sarah said, "I'll have Lizzy ready."

As Sarah told Elizabeth, a squeal erupted from the other end of the phone.

A motorcade came up behind him, and he pulled to the side to let it pass.

When he arrived, Elizabeth sat on the porch with her flamingo.

He got out, and she ran to the car.

"Daddy," she squealed.

Jax picked her up and carried her towards the front door.

He set her down, and Elizabeth pushed on the front door. Her My Little Pony carry-on sat next to the door.

"Jax, can we talk?" Tom asked from the stairs.

"I was just leaving with Lizbeth," Jax replied.

"It will only take a minute," Tom said.

Jax followed him towards the office next to the dining room. It had once been his room, though it was much more of an office than it had been when Jax used it. Books and papers lined a large desk, and documents with labels sat next to them.

Elizabeth had followed them into the room, and she stood in the doorway.

"Daddy, I thought we were going?" she asked.

"We are. Give me a minute to talk to Tom," Jax replied.

She hung her head and walked out the door.

"What is it?" Jax asked.

"I wanted to see how things were going," Tom said.

"They're okay. Doing the best I can," Jax replied.

"I wasn't talking about that. I was talking about the other thing."

Jax stared at him, "I can't talk about an ongoing investigation with you. You know that."

"Elaine wants to know what's going on," Tom said.

"We're still trying to figure that out for ourselves."

Tom sat in his chair.

"Look, I know you don't like me, but this is how things are. Elaine Franklin will be President soon. She wants people on her side that will do their jobs and report to her."

Jax could only stare at him. This man was asking him to break the rules. Rules that he knew and that the woman who would be President knew.

"You're asking me to bend the knee? My job is to find out what's going on, and I'm not going to give her a personal update.

She's not my CO, and she's not my boss. I have to go. My daughter is waiting."

He stormed from the room. He grabbed Elizabeth's carry-on and her hand and walked out the door.

"Go get in the car," Jax said.

Jax turned around, and Tom stood next to the stairs. His eyes were unwavering.

"Tom, I don't know what she thinks I can tell her. I know she has clearance for a lot of things, but—"

"No, she knows what you're looking into. She told you that. She wants to know what you find."

"I'm hoping to be done by the inauguration," Jax said.

He hurried to the car, where Elizabeth stood next to the door.

"You didn't unlock it," she said.

"Sorry," Jax replied.

He unlocked the doors and stared at Tom standing in the doorway.

I will not have a working relationship with my ex-wife's fiancé.

He pulled out of the driveway and drove down the road.

* * *

In a small black car up the street, Drake watched him and wondered what type of conversation he had had with Tom.

He opened his phone and dialed the number of the voice.

"I've been following Agent Reed. Did you know his ex-wife is engaged to Elaine Franklin's Chief of Staff?"

The other end went silent.

"I'd heard rumors, but that's it." The voice said.

"I don't know what they discussed, but Reed didn't look happy when he left. Do you think they talked about our plans?"

"I don't think they're far enough along to be able to do that. Elaine Franklin is not the President yet. It would break protocol for him to do that, and Reed is a by-the-books type of person."

"What do you want me to do?" Drake asked.

"Keep watching them. Reed is the main target, but keep an eye on Griggs. She seems to know what she's doing."

The call ended, and Drake started the car.

He returned to his office and pulled the car into the garage beneath the building.

CHAPTER SIXTY-FOUR

GRIGGS SAT in a car across from where Drake had gotten out. A camera sat on her lap.

Instead of staying at her mom's, she'd gone there, grabbed her camera, and sat waiting in the darkened garage for the man to return.

She held up the camera and took a long-range shot of Drake as he walked from his car to the elevator.

He'd given them his name, but she knew pictures were a better way to identify someone.

She held the button down, taking numerous pictures of him. She wanted to make sure there were enough from various angles to submit them to the computer.

She drove home afterward and walked in the door. She carried her bag with her laptop downstairs and set it up at the kitchen table.

"What are you looking at?" her mom asked.

"I can't talk about it," Griggs replied.

"You sound like your dad," her mom said.

Her mom sat down at the table across from her.

"Mom, can I ask you a question?"

"Okay, what about?" her mom asked apprehensively.

"About my biological dad," Griggs said.

"I'll answer if I can," she replied.

"Something came up with Agent Reed about when he was flying in Iraq. Did dad have any issues with his CO?"

Her mom only stared at her; then, her eyes moved away.

"How did you know that?" her mom asked.

"Just something that Jax said. He flew with my dad. They were on opposite rotations, and Jax had a few issues with his CO. I'm trying to narrow it down to specifics."

"Don't try to fix him, Vanessa. That man is almost twice your age."

"I know, but he's a nice guy, and it seems like he's been screwed over a few times. I want to find out if there's something more to it. Like with dad."

"You think they're connected?" her mom asked.

"I don't know. I need someone to talk through this with."

"Okay, but why do you want to help him?" her mom asked.

"What do you mean?" Griggs replied.

"Vanessa, I may be your mom, but I'm not blind. He's a good-looking man, but he's your superior, at least in this matter. I don't want you to get hurt."

Griggs smiled, but she averted her eyes from meeting her mom.

"I'm not asking for dating advice. But what if there's a connection to what happened to him and the intelligence failure that got my dad shot down?"

"You should look at the records and see if there were any discipline issues with your dad. He didn't say there were, but he was deployed, and we didn't talk as much as either of us would have liked. You were little at the time, and he cared for you. He called when he could but didn't like to talk about work. He wanted to know how his girl was and how life was on the other side of the world. He avoided all talk about work."

"But you said something about him having trouble with his CO?"

"You can look for it, but I don't want whatever he got into to cloud your mind. He was a good man. What those barbarians did to him was horrible. Now that it's been a while, I've looked at how we treated the Iraqis. Your father didn't deserve what happened to him. Many innocent people died, more on the Iraqi side, but still many people."

"So, if I did find something, you would want me to keep it to myself?"

"I'd rather remember how he was on his last rotation. He was in good spirits, but he was cloudy."

"Any idea what it could've been?"

Her mom stopped and stood up. She went up the stairs, and Griggs heard her rummaging around in her bedroom.

She returned a few minutes later with a letter.

"What's this?" Griggs asked.

"A letter I got from another pilot. Your dad didn't want to send it by mail. He was worried about security. If it were opened, he would be in trouble."

"Why would he have been in trouble?"

"Read the letter," her mom said.

Griggs took it, and her mom left the room.

* * *

Dear Carol,

If you're reading this, I've been killed in action. I didn't want to write one of these letters, but it's something that's required.

I wanted to tell you how much I love you and our little girl.

If I've been killed in action, I want you to know it may not have been my fault.

Our CO has been sending us up on missions that don't have a focus. We're doing runs, but we're dropping bombs. I didn't know why until recently. If we keep dropping them, someone gets paid. If the war stops, the money stops.

I was recently brought into my CO's office, and they talked to me about what I found.

I found it by chance. I was walking by his office and heard him on the phone with someone. They were talking about the need to drop more bombs because the money wasn't coming in the way it should be.

I was told not to say anything at his meeting with me.

The CO was pretty pissed when I filed a paper about what I heard.

That paper disappeared.

I'm worried about the next time I go up.

This is the third or fourth time I've written this letter. None of them have reached you. I ensured Captain Webb would bring this one home on his next rotation if I were killed. He promised not to open it.

I will miss our conversations. I will miss watching our daughter grow up.

She is quite beautiful, and I hope you find someone that will help you after I'm gone.

You are such an amazing woman, and making you laugh during our calls brought me joy.

Love,

Marcus

* * *

Griggs stared at it and wiped her eyes.

Her mom came up behind her and hugged her.

"I'm sorry, Vanessa," her mom said.

"Why didn't you show this to anyone?" Griggs asked.

"I tried but was told it would open a wound that the military didn't want to be opened."

"So you held onto it until you thought it could bring something out?"

"Well, I hoped our daughter would grow up and find a way to honor her father. I've never shown that to anyone, not even your stepfather. Webb never opened it."

"So, this Webb, is it the same one who died in Las Vegas?"

"When I saw the video, I was angry at Agent Reed. When I found out you were in the room. I hid it from Thomas because he wouldn't understand. I breathed relief when the news came that the video had been edited."

"Mom, I talked to him. He didn't mention dad."

"He wouldn't. We lost touch after he brought that letter. He said Webb didn't feel good about spending time with him. So we had our lives, and he had his. I met him once at an Air Force function. I didn't like the way he looked at me."

"What do you mean?" Griggs asked but already knew the answer. Webb had given her the same feelings.

"He made me uncomfortable," her mom said.

"I understand that," Griggs replied.

"You do whatever you need to do with this." Her mom said.

"I have to show this to Jax," Griggs said.

"I don't know if that's a good idea," her mom said.

"I think they had the same CO. If I can bring dad justice, then I will."

"Okay, but be careful. His CO is in a very powerful position."

"Who was he?"

"Miles Frank," Carol said, "he's the CO your father referenced in the letter. I'm not sure who else knew about the money your dad talks about, but I don't believe in a coincidence."

Griggs put the letter away, and her mom hugged her.

"He was a good man, Vanessa. He loved you a lot."

Griggs wiped a tear away, and her mom walked out of the room.

She knew she couldn't talk to Jax. He was with Elizabeth, and she didn't want to disrupt that.

It was getting late, but she called for a car and had it take her to the FBI building.

She walked inside, flashed her temporary badge, and went up the elevator.

A few other agents were burning the midnight oil, and she walked to the desk she'd used the day before.

She turned on the computer and searched through all the information about Miles Frank and where he'd been stationed.

She found the information about the CEO of Executive Actions. Their employee records were in the IRS database.

The company had buildings around the world, as she'd told Jax. She fed the picture she'd taken into the database of ex-military personnel. It ran through the whole database.

She watched it run, got herself coffee, and candy from the machine, and nodded off a few times.

When it stopped searching, the sun was coming up.

CHAPTER SIXTY-FIVE

AS THE NAME on the computer came up, the sound of Elizabeth in the kitchen roused Jax from his sleep.

He pulled on his pants and shuffled into the hallway.

"Daddy, I made you coffee," Elizabeth said.

"When did you learn to do that?"

"Sometimes Tom stays up late working. Mom showed me how, so I can help her in the kitchen."

She'd poured it into a mug; the light brown color of the liquid swirled around.

He took a sip.

"You made it perfect. How did you know how I drink my coffee?" Jax asked.

She squealed in delight.

"I've watched you drink it since I was little. I paid attention."

"Okay, so what are we doing today?" he asked.

"You don't have to be at work?"

"Not for a little while. Do you want to get breakfast or play another game on the console?"

Elizabeth shrugged.

Jax had beaten her in the flying game numerous times the night before, and they finally turned it off after he let her win a dog fight.

She knew he'd let her win.

"We played a lot last night."

"Okay, we'll get cleaned up, then we'll get breakfast. Where did you want to go?" Jax asked.

"There's a cafe by mom and Tom's. Can we go there?" she asked.

"Sure, if that's what you want to do," Jax replied.

"Yay," she yelled and ran down the hallway to her room.

Jax sipped on his coffee and listened to the shower turn on.

He picked up his phone for a minute.

Griggs sent him a couple of texts:

I need to talk to you. I found something interesting.

Then another:

I know you're with Lizbeth, but I need to talk to you.

He replied:

I will after I drop her off.

The water turned off. Jax got up, walked into his room to grab a set of clothes, waited until Elizabeth closed the door to her room, then hurried through his shower.

When he finished, he found Elizabeth on the couch, a controller in her hands.

He grabbed his keys. Elizabeth held her bag and stared up at her dad.

"I thought you would take me to Mom's house after breakfast. Your phone buzzed when you were in the shower, and I looked at it."

Jax picked it up and stared at it.

"Okay, is that okay? I know your mom was expecting you back today," Jax said.

"It's okay. Dad, who is Griggs?"

"She's the person I'm working with right now."

"Like your partner?"

"Sort of. She's with the Air Force and—"

"Like you were?"

"Sort of. She works for the police in the Air Force. It's called OSI, or Office of Special Investigations."

"Are you dating her?"

"No, I'm just working with her."

"You should date someone. Mom is happy with Tom. I want you to be happy too."

Jax smiled, and they hurried out the doors.

By the time they reached the restaurant, the wait was nearly an hour, and they stood inside while the snow fell. The hostess led them to a table in the back. Jax ordered a coffee for himself and hot chocolate for Elizabeth.

"What?" Jax asked.

"It's nice to see you, Dad," Elizabeth said.

"You too, little bug," he said.

"Dad," Elizabeth said, "do you like Griggs?"

"Yeah, she's good at her job," Jax replied.

"That's not what I meant."

"Is this like what you said before we left the house?"

She smiled.

When their food arrived, Jax could only stare at the portions overflowing his plate.

"How often does your mom bring you here?" he asked.

"Once a month," Lizbeth said, "I have enough for a few days afterward."

Jax glanced at her plate; three pancakes covered her plate.

His plate was loaded with potatoes, eggs, and five pieces of bacon.

"I'll need a box for this food. I can't eat all of it."

"Dad," Elizabeth asked, "do you like Tom?"

"Yeah, he's okay," Jax replied.

"What did you talk about?"

She was getting more intelligent and more observant.

"You know who Tom works for?"

"Yeah, she's going to be President. He got us tickets for her inauguration thing. She's nice. She's been over to the house with all of her people. Those people in suits are nice. I text her sometimes."

Jax smiled at the last comment. How many kids can text the President-Elect?

"We were talking about work stuff," Jax finally answered.

"What work stuff?"

"I'm working on something, and he had a couple of questions about it."

"Did you tell him?"

"I told him what I could. It's a big thing Griggs, and I are working on."

"That's what mom told me. I love my flamingo. You got that from where we used to live?"

"Yes," Jax said"

She stopped and stared at him, "Why aren't you and mom together anymore?"

The question stopped him in his tracks, "Have you talked to your mom about this?"

"Yes, but I wanted to ask you too."

"Okay. Sometimes people drift apart. I was gone a lot when we moved here, and we weren't who we thought we were. Does that make sense?"

She shook her head.

"When I was gone a lot for work, it didn't work out well. We missed each other, but when we moved here, I was home, but not. My mind was on work when I started. I had a big case when I started this job. It took a lot of time, and I didn't make time for you and your mom."

"Okay," she replied.

"Did you think there was something else?"

"No, that's what Mom said, too," she replied.

They finished their meal, and Jax drove her home. They reached the end of the street, and it was blocked off by police vehicles.

He pulled up next to an officer.

"I'm trying to get to my ex-wife's house," Jax said.

"Which one is it?" the officer asked.

Jax pointed to the house.

"I'll have to get clearance to let you through," the officer said and talked into his radio.

A police car in front of him moved, and the officer waved him through.

The place was crawling with Secret Service. An agent approached him and asked for his ID.

"Elaine is here," Elizabeth said from the backseat.

"I think so," Jax replied.

The agent led him to the house, where Secret Service patted him down, and Jax forgot he had his firearm.

He showed his FBI credentials, but the agent didn't care.

"I'll hold onto this until you leave, Sir," the agent said.

Elizabeth opened the door, and Jax followed her inside.

He was led to the living room, where President-Elect Franklin sat in one of the flower-printed chairs.

"Hello, Agent Reed," she said.

Jax smiled, "I was bringing Lizbeth back. I wasn't expecting you to be here," Jax said.

"All the more reason for me to be here," she replied.

She motioned for him to sit down.

Tom walked into the room, Jax gave Elizabeth a kiss and

hug, and she hurried into the kitchen as Sarah closed the doors to the room.

"I felt it would be better to do it in person. I thought you'd bring your daughter back. It is fortuitous."

"For whom?" Jax asked.

"I know Tom asked you a few questions about your case, but I want to ask the same ones."

"I can't talk about the case. Maybe after the inauguration, but it's an open case, and it wouldn't be appropriate."

"Do you know where the drone is?"

"We think it was sold. It's probably in the hands of the Russians or the Chinese," Jax said.

It was a complete dodge, but he smiled.

"Okay, I hope you're right," she said.

His phone buzzed, and he stared at it.

It was Griggs: *Where are you?*

He tucked it away.

"I have to go," Jax said and hurried to the door.

Sarah stopped him at the front door, "What was that all about?"

He scanned the space around them. Four Secret Service agents stood in the house's foyer, but he didn't think they could hear him.

"It's a long story," Jax said, "I have to go."

"Jackson," Sarah said, "Be careful, okay?"

He smiled at her, "I'll do my best, Sarah."

The agent outside returned his firearm and walked Jax to his car. Jax drove to the Hoover building.

Once in his cubicle, he glanced around for Griggs.

"She's in the cafeteria," an agent said.

"Why?" Jax asked.

"Probably for coffee and food," the agent said, "she was here when I got in at six-thirty. Her head was down on the desk."

"Okay," Jax replied.

He went to the cafeteria and found Griggs at a table with two cups of coffee and a couple of pastries in front of her.

"You hungry?" he asked.

She glanced up from her food.

"Just a bit," she replied.

"Need some help carrying that?"

"That would be great," she replied.

Jax grabbed one of the coffee cups and a bag of food.

They returned to the office, and Griggs flopped down in her chair.

"Been here all night, I hear?"

"Yes, I did a little work since we last saw each other."

A camera rested on her desk.

"What did you use that for?"

"For this," she said and handed him a copy of her picture.

"How?" Jax asked.

"When you got Elizabeth, I decided to camp at his office. I got this in the parking garage."

"What did you do with the picture?"

"I ran it through the military service database."

"And?"

"It came back as someone reportedly dead," Griggs said.

"Explain?" Jax said.

"The computer kicked out a name to go with the face. I did a bit of searching to figure it out because the computer said he was dead."

"Dead from what?" Jax asked.

"He was supposedly killed in a firefight in Syria. They never found his body, but they found his tags. The records of the incident assumed he was killed by enemy fire."

"Those guys don't just leave their buddies on the field," Jax said.

"I know, so I did some digging. He was with a group that was beyond Delta. They're called Task Force Black. They do insertions in hostile areas and answer to the President and Chairman of Joint Chiefs. It is a covert program implemented by Reagan, and it's still going. They are a quick insertion team. If they die, the whole place is obliterated."

"How the hell did you find this out?" Jax asked.

"You have your contacts. I have mine," Griggs replied.

"Okay, so what's his name?"

"Brad Drake, Jax, he's a badass. He was a multi-task team member. He could do it all."

"So this is the big thing you found?"

"It's the small thing that led me to other things."

"Like?"

"I was up talking to my mom last night."

She handed Jax the letter.

He sat quietly reading it.

When he glanced up, Griggs was watching him.

"He found something, and they killed him for it and blamed bad intelligence?" Jax asked.

"I looked into what happened to my dad. The intelligence was off. There wasn't supposed to be an anti-aircraft battery where he did the strike. It had supposedly been knocked out before then. I dug some more. They never had proof it was knocked out. It was an intelligence assumption."

"This is good work, Vanessa," Jax said.

Griggs stopped and smiled at him.

"Thanks, but that's not the biggest thing I found." She said.

"Okay," Jax said.

His curiosity was piqued.

"You were over there. Did you ever hear of anything like this?" Griggs asked, pointing to the letter.

"We heard all kinds of things. It was just a rumor, but it wouldn't surprise me. There was a lot of money in that war."

"Okay, so we have my dad. We have you, and we have Webb over there, as well as Miles Frank."

"Webb was my superior, and Aaron Williams was my Superior Officer. Miles Frank was over all of us. He was a two-star or something. He doesn't like to be called a General."

"Right. I did more looking." Griggs replied before continuing her findings.

"Miles Frank, Webb, and Brad Drake were over there simultaneously. Drake was with the Teams at the time. He would have had some interaction with people. I looked at his file. He had some big beef with a few people. From what I read, I'm surprised he made it through BUDS."

"All of these guys who are players were there at the same time. And you think they may have known each other?"

"You know who else was stationed over there?" Griggs asked. She shuffled a piece of paper towards him.

A man in his Air Force blues smiled out from a picture. The picture said the name of the man.

"Johnny Milburn," Jax muttered, reading the label.

"Yes, we have all of our major people over there simultaneously. They would've at least run into each other. I don't know how you didn't run into my dad. He was a five-nine, big, black man," she said.

"I probably did, but I don't remember. You think these people knew each other, though?"

"It's entirely possible," Griggs said.

"Is there anyone we can talk to about Drake?" Jax asked.

"We can go to his old training ground. It's at Fort Dawson," Griggs said.

"Okay, I guess we're driving to West Virginia," Jax said.

"Do you still think this is going where we think it is?" Griggs asked.

"It may, but we need to find Johnny Milburn," Jax said.

They took the elevator to the garage.

"Right. Well, I still want to dig into Drake. He grew up in West Virginia. Maybe he has family up there?" Griggs suggested.

"We'll have to look into that. It would be a perfect place to launch the drone from." Jax said.

"From what I read, he's had family in the service for a long time."

"So, what are we doing?" Griggs asked.

"We're going for a drive to Fort Bragg," Jax replied.

THEIR CAR REACHED the front gate of Fort Bragg, and Jax showed his badge.

"Hold on, Sir," the guard said.

He waved them to the side of the gate, and Jax waited.

Another vehicle pulled up behind them.

Another guard got out of the vehicle.

"You can follow me to the base commander's building," the guard said.

Jax did as he was told. It was a ten-minute drive through parts of the base near the front gate.

The guard parked and led them into the building.

"Take a seat. He'll be with you shortly," the guard said.

Jax and Griggs sat down in the small waiting room of the building.

A tall man, his hair cut short with grey stubble along the sides, walked out of a room.

Griggs was in her uniform, and Jax wore his suit.

"The FBI and OSI are working together?" he asked.

"Just on this one, Sir," Jax said.

Griggs saluted the man, and he returned it.

His uniform was not the greens of the Army but the Marine MCCU uniform.

Jax stared at the rank on the man's shoulders, and his back went a little straighter.

"Come into my office. We can talk about this," the man said.

They sat in the two chairs in front of the desk. Jax wondered why the chairs across from a CO's were always the most uncomfortable.

"I am General West," the man said, "this is my installation. What can I do for OSI and the FBI?"

"We're actually looking into something else, but our case led us here," Jax said.

"Really? What could have led you to Fort Bragg?"

"Brad Drake," Jax said.

West's eyebrows went up, and he glanced from both of them to the open door behind them. He stood up and closed the door.

"What could a dead soldier have to do with this?"

"Well, the only thing they found was his tags," Griggs said.

West's eyes darted to her, "How long you been in," he glanced at her name, "Griggs?"

"Six years, Sir," Griggs replied.

"In those six years," his eyes darted around the room, "have you done a good job."

"Top of my class at boot compact. Top at school as well, Sir," Griggs replied.

"Well, I've been in a lot longer than that, and I'd have to say you're very pushy for someone who hasn't seen that much of the service," West replied.

"Her father was Air Force," Jax said.

"What did he do? Same as you?"

Jax glanced over at Griggs. He knew she was getting dressed down, and he didn't much like it.

"Her father was Marcus Griggs, Sir," Jax said.

West froze and stared at Griggs.

"I'm sorry about your father. It was a dark day for the service when that video went up. All of us felt something for him. We may not have known him but felt for his family."

"Sir, our trail has led us to Drake. We want to keep going with it," Jax said.

"Very well. I was his CO, but you'd be better off talking to his group. They're farther out. I'll have someone escort you."

"Is there a name for his group?" Jax asked.

"He was a part of Task Force Green, as far as I knew," West said.

Jax knew he was lying to them, but the hard-ass Marine played his hand well, and Jax let it alone.

Griggs saluted him. Jax went to do the same but remembered his place and lowered his arm.

The same guard who'd escorted them stood outside the door.

They got in their vehicle and followed the guard past soldiers on obstacle courses, then the base disappeared, and they reached a section of the base covered in trees. Across a creek stood a few small buildings set back against some hills.

The guard stopped and got out.

"That's where you need to go," the guard said.

He got back in his vehicle and sat there.

Jax and Griggs stared at each other, got out, and walked toward the guard's vehicle.

"We can find it from here," Jax said.

"The General asked me to wait for you. This group can get rowdy. West wanted to ensure you made it off base in one piece." The guard said.

Jax and Griggs crossed the bridge separating the two pieces of land.

Long grass grew around the buildings, and it looked like no one was home.

"You thinking what I'm thinking?" Jax asked.

"We've got a rifle aimed at our heads?"

"Yep," Jax replied.

They walked up the steps, and Jax pushed on the front door.

Ten men lay on bunks. Jax and Griggs felt all twenty eyes on them.

"West sent me here to talk to one of you about Brad Drake."

The room turned cold, and Jax was confident it had nothing to do with the wind blowing outside.

"Drake's dead," a voice said.

Jax glanced in the direction of the voice. The man stood six feet. His shoulders stuck out like boulders on a mountain.

"Well, we seem to think differently," Jax said.

He pulled the picture Griggs had taken from his pocket and flashed it around.

The mountain walked towards them, "Where did you get that?"

"I took it last night," Griggs replied.

He glanced from Jax to Griggs.

"So, he's alive?" the Mountain replied.

"It appears so."

"Did you show that to West?" the Mountain asked.

"I was hoping one of you could talk to me about him. We know a few things, but there are some we can't put together."

"And what? You want our help?" the Mountain asked.

The others in the bay were quiet. None of the others moved from their bunks, and besides their eyes, they didn't acknowledge that Jax and Griggs were there.

"You know he's alive. Maybe you can tell us about him?" Jax said.

"I can tell you," a voice said from the back.

"Sit down, Phillips," the Mountain said.

A man about five-nine, lithe and fit, walked towards them.

"We all knew he skated off. Don't act like you didn't," Phillips said.

The mountain walked back to his bunk and stared at Phillips, who may have been younger and smaller than the Mountain, but held a lot more sway in the group.

"Drake was a good soldier, but he wanted more. A few people had contacted him. Once you're in this game for a while, your name gets out. You get all kinds of phone calls, emails, and all that shit. This group wanted to hire him, but it wouldn't do it while he was on active duty. So he made it look like he got blown up. A few of us thought of doing the same with the money they offered."

"Why?" Jax asked.

"Man, we are the meat grinder. We are the only ones they send in for the bullshit no one wants. We get the things Delta and Teams won't get approval for. Don't get me wrong; we're all from the Teams and Delta. We're just another prong on the spear. But the shit we've seen and done, those boys say no," Phillips said.

"I understand he was big on the mental side?" Jax said.

"You have to compartmentalize what we do. It's the reason most of us are divorced. We take care of each other. Drake did some things that weren't cool. I was happy to see him disappear."

"You know anything else about him?" Griggs asked.

The man's eyes darted to her as if he'd forgotten she was there.

"Look in coal country. Drake's family had land in West Virginia. He wouldn't shut up about it. He said he was going to make a lot of money. Said there was coal in those mountains. If you are hunting the person in that picture, you'll need Kevlar."

He turned and walked to where he'd been in the back of the room.

Jax and Griggs walked to their car and stared at each other.

"Did everything go all right?" the guard asked.

"Fine, just fine," Jax replied.

They got in their car.

"So it appears he wasn't well-liked by his peers," Griggs said.

Jax nodded.

They followed the guard back to the Commander's office.

West was waiting for them when they walked in.

"I see they didn't kill you. That's a positive sign. Did you get what you needed?" West asked.

"I think we did," Jax replied.

"Those boys know each other well. If he is alive, I can guarantee one of them is in contact with him. You best wear Kevlar from now on," West said.

"They said something similar," Griggs replied.

"I hope you get your man and find out what you need, too," West said.

Jax nodded, Griggs saluted, and they returned to their car.

He started the car, and they drove toward DC.

"I get the feeling we're going to be the ones hunted," Griggs said.

"Nope, we're the hunters," Jax replied.

CHAPTER SIXTY-SEVEN

THE ROAD WOUND through the city, and Drake's phone buzzed.

He didn't recognize the number and ignored it until it rang two more times.

He pulled over and answered it.

"Hello?" he asked.

"Hey, it's Morris," the other end said.

"I don't know anyone by that name," Drake said.

"Wait, don't hang up. There was an FBI agent and an Air Force woman out here."

"What did they ask?" Drake asked.

"They know you're alive, or at least believe you are."

The call ended, and Drake stared out the window of his vehicle.

Anyone who'd walked by would have seen him assaulting his steering wheel. A cop would have pulled up behind him.

Shit. Fuck. Damnit.

He pulled back on the road and drove to his office.

The garage opened, and he went up the elevator.

"Mr. Warren, I have something I'd like to show you," a man said.

"I'm in a bit of a hurry," Drake said.

The guard pulled a picture from an envelope in his hands.

It was a picture of Griggs in her car from the night before, the camera resting on the edge of her window.

"Where did you get this?"

"We reviewed a video from yesterday, and this caught our eye. You told us to report anything out of the ordinary." The guard said.

"Thank you," Drake said.

He took the picture from the guard and walked back to his office.

Drake sat down in his chair and stared at the picture.

He pressed a button on his desk. The room buzzed slightly, then went silent.

Drake dialed the number and waited.

It rang three times.

"I'm a bit busy right now. I need to call you back," the person on the other end said.

"This is important. I think I've been made," Drake said.

"What the hell are you talking about?"

Drake told him about the picture and the phone call.

"Fuck me. She is persistent, isn't she? Do what needs to be done."

Drake stared at the wall behind his desk.

One of the pictures drew his eye.

It was of himself, Miles Frank, David Webb, and Aaron Williams.

"I don't know how they didn't see this picture?" he asked the empty room.

He took it down, slid it into a drawer, and walked to the wall where it had been.

Drake ran his hand over a small notch in the wall and pressed down.

The wall folded out and opened up.

A large sniper rifle sat on a pedestal with an MP5.

He grabbed both of them, set them on the ground, and stripped them.

It had been a while since he'd done it, but it was like he'd never stopped.

The action calmed his mind and gave him something to focus on.

He lubricated the pins, replaced everything, and slid the cartridges into place.

The disassembled sniper rifle lay on the floor. Drake put it into a duffle bag. He slid the MP5 in as well and zipped the bag.

He walked out of his office and stopped at his secretary's desk.

"I will be out of town for a while. Please call the other numbers on your list if you have any problems."

"Is everything okay, Sir?" she asked.

"Yes, it's fine. But if you need anything, please call the numbers." He said.

He took the elevator to his car and drove out of the city toward West Virginia.

Johnny Milburn would have a roommate.

CHAPTER SIXTY-EIGHT

"YOU KNOW, we may want to put someone on Sarah or Elizabeth," Griggs suggested.

"I don't know. I hope this doesn't pull them into this. I have so much on my mind right now," Jax replied.

He pulled papers from his pocket and laid them on the desk.

"What's that?" Griggs asked.

"Divorce papers," Jax replied.

"Oh, shit. You carry those everywhere?"

"They were delivered this morning," Jax said.

"She had them delivered while Elizabeth was there?"

"They arrived when I went back after dropping her off."

"Why'd you go back?"

"I don't know. I just felt like going back to my apartment," Jax said.

"How long were you there before they showed up?"

"They stopped me on the street as I was walking in."

"Sorry," Griggs said.

"It's fine. Not much I can do about it now."

"Your ex-wife is engaged to the Chief of Staff for the President-Elect, and you didn't think they'd want things to be handled before she took office?"

"When you put it like that, it makes me look like an idiot," Jax said.

Griggs shrugged.

"You think I'm being an idiot, don't you?" Jax asked.

"You've been separated for a couple of years, right?"

"Yes, but—"

"You've been separated for a couple of years. She's moved on. Why can't you?"

Jax didn't answer.

"You need to let it go, for Elizabeth's sake. She doesn't want her dad to be filled with regret. She wants him to be happy."

"Was Decker there for you?"

"He tried to be. He wasn't my dad. I was an asshole to him. I've made up for that. His kids and I didn't get along at first. They'd had him to themselves for a long time."

"Right. His first wife died from cancer?"

"Yes, Jackie died of cancer. His daughter looks just like her. The other thing was raising me, a black girl, in a white household. I was pissed about my mom dating a white guy after my dad."

"But your mom is white?"

"That has nothing to do with it. I could try and explain it, but it would come off wrong. So let's move on."

"So, you're saying I should sign them and shut up?"

"Unless there is something wrong in the custody agreement," Griggs said, "If not, sign them and be done with it."

Jax stared at the papers in front of him, ran his finger over his ring, and pulled out a pen. He signed them and put them back in his jacket pocket.

"Okay, that's done. Let's get some real work done. You want to go and talk to Brad Drake?" Griggs asked.

They walked into Decker's office.

"We have a lead on something, and we'd like to take a couple of agents with us as backup?" Jax asked.

"You think there's going to be a problem?" Decker asked.

They told him all they'd learned about Drake. Decker didn't look excited.

"You have this badass ex-special forces guy that you're looking for. You discover who he is and talk to some of his war buddies? Put on a jacket before you leave, both of you. There are a couple of agents you can take. Mirello and Lyons are right there. Take them."

Jax and Griggs stopped and talked to Mirello and Lyons before heading downstairs to get jackets for the four of them.

Jax and Mirello had been partners when Jax arrived from the academy. Their first case soured their relationship.

They all left and drove to the Executive Actions offices.

The same secretary who'd been there the last time stared at them.

"We're looking for Oliver Warren," Jax said.

"He left a little while ago. Said he had to go out of town for work."

"Is that normal for him?" Jax asked.

"I think I should call the company lawyers," the secretary said.

"Did he say anything else?"

"No, he left with a couple of duffle bags. They were loaded down. He was almost dragging them."

"How long have you worked for the company?" Griggs asked.

"Six months," she replied.

"He always leaves with big duffle bags?"

"No, never, When he came back last time, he brought them in. At first, I thought they were clothes, but—"

"But what?" Jax asked.

"They were weighted down. Like there was something heavy in the bags."

"You mind if we look around?"

"I'm going to call the lawyers," she said.

"You do that," Jax said.

He and Griggs walked down the hallway. The door to the office they'd sat in was open and empty.

Mirello and Lyons were close behind them.

"Shit," Lyons said.

"This is your show, Jax. You want to call for the warrant?" Mirello asked.

"Yep," Jax replied.

He called Decker and asked for a warrant for the Executive Actions offices.

The secretary had picked up the phone. Jax glanced around at the cameras in the lobby.

"I think it would be best if you didn't call anyone," Jax said.

"But you're getting a warrant. I was told to call these numbers if anything goes wrong while Mr. Warren is away," she said.

"Could I see those numbers?" Jax asked.

"When you have a warrant, you can," she said.

The warrant showed up just over an hour later.

Jax walked into the office and stared at the rows of pictures along the walls. A small caliber handgun rested on the desk.

"Why didn't we notice these pictures last time?" Griggs asked.

"I don't know, but it looks like there's one missing," Mirello said, pointing to an empty spot on the wall.

The secretary came in and handed Jax the numbers.

"Thank you," Jax said.

She turned and stormed out.

Jax looked around the desk and found an empty picture frame in the waste bin.

"Why would he take one down?" Jax asked.

There were two other offices, and Mirello and Lyons were searching them.

The other offices were empty of furniture.

"Please bring her back in here," Jax said.

Griggs brought the secretary back to the room, "What?"

"Did anyone ever use those other offices?"

"I never saw anyone. Mr. Warren said someone was using them at night, but I never saw anyone."

"Thank you," Jax said.

She walked out of the room.

Griggs stared after her, "That girl is pissed."

"Yep," Lyons said.

Jax stared at the space on the wall and ran his finger along it.

"What are you looking for?" Griggs asked.

"This wall doesn't look right," he said.

He continued to run his fingers along the edge of the wall panels until there was a click and the panel moved to the side.

They stared into the space where the rifles had been and a picture left on the racks.

"Those racks look as if they held firearms," Mirello said.

"Yes, they do. Can you get someone in here? I want this whole place dusted," Jax said.

Jax walked out of the room.

He held the picture in his gloved hands.

Griggs stared at it. It was the same picture the security guard had given Drake.

"Is that a threat?" Griggs asked.

"Looks like one to me," Jax said.

"Fuck," Griggs said.

"Call Decker," Jax said.

Griggs picked up her phone and dialed. She relayed what they'd found.

CHAPTER SIXTY-NINE

DECKER SLID his coffee out of the way and glanced at his daughter.

"Vanessa, you're out. I want you to go home and stay there. I talked to your CO when you were on your way back. He agrees. He wants you laying low."

She looked at the floor, then at Jax.

"What did you think he was going to do? It was a threat. I'd pull you off, too," Jax told her.

"I wanted to keep working," she said.

She stood up and walked out of the room.

"That went well," Decker said.

Jax nodded and hurried after her.

He found her next to the elevator.

"He's doing this to protect you," he said.

"I don't need protecting," she said.

"Right. You're just going to keep doing what you're doing," Jax said.

The elevator doors opened, and they stepped in.

"What are you talking about?" she asked.

"You can do work from your laptop. I can do the footwork if you can do the technical stuff?" Jax asked.

"You're not throwing me off?"

"According to your dad, you're off. I agree. I don't want you leaving the house, but you can do it from there."

"What about my dad?"

"I'm sure he knows you'll be working this from home. Just do that," Jax said.

He left her in the lobby and took the elevator back up.

Jax went to his desk as Decker walked up.

"She's going home?" he asked.

"Yes," Jax replied and shuffled some papers around his desk.

"I've never seen Vanessa so involved in something. Her mom told me she has a lot of respect for you. Don't let me down on this. I'd be stupid to think she won't work on this from home, but keep her out of the field until we catch this guy."

Jax nodded and stared at his laptop.

"What did you find in those offices?" Decker asked.

Jax took a look around the room.

"Care for a walk in the snow?" Jax asked.

Decker frowned and went back to his office.

He returned with his coat.

They rode the elevator to the ground floor and walked out the doors into the blowing snow.

Jax led him towards The Mall and across the Smithsonian Castle.

They sat on a bench just inside the doors.

The crowds hadn't started yet, and Jax wasn't sure if they would, considering the snow.

"So, what is it?" Decker asked.

"What I'm about to tell is our theory. We've done a lot of work on it," Jax said.

He relayed all of their theories about the drone, Miles Frank, and the intentions of the drone pilot.

When he finished, Decker could only stare at him.

"You think this is what's going on?" Decker asked.

Jax glanced around them and stopped as a couple walked past them.

"It's the only thing that fits all that we've looked at. This drone was stolen by Johnny Milburn, who is still alive. He was the only one who could fly it besides the two dead pilots."

"But why does Miles Frank hate Elaine Franklin this much?" Decker asked.

"We haven't looked into that. I was going to do that today. They were both in the house. He wouldn't be the first politician to hold a grudge."

"Do you think there is anyone else involved in this?"

"Maybe, but I'm not ready to talk to that person yet. I need to get access to Miles Frank, though."

"You want to interrogate the Speaker of the House?"

"Not interrogate," Jax said, "ask some pointed questions. He was my CO at one point. There's some bad blood between us. I think he's the reason my intel was bad."

"You think he set you up to fail?"

The wind rattled the doors, and more people hurried into the building.

"Webb said as much before his head exploded."

"Okay. You have my support. But keep this quiet. This is big. It needs to be you, me, and Vanessa."

"So, she's still in?"

"I would expect nothing less from you or her," Decker said.

CHAPTER SEVENTY

JOHNNY LAY on the couch across from Drake.

When he'd arrived the night before, Johnny had been asleep in his room.

Drake had looked at the mess around the cabin and started cleaning.

The place was spotless when Johnny woke up.

Johnny had walked into the living room and stopped when he saw Drake.

"You sleep pretty soundly," Drake said.

"I was up late doing things," Johnny said.

"So was I," Drake said.

Johnny took in the cleanliness of the place and glanced at Drake.

"When I suggested this place was somewhere to use as a base. I didn't think you'd let it go to the birds." Drake told him.

"I didn't. I cleaned it last week."

"Right. That's why there were maggots on the meat in the sink?"

"What the hell are you doing here?" Johnny asked.

"I needed a place to stay for a little while."

"Why?"

"Some things have happened. I had to get out of the city," Drake said.

"They on to us?"

"No, only me," Drake said.

"I'd hate for them to have to come up here. I'd have to blow them all away."

Drake smiled, "You taking it up today?"

"Nah, I'm just checking the ordnance, cleaning the wings. All of it is regular maintenance."

"You need help with it?"

"Sure, if you're into helping," Johnny replied.

"I need something to do," Drake said.

Johnny ate a bowl of cereal and sipped on the coffee Drake made.

"How come I make coffee, and it tastes like shit? You come here and make it, and it tastes like this?"

"I have no idea," Drake said, sipping his cup.

Johnny grabbed his coat, and Drake followed him to the garage.

The drone sat in the middle of the garage. The ordnance around it gave off a smell that Drake didn't like.

"Are these all sealed?" he asked.

"Of course. I also thought the smell was weird, but they're sealed."

Each of the bombs and missiles sat on their racks, ready to be loaded. The control tags were still on them, marking them safe until removed, which Johnny would do in a few days, so they were ready.

"The wings fluttered a little the other night in the snow. I wanted to check the ailerons for ice issues." Johnny said.

He pulled a few tools from a chest along the wall in the back of the garage. He turned on the heater, and the room warmed up so that it was more tolerable but not hot, as that would damage the aircraft.

Johnny turned his attention to the ailerons or flaps along the edge of the wings and tail section of the drone.

He moved them gently with his hands. The one on the left wing moved slower than the other. He adjusted the tension on it, checked how the right one moved, and made minor adjustments.

Drake stood back and watched the man work.

Johnny didn't look up or ask for help as he moved from one part to another on the aircraft, finally ending with a check of the engines. These he checked for airflow issues, both in and out of engines, adjusting the intake, so the air moved more smoothly across the front of the aircraft and through the air intake ports at the front.

It was a minor adjustment but pulled more air in and gave more thrust, which Johnny had worried about, though he hadn't told Drake or anyone else.

Once finished with the main parts of the aircraft, he moved to the camera. It was stable, but he took apart the lens. He checked it for cracks, cleaned it, and checked the housing for cracks. Finding a replacement lens would be impossible this close to their action date, and he didn't need a lens malfunction while flying. It would cause him to be blind.

He looked up from his work; sweat rolled off his face and chest onto the floor.

It took four hours from start to finish. Drake returned to the house twice in that time. He returned only to see Johnny on his hands and knees, adjusting this or tightening that.

"You do good work," Drake said.

Johnny glanced up at Drake as if he'd never seen him.

"I guess I zoned out. I forgot you were there," Johnny said.

"It's fine. Your meticulous nature is one of the reasons we wanted you for this job. At least that's what I was told."

"Yes, I modified a few things to get more thrust. Adjusting the ailerons for more lift. Things like that."

Drake stared at him as if he were speaking another language.

"They're the flaps on the back of the wings. The last time I took it up, I was getting a bit of drag. I was worried the cold weather damaged them."

"Did it?"

"No, it was just tight. I made it better."

"So, we have a week?" Drake asked.

"Yes, on the twentieth of January," Johnny replied, "I'm glad it's in the middle of the week. We couldn't do it if it were on a Sunday."

"Why not?"

Johnny smiled, "When the inauguration is on a Sunday, they swear the President privately, but the spectacle is done the following Monday. It being on a Thursday helps us."

"I see. Have you checked out everything on The Mall?" Drake asked.

"I'm going to DC today. I know the procession route in case there is a problem and we have to do something else. I should be able to hit the target. I don't want to worry about taking out the Beast."

"Be careful while you're there," Drake said.

Johnny returned his tools to their places in the chest along the wall, turned off the heater, and walked to the door.

"Aren't you going to check the ordnance?"

"I did it last night before you arrived."

They walked out; Johnny grabbed the keys for his vehicle and headed back outside.

"You going now?" Drake asked.

"Might as well get it done," Johnny said, started the car, and pulled out.

WHILE JOHNNY LEFT the cabin headed for DC, the Speaker of the House was in his office.

Miles Frank walked out of his office into the hallway, separating his office from his secretary's.

"I need to see the President," he said.

His chief of staff was close behind him.

The man dialed a number on his phone and sputtered into it.

His detail led him through the hallways, to the elevator, and down.

"It's done," his chief of staff informed him.

They reached the bottom and got into a black SUV. The drive to the White House is short, but Miles Frank always liked it. He watched the snow fall beyond the blackened windows and the White House grow in his field of view.

He was hurried inside by his detail and ushered towards the Oval office.

"What is it, Miles?" President Thompson asked.

"I have something that needs to be put down," Miles said.

President Thompson stared at him.

"What are you talking about?"

"An investigation is going on that is affecting my ability to work. I would like to see if there is anything you can do about it."

"You're asking me to do this for you?"

"The President always does things in the last week that are questioned later. There was a downed drone at Creech Air Force Base in Nevada. I want to see if that investigation can be shut down?"

President Thompson frowned, "Miles, I want to help you. You know that I do. But this is a big ask. Elaine Franklin has asked about this drone as well."

Miles glanced from the President to the Marine stationed outside the Oval, "I understand."

"Look. I can do many things, but interfering with an FBI investigation is not one of them. I can't do anything that would jeopardize my legacy."

"I understand, Sir," Miles replied.

"Is that the only reason you came over here?"

"Are you attending the inauguration?"

"I've been fighting with myself over this. The First Lady wants me to attend. She said it would look good on the news."

"But?"

"I don't want to watch that woman take the oath."

"Where are you leaning?"

"What does this have to do with anything?"

"You know I won't be attending. Have to keep that line of succession going."

"Right, forgot about that."

"I will leave you then," Miles said.

"I'm sorry, Miles," President Thompson said.

Miles nodded.

You're not right now, but you will be.

CHAPTER SEVENTY-TWO

GRIGGS STARED at her laptop's screen. She'd been going at it since she woke up, and her eyes had started to water.

"You know he's doing this for your safety?" her mom said.

"I know, but it still sucks," she replied.

"Well, look at it this way. We can have lunch together," her mom said and set a bowl in front of her.

"Is that chicken soup?"

"Yes, I thought it would be a good thing on a cold, snowy day."

"It's snowing again?"

"Yes, it has been since this morning. You haven't looked up much today, have you?"

Griggs sipped at her soup and glanced at the patterns of snowflakes striking the window.

"I'll leave you to work," her mom said and hurried away.

Griggs stared outside and wondered if their theory was correct.

She'd been looking into Drake's family and finally found the name in a listing for a small West Virginia town.

She looked at the website for the town. It looked like a late oo's relic.

Griggs dialed up Jax and waited for him to answer.

"I think I have a lead on Brad Drake's family," she said.

"It's in West Virginia. It's a little town. One of those that won't like an FBI agent snooping around, but if I go there, I'll have an easier time."

"I don't know, Sarah. Your dad would be pretty pissed about it," he said.

"I'll handle him. I'm already headed for the door," Griggs said and ended the call.

"Mom, I'm going out for a few things. I'll be back later." She said.

Her mom came out of the kitchen and stared at her.

"Vanessa Griggs, you don't go chasing things unless you're ready for them."

"I'm just going out," she said and hurried out the door.

She held her mother's car keys and got in her mom's Range Rover.

There was little traffic on the road, and she put in the directions on her phone. The car gave her the directions, none of them worth anything until she got out of the city.

CHAPTER SEVENTY-THREE

JOHNNY PULLED into the garage on Ohio street, got out, and made his way towards The Mall.

It had taken him longer than he thought to reach DC. There had been an accident coming in that delayed him, and he'd have less time than he wanted along The Mall.

As the snow continued to fall, he grabbed his coat from the car.

The crowd of people moved along The Mall. Some stopped at the museums. Others took in the sights. It was busier than he'd anticipated. He'd hoped the weather would hold them off.

He walked the path the drone would take down The Mall, noting obstructions along the way. There were a few trees and things like that, small things, but he made a mental note of each one.

There would be more people along The Mall and near the Capitol on the day of the inauguration.

He noted the height of the scaffolding and noted where everyone would be seated.

The videos he'd watched online of past inaugurals were perfect for helping him identify where some would be sitting.

Though the rounds would take out numerous people, he would fly the drone down from the mountain as the President and President-Elect were en route to the Capitol complex.

He still wasn't sure if President Thompson was attending, not that he would be the first to miss it. He knew there'd been four others who'd missed the inaugurals of their rivals.

Would Bill Thompson be added to that list?

Johnny took pictures along the route with his camera, and a Capitol police officer walked up to him.

"Could I help you, sir?" the officer asked.

"My wife is coming for the inauguration. She wanted me to update her on how it all looks," Johnny replied.

"Could I see some ID?" the officer asked.

Johnny acted offended.

"I'm just looking at the construction," he replied.

"I understand that. It's just routine," the officer said.

"Mr. Jones, how long will you stay in our nation's capital?"

Johnny stared at him. He hadn't expected to be interrogated.

"I'm just here for work for a couple of days. Then my wife is flying in for the festivities. She's a big donor to the Franklin Campaign."

"I see. Enjoy the rest of your stay, and please, no more pictures of the scaffolding."

"Yes, sir," Johnny replied.

He put away his ID and walked away.

Johnny didn't have to look back to know the officer continued to watch him. He felt the man's eyes burning through his skull. He crossed the street, heading towards the Holocaust museum and the Jefferson Memorial.

When he reached his car, he dialed up Drake.

"There sure is a lot of security down here. You think someone knows something?"

"It's getting closer to the date. They're just tightening things up. The usual stuff."

"Okay, well, I'm heading back. See you in a while." Johnny said.

On the drive, he thought of the officer who'd stopped him but didn't tell Drake about that.

CHAPTER SEVENTY-FOUR

JAX WALKED up the steps to the side entrance to the Capitol. He showed his badge, and security let him through.

He called earlier about having a meeting with the Speaker but had been rebuffed. Decker called a couple of people and landed him the appointment. There had been assurances that it was only a formality.

Jax smiled his approval at being led inside.

He knew Miles wouldn't be looking forward to the meeting, and he wanted to see the man squirm for once at his behest.

Jax took the elevator to the floor of the Speaker's office, got out, and was patted down by Secret Service.

They stared at him when they felt his weapon. He showed them his badge.

"The Speaker wishes your firearm to remain outside his office." The agent said.

"Doesn't trust me, eh?"

"He made it clear he would feel better if it were left with us," the agent replied.

Jax handed his firearm to the agent, who put it in a lockbox.

The door was opened by an older woman Jax took to be the Speaker's secretary.

"You must be Jackson Reed," she said, "I read about you on the internet."

"It's all one-sided," he replied.

"The Speaker is getting off a call. He'll be with you shortly." She said.

"Is it okay if I make a call?" Jax asked and pulled out his phone.

"That's fine," she said.

He dialed Griggs's number.

It rang a few times, and he almost hung up.

"What is it?" she asked.

"It's me," he said.

"I know. I put your number into my phone."

"Oh, I'm at the Speaker's office," he said.

"What are you doing there?" she asked.

"Asking a few questions," he replied.

He spoke quietly not to disrupt those in the office.

"Shouldn't we wait before approaching him?" she asked.

"No," Jax replied, "I think it would be good to get in now. Where are you?"

"I'm home," she said.

"Are you sure?" he asked.

"Yes," she replied.

"Okay, I'll talk to you later," he said.

"Girlfriend?" the secretary asked.

"No," Jax replied, "My partner."

"Same thing," she said.

"I work for the FBI. She's my partner at work," he said.

The woman stared at him.

She hadn't been told I work for the FBI.

Her phone buzzed.

"He's ready for you," she said.

Jax walked to the door, and Miles Frank met him at it.

"Ah, Jackson," Miles said, "it's good to see you."

The doors closed behind him, and Jax stared at the white walls and numerous pictures. President Thompson's photograph sat in the middle of the wall behind his desk.

"I assume you'll have one of Elaine Franklin after her swearing-in?" Jax asked.

Miles didn't reply.

"Don't assume anything. That always got you into trouble," he replied.

That bit hurt, and Jax's eyes glazed over for a minute. He assumed the intel on his flight was correct. He never thought to question it.

"Yes, assumptions are a bad thing. I want to ask you a few questions about things over there," Jax said.

"Okay," Miles replied.

"Do you remember David Webb?" Jax asked.

"I remember him quite well. It's a tragic thing that happened to him." Miles said.

"It is quite terrible," Jax said.

"I was very disheartened to learn you were involved in such a thing," Miles said.

"I've been exonerated, as I'm sure you're aware."

"But to see his head explode in such a way. It must have been terrible?" Miles asked.

"It was, but how did you know Webb?"

"He was under my command in Iraq and Afghanistan."

"From what I understand, you were demoted in Iraq after the loss of a pilot; then a bombing went wrong?" Jax asked.

"The pilot was a horrible thing. Having him captured, and that video. It was terrible. But the bombing, I believe you were involved with that?"

"I was the pilot and lost my flight status due to an error in intelligence. I lost my flight status afterward," Jax said.

Miles smiled at the last part, and Jax wanted to reach across the man's desk and strangle him but resisted the impulse.

"I believe the reason for your disciplinary hearing was mental issues associated with that bombing."

This mother fucker.

A salty taste filled Jax's mouth, and he realized he'd bitten the inside of his mouth.

"Yes, but it was called an intelligence failure as well. Am I correct?"

"So, is Webb all you have for me?"

"There is the matter of someone else. Do you know a man named Brad Drake?"

Was that a flinch?

Jax watched the Speaker for a moment.

"I have no idea who that is," Miles said.

Jax had seen him flinch at the name.

"What does this have to do with?"

"The lost drone at Creech Air Base," Jax said.

"I thought the case was closed after Webb died?"

"We're looking into new developments."

"I hope you find what you're looking for," Miles said.

"I haven't lost a case yet," Jax replied.

Jax walked to the door and turned around, a thought occurring to him.

"Are you attending the inauguration?"

Miles only stared. He was not prepared for that question.

"I'll be away from the Capitol. Have to keep the line of succession going in case of an accident," he said.

"I see. Will you be watching it?"

Miles smiled, "I wouldn't miss it."

"That's good to know," Jax said.

He walked out of the office, nodding to the secretary as he made his way out.

Jax retrieved his firearm from the agents and took the elevator.

When he'd returned to his car, he dialed Decker's home number.

A woman, whom Jax assumed was Decker's wife, Griggs's mom, answered the phone.

"Vanessa Griggs, please," Jax said.

"Is this Agent Reed?"

"Yes, it is."

"Vanessa left over an hour ago. Said she was going shopping."

"Okay, thank you," Jax replied.

He ended the call and dialed Griggs.

It went to voicemail.

CHAPTER SEVENTY-FIVE

GRIGGS STARED at the people in the diner. None of them looked like Drake.

She'd worn her uniform and received the customary 'thank you for your service' greetings from numerous people when she'd sat down.

"You look like you're searching for someone," the waitress commented.

"I was thinking of buying land up here. I came into money and thought I'd take a look. I thought there was land for sale."

"Raven Hill is a mountain. Some company bought it after the owner died."

"Do you know the name of the company?" Griggs asked.

"Oh yes, it was a big stink. The town got the land when the man died. They sold it to this company. Called themselves 'Executive Actions.'"

Griggs tried not to show her surprise.

"Could you tell me how to get to Raven Hill?"

"Sure, you go down the road a piece. You'll see a white billboard on the left. To the right is the road that leads up. There's a gate at the top of the hill. No one can get in. Not sure what they did up there, but people around here thought it would be a coal company. People returned to their lives when that didn't happen, though they were a bit upset about it."

"Not much going on in this town," Griggs said.

"Not really. Most people work in the cities now. We're one of the last places to survive."

"Looks like you're doing good business?"

"It's the only restaurant for miles around. We get a good Sunday crowd. People come in after church and things like that."

"Any land close to Raven Hill?"

"There were a few construction trucks up there after that land was sold, but nothing came of it, as I said. We could use the money around here."

"They put a fence around the property?"

"Yes," the woman replied, "it's not electrified, but it will almost kill you if you try to climb it."

"Anyone done that?"

"A few kids went up looking for things. There are a couple of old mines on the property. They went up looking and said someone was shooting at them."

"That's crazy," Griggs said.

"Sheriff got ahold of the company. I told them they couldn't be shooting at kids. The owner told them they shouldn't be trespassing then."

"Did any of those workers come in here?"

"They were told not to."

Griggs thanked her, paid for her food, and walked out to her mom's Range Rover.

CHAPTER SEVENTY-SIX

JOHNNY PULLED off the side of the road and stared across the street as a Range Rover pulled onto the road.

He'd seen the driver come out of the diner and get in her vehicle.

She was a Black woman wearing an Air Force uniform. Her hair was pulled into a tight bun. He took a picture of her with his phone as she drove away.

He'd seen a picture of her on the TV and wanted to ensure he was right.

Johnny watched her drive away towards the interstate.

He drove up the mountain and through the gate.

The road was slushy from the snow, and his jeep slid a bit as he made his way up.

Drake stood on the side of the house, bent over and looking at something.

Johnny pulled in and jumped out of the jeep.

"What are you doing?" he asked.

"Looks like we have a few raccoons or something," Drake said and pointed to some scat on the ground near the house.

Johnny took a look at it and frowned.

"It's a raccoon. I grew up with raccoons. They're all over Utah."

Drake stepped back and looked at Johnny. His hair was messed up, and mud clung to the outside of the jeep.

"You came up pretty fast. What's the hurry?"

"I think I saw that woman. The one who's working with that FBI agent. She was down at the diner."

"She wouldn't be up here. There's no reason for that." Drake said.

Johnny held up his phone to show him the picture he'd taken.

"Shit," Drake said after looking at the picture.

"It's her, isn't it?"

"Yeah, it's fucking her," Drake said.

"What do we do about it?"

"You don't do anything. I need to call our friend. Maybe he has some ideas."

Drake hurried to the door.

"Where are you going?"

"To take care of it."

He got in and pulled away from the cabin.

Johnny watched him go and glanced at the blue sky overhead. There were clouds around the fringes of it, and he worried about the drone.

* * *

Drake reached the main road and called Miles.

"We have a big problem, Mr. Speaker," Drake said.

"You have one? So do I. Jackson Reed visited me."

"His partner was at the diner not half an hour ago. Where are they getting their information?"

"I have a good idea. When is he taking it up again?"

"Probably tonight," Drake said.

"If they have what I think they do, they'll need confirmation. I know where they'll be going."

"You think he'll be alone?"

"Does it matter?" Miles replied.

"Not really, but I'd rather take him out than his whole family. It will look better to the press."

"Always a politician," Drake said.

"Once you get into this, it's hard to get out," Miles said.

"I know the feeling," Drake replied, "so, what's your plan?"

Miles laid out his plan. Drake smiled, turned around, and drove back to the cabin.

CHAPTER SEVENTY-SEVEN

JAX'S PHONE RANG. It was Decker.

"What's up, Boss," Jax answered.

"I have some information you may be interested in," Decker said.

"Okay?"

"The Navy has procured that other drone. They're moving it out here." Decker said.

"You're kidding?"

"I heard it from someone."

"Thank you," Jax said and ended the call.

He dialed a number on his phone he hadn't used until that moment.

"This is Gonzalez," the person answered.

"I hear you have the drone in Virginia?" Jax asked.

"Jackson Reed," Gonzalez said, "it's good to hear your voice. Yes, I brought the drone out for the Navy. They're having me test it for them. "

"I need to talk to you," Jax said.

"You're talking," she replied.

"No, in person," Jax said, "I have a few questions I need to ask."

"Okay," she said and gave him directions to the base.

He drove to the base, pulled up to the gate, and showed his ID.

"Your name was added to the list. Thank you, Sir. Follow the road back. You'll see the tarmac and hangar. That's where she'll be."

Jax followed the directions, reached the tarmac, and parked his car.

Victoria Gonzalez walked out to meet him.

"Good to see you again," she said.

"You as well," he replied.

"Are you any closer to finding my aircraft?" she asked.

"That's the reason I'm here."

"I assumed so. What can I answer for you?"

"First, where are you storing the other one?" Jax asked.

"Follow me," she said.

They walked past a gate next to where he'd parked and through another checkpoint.

Jax stared at her uniform for a minute and smiled.

She glanced back at him.

"What's with the smile?" she said.

He pointed to her shoulder.

"You added another stripe," he said.

"Yes. I got a promotion. I wasn't expecting it. I expected a demotion. I was told I'd done good work. Some things were out of my control, and I handled them as well as anyone could. The lost aircraft wasn't my fault."

"Did you find the problem with the update?" Jax asked.

"We did. A few strings of code allowed it to be taken over."

"And you just happened to see it?"

"We looked at it and ran it on the simulator. We figured it

would have been easy to take the drone with the code's structure."

"Where did the code originate?" Jax asked.

She led him into a hangar. The drone sat in the middle of the room with guards.

"So, you remember me saying the update came from the manufacturer?"

"Right. I remember you saying that," Jax replied.

"I checked with them. They didn't have a record of sending an update for the drone."

"So, what are your thoughts?"

"It was brought in from someone on the outside."

"You think Webb installed it?"

"He could have. I don't know who could have written it. It wasn't Webb."

"What are its capabilities?" Jax asked, changing the subject.

"I told you it's virtually invisible to radar, but we found a few things that make that less evident as we tested it." She said.

"Like?"

"What's the point of this inquiry? Is there something you're not telling me?"

"I'll get to that, but I need things answered first," Jax said.

"Okay, so like any aircraft, it's susceptible to the cold. Ice can form on the wings. We've found that the ailerons stick a bit in cold weather. But that may have something to do with the unboxing of it. It was accustomed to the desert weather, and it's fucking cold here. The crew is working on that."

"You mean it's not acclimated to this weather?"

"Something like that," she replied.

"So, have you found a new pilot?"

She smiled.

"That's the other reason for the extra stripe. There is no one else who knows the aircraft as I do. I've watched flight videos until I can do it damn near with my eyes closed. I took it up a few times at Creech before the Navy called. But don't go spreading that around."

"Gotcha," Jax said.

"What other questions do you have?"

Jax knelt and looked at the front gun ports, the wings' missile racks, and the bomb clips on the aircraft's undercarriage.

"These gunports work as well?"

"Yes," she said and stared at him. "There's a question you want to ask but are afraid to do so. Just ask it, Agent Reed."

Jax took a deep breath and led her away from the rest of the crew.

"I think we know what the other drone will be used for. We don't have real evidence, just opportunity, and circumstance," he said.

"Tell me your theories, and I'll explain how it could be done. I might be able to tell you what ordnance they're using as well," Victoria said.

Jax walked with her around the building, laying out his and Griggs' theories. It took the better part of an hour for him to explain it all.

When he finished, she sat down on a bench outside the hangar.

"Well, damn, that's a hell of a theory," she said.

"Yes, but is this thing capable of pulling that off? And if it's in the air, does what you said about being able to track it come into play? I need to know if there is a way to shoot it down," Jax said.

"I know the White House has a team tracking lasers on the roof. But this thing works differently than that. It reflects all of that back at whoever is sending the signal. It isn't very easy, and I don't fully understand all of the technical aspects of it myself, but that's what I've been told. Those lasers on the White House won't stop this thing." She said.

"This drone can accomplish this, though?"

"Definitely. It's more than capable of it."

"If I can get a bead on it, do you think you could instruct a tower how to do that?"

"I've worked with this tower to do that. I needed to know its capabilities, and when we discovered it wasn't completely invisible, I showed it how to track it. After seeing the other one, I thought it was a good idea. I showed the tower at Creech."

"Great, that's all I needed to know."

"Jax, if this is going down, I want to be the one to take the aircraft out." She said.

"I get that. When we find it, I want you to pilot it. It may be on a moment's notice," Jax said.

"That's fine; I will continue what I've been doing with the Navy," she said.

Jax nodded and walked towards his car.

She followed him.

"You know," she said, "if what you're suggesting is real, we need to notify someone."

"Griggs and I are working on that. I needed to come out and talk to you about this drone."

She smiled.

"Take care, Jax," she said.

"I'll do my best," he replied.

CHAPTER SEVENTY-EIGHT

AARON WILLIAMS CALLED a number after having ended the previous call with Jax.

"It's all set. They'll be there later," he said.

"Fine. I'll make sure everything is ready," the voice on the other end said.

Williams ended the call, then told his secretary he was done for the day and that she should call for his car.

He had an appointment with Miles Frank. It would be the last meeting the two would have before the inauguration.

His car took him the short distance to the Congressional office building. The driver parked in the underground parking structure, and Williams took the elevator that various people had used numerous times over the last week.

Miles's secretary smiled at him as he walked in.

The Speaker himself stood in the doorway to his office.

"Glad to see you, Aaron," he said.

"I received a phone call from Reed. They're coming over for dinner. My wife is out of town. I thought I could persuade him to stop the investigation."

"What on earth made you think that?"

"I'm having our friend handle this. They will arrive and leave. What happens between those two points is not my concern." Aaron said.

"This isn't usual. You like Reed. You made sure he got into the academy and landed on his feet. Why the change of heart?"

"They're getting too close. I thought you'd understand."

"I see. So the aircraft is working properly?"

"It's ready to go. Where will you be when the inauguration takes place?"

Miles stared at him, "I'll be making sure my speech is ready. One can't be too ready for terrible things to happen."

"I understand, but I need to know where you're going to be in case anything arises."

"Right. You're saying you'll have to find a way to get me safe if you miss them tonight?"

"That's exactly what I'm saying."

Miles stood up and walked to the window.

"You know, this place has grown on me. I've always wanted to sit in a big chair. It's something I've worked on for years. I won't have someone screw it up."

"It won't be screwed up," Williams said.

"Yes, I will be sworn in by the end of the festivities. I'll handle whatever comes afterward." Miles said.

"Was there something else, Mr. Speaker?"

"No, but the next time you see me, it will be Mr. President," Miles said.

Williams adjusted his jacket as he stood and walked to the door.

Miles watched him walk out.

He returned to his desk and picked up the phone.

"I know you've been told to handle those two, but I no longer trust Williams. Handle all of it then." Miles said.

"It will be done," Drake said on the other end.

CHAPTER SEVENTY-NINE

JAX GLANCED ACROSS THE ROOM.

The other agents had kept their distance since he and Griggs had arrived.

"I need you two to come with me," Decker said as he walked past their desks.

He didn't stop; he only kept moving.

"Someone in the garage needs to speak to you," he said.

"Who?" Jax asked.

"Just go," Decker said.

They took the elevator, and a black SUV sat just beyond the doors when they opened. It was flanked on all sides by Secret Service. Jax watched them fidget. They did not want to be where they were.

An agent opened the door to the SUV. Elaine Franklin waved them into the vehicle.

They got in and sat down.

Jax glanced from the President-Elect to Tom.

Tom was buried in notes on his lap. He didn't look up until the vehicle was moving.

"I understand through the grapevine you two are involved in something."

"Where did you hear that?"

"I have my little birds everywhere in this town. It's what happens when you're in politics as long as I have been. They say you are still looking for that drone on US soil."

"Okay," Jax said.

"If you're still looking into it, you believe there is a chance it will be recovered. Because let's face it, you wouldn't continue to look for it here if the Russians or Chinese took it."

Jax stared at Griggs.

Tom smiled at Jax.

"What we're wondering," Tom said, "is why you're still looking? We know you took a trip to Groom Lake. You must have found something out there because we heard about the raid on Executive Actions. That ruffled some feathers."

"I've had people looking into that company before. I always got stonewalled." Elaine Franklin said.

"It looks like a shell company for doing other things. I think it's used for laundering money." Griggs said.

"I believed that as well. It's why I pursued it while I was on the house finance committee." Elaine said.

"We found a few things with it overseas," Jax said.

"What were those things?" Elaine asked.

Jax paused and glanced at both of them, then at Griggs.

"I have clearance, as does Tom. You found something overseas that you couldn't explain or scared you. It's the only reason I have for you why you won't tell me what you found."

He explained to her the pictures they'd found from India.

"This company is building an army? For what purpose?"

"We're not certain. What we're looking into may have nothing to do with that. Or it could be the first volley of their intentions. We're not certain on either point."

"But you think it's one of those?" Elaine pressed.

"What is your theory on this first volley?" Tom asked.

The window was up, but Jax took a look outside. Snow was falling, and though he knew they were secure in the vehicle, the slick, wet roads made him uncomfortable. It had nothing to do with the surface of the streets but the direction the questions had taken.

"We're not at liberty to say yet. Before broaching it with anyone, we want to ensure our theory is correct."

"I will be President in a few days. Will you tell me then?" she asked.

"It would be my pleasure to tell you then," Jax replied.

"But you won't tell me now?" she asked.

"Madame President-Elect, I would love nothing more than to tell you now. But until we're certain of what is going on, we don't want to cause any problems. I will let you know when we have certifiable information, but until then, I'm afraid I have to keep you in the dark."

"I understand," she said, but Jax thought she did not understand.

"Thank you," he replied.

Jax glanced out the window again, and they'd arrived at her residence.

"I must get out and play with my grandchildren for a while. Their laughter and smiles keep me young and wise."

She got out, and her team escorted her into the house.

Jax noticed Tom did not get out of the vehicle.

"Jax, if there is something you need, let me know. I wish you would tell us your theory," Tom said.

"I wish I could as well, but as I said," Jax said, "we want to make certain before we say anything."

"Okay, will you be getting Elizabeth this week?" Tom asked.

"I won't be able to until after the inauguration," Jax said.

"I will let Sarah know," Tom said.

"Could you also let her know my lawyer has the papers?"

Tom flinched and stared at Jax's ring.

"I will, and Jax, I'm sorry," Tom said.

"Don't be. You're getting a hell of a woman. Treat her right." Jax said.

"I will. You have to get out now. They aren't your chauffeur," Tom said.

They got out and realized they were farther away from the Hoover than they wanted.

Jax called for a ride, returned to the Hoover, and spent the rest of the day organizing everything for their meeting with Williams.

CHAPTER EIGHTY

JAX GATHERED ALL the evidence they had and stood up from his desk.

Griggs glanced at him.

His phone buzzed.

"Jax, I've sent a car for you," Williams said.

"Okay," Jax replied and hung up.

Jax glanced at Griggs.

"It's time," he said.

"I hope we have everything we need to convince him and show him that we're right," Griggs said.

"It's not the convincing thing I'm worried about. I believe he already knows it all. He's playing coy and doesn't want the others to know what he's doing."

"So, we have to make him give himself and the others up?" Griggs asked.

"Something like that," Jax said.

Jax and Griggs walked into Decker's office and told him the news.

"You two, be careful. I don't like this. In case you need me, call me on my cell," Decker said.

"We'll be careful," Griggs said.

Decker smiled at her as they walked out of the room.

He glanced at the pictures on his desk. One of them was Griggs in a soccer uniform when she was little. He thought of that day. It was just after her mom, and he had been dating for a while and moved in together.

Vanessa was small then. Her mom had braided her hair with beads, and they made a noise when they struck the back of her uniform.

Decker thought of the girl she was then and then the woman she'd become. He smiled and watched them step into the elevator.

Jax stood holding the elevator for her.

"Be careful," Decker whispered to himself.

They slipped into the elevator and were gone.

CHAPTER EIGHTY-ONE

DRAKE SAT along a hill overlooking a large house.

Numerous guards walked the perimeter with their rifles held low as if anticipating trouble.

He watched them make their patrols. Chatting with each other and quietly staring off in the distance.

Drake, his rifle ready, picked up his phone.

"They're on their way. It would be best if you headed in," he said.

"Roger that," Johnny said on the other end.

Drake continued to watch Aaron Williams pace the living room floor.

He knew the man's wife and kids were gone for the night and that he made an excuse to his wife to stay back.

Williams glanced at the same guards' Drake watched from his vantage point on the hill.

Williams took a couple of sips of whiskey and waited.

* * *

The countryside moved smoothly for Jax as he watched it from inside the car. The rain pattered the windows as the car moved along, and Jax realized he'd never been to Williams's house but was sure it was more significant than the small apartment he lived in.

He knew the man had money from his job and some he'd put away for rainy days.

He glanced at Griggs; a stack of papers rested on her lap. It was everything they had about their investigation.

"It's fine," Jax said as she shuffled the papers around for what could have been the hundredth time.

She relaxed and watched the countryside as he'd been doing.

The car reached the house at the end of a cul-de-sac and stopped at a large iron gate. They were waved through, and the car rolled to a stop near the house. A guard with an MP5 opened the door on Jax's side and waved them out.

"He's inside," the guard said.

Jax and Griggs walked to the door, and Aaron Williams opened it wearing a smile.

"Glad to see both of you. Please come in," Williams said.

Williams nodded to the guard, and the man returned to his patrol.

The house's high ceilings drew Griggs's eyes and the multiple art pieces on the walls.

"I had no idea you had all this stuff," Jax said.

"I didn't decorate it. My wife did. I don't have the style she does," he said.

Williams led them towards a room with a long dining table. And waved for them to sit. Bottles of wine sat on the table, and Williams offered them to his guests.

Jax grabbed a red and poured himself a glass. His attempt to pass it to Griggs failed, as she opted for the white.

She poured herself a glass and glanced at Williams.

"Where are your wife and kids tonight?" Griggs asked.

"My son had something at school. I rarely miss those things, but I needed to speak with both of you." He said.

"Sorry you're missing it on our account," Jax said.

"It's fine. Work is important. What you two are doing is important too. I will bring the food out." He said.

Williams disappeared, and Jax and Griggs sipped on their wine as they stared at their palatial surroundings.

"You grabbed the papers?" Jax asked.

"Yes," she said, showing him.

* * *

"I know you're wondering why I asked you here," Williams said.

"We were a bit curious," Jax said.

"In this case, with the drone, I put you on it for a reason. I know your mind, Jax. I thought I'd have to do so much lifting. I know you have questions, but I have something better."

He pulled his phone out and sat it in the middle of the table.

"I went to see Miles Frank today. That man is not very bright. He plays like he is, but he isn't."

"Explain?" Jax said.

Williams pressed play on his phone.

They listened to the conversation earlier that afternoon in the Speaker's office.

When Williams stopped it, Jax and Griggs stared at him.

"That's an admission of guilt from both of you and a threat against both of us," Jax said.

"Why do you think I have so many guards tonight," Williams said.

* * *

Johnny had prepped the drone before nightfall. It sat on the patch of tarmac outside the small cabin in the West Virginia Mountains.

Johnny checked each part of the drone individually, ensuring the belt-fed guns were secure, that he'd attached the missiles properly and removed their plugs to make them live.

He got up from the couch, where he'd been watching TV in anticipation of Drake's call.

Johnny walked out the door, did one more pass on the ordnance attached to the aircraft, and returned to the warmth of the cabin.

He opened the door to his operations room and flicked on the lights. The whir of fans started up, followed closely by that of electronics.

The flight controls turned on, and he sat in his chair. The view from the camera was of the cabin. The engines turned on. He maneuvered them vertically, and the drone rose again over the treetops.

A light rain fell, a massive difference from the snow he'd been flying in the last few times. The change in weather was a relief, as he'd become worried about the ice on the wings.

The engines realigned, and the aircraft took off towards Virginia.

Johnny was light on the stick, and the drone moved smoothly over the countryside.

* * *

Drake sat on the hill, adjusted his rifle, and watched Williams in the kitchen.

Williams plated food for the three of them and carried it into the other room as Drake scanned the perimeter again.

He watched the wind blowing off the coast, stirring the

blades of grass in the backyard, and adjusted his sites to account for it.

The temperature dropped, and he had to account for that.

He moved an inch forwards and picked off the first guard near the back wall, then the next as he was about to raise the alarm.

Two guards were down in a matter of seconds, and he moved to the other four.

One of the patterns of their paths crossed, and he'd have to wait. Then he watched as a guard approached the front gate, where he'd dropped the first two.

The man was running, but Drake dropped him before he could alert the others.

Three to go.

He moved his rifle to the left of the gate as another guard was making a path, dropping the guard.

Drake continued this until all the guards were down.

There would be no return fire on him or anything else.

* * *

The drone flew higher, avoiding the lights of DC.

He practiced the run the night before, unarmed.

There would be no mistakes.

The aircraft rose over the hill, and Johnny watched the infrared flare in front of him.

Eight cold bodies were lying on the ground throughout the compound.

He floated higher and saw the lone man on the hill.

Johnny knew who that was.

He hovered in the air for a minute. The activity in the house intrigued him. He wondered what they were saying and wished he could read lips.

Three people sat at a long table in the corner of the house.

He adjusted his controls, sighted the room, and pressed the trigger.

The missile locked onto the only heat source in the house, the kitchen stove.

* * *

"Get down," Jax screamed.

The missile blew out the windows sending glass, concrete, and wood into the air.

Jax stood up and stared out the shattered window.

He scanned the debris field for Griggs. She lay on her side against the wall.

His chair had been furthest from the blast, and he'd merely been knocked out of it.

Jax crawled towards Griggs and roused her. A part of her left arm was twisted in a way he didn't like.

He moved her, and she screamed.

"Good, you're alive," he said.

"Where is the phone?" she asked.

The phone lay on the floor, next to the overturned table. Williams lay next to it. A large shard of glass jutted from his side.

Jax moved towards him.

"I'm sorry," he said, "tell my wife I'm sorry."

Jax helped him up, and Griggs stared at them both.

"Help me get him out of here," he said.

She nodded, tucked her left arm to her chest, and hobbled over as Jax stared at the broken glass.

"It's still out there. I can hear it." Jax said.

Shells ripped through the building as they hurried to the front door.

The wind blew Jax's hair. He knew it wasn't natural wind but shells missing his head as they buzzed past.

He carried Williams out with Griggs's help.

They reached the front door as something struck the interior of the house.

It sent Jax and Griggs end over end into the front yard.

Jax raised his gun as the drone moved around the house for a better shot.

He aimed where he knew the camera would be.

The shot clipped it, and the drone took off.

Jax pulled out his phone and dialed Gonzalez.

"What's up?" she asked.

"How soon can you get that drone in the air?" he asked.

"I was ready to send it up in a couple of minutes. I stopped because you called."

"The other drone is up. I need the tower to track it." Jax said.

"Okay," she replied.

Jax set his phone down and stared at the bodies of the guards.

"Griggs, Drake is out there," he said.

She only stared at him.

"Are you okay?" she asked.

"I'm okay," Jax said.

"Who did you call?"

"Gonzalez," Jax said, "she's getting the other drone up to go after him."

He studied Griggs again.

"I'm going after him," Jax said.

He stood up and ran to the side of the building. He fired into the night where he thought Drake had been. He knew he'd miss but had to risk the shots.

He returned to Griggs, who held Williams, "He's gone."

"I have to make a few calls," Jax dialed Decker and told him what had happened. Before the man could get into it with him, he hung up.

Gonzalez called back.

"Sir, I'm relaying this message from Gonzalez. She's in the air, and the tower is tracking the aircraft."

"Let me know what happens," Jax said.

CHAPTER EIGHTY-TWO

VICTORIA GONZALEZ BANKED the drone to the left as it crossed a hill.

A similar setup to what Johnny Milburn used, though more features weren't available in the black market version he'd been using. Mainly there were cameras installed on the left and right sides of the rig; to give whoever watched her pilot the aircraft a better view of what she saw and how she handled the controls.

It was an added feature the Navy required after the crash of the previous version.

The hill she'd come over was slightly behind where the other drone was.

She heard the direction she should be flying from the tower in her ear. As the drone crossed a set of trees, she saw the other drone ahead of her.

She'd taken it up earlier in the day with total armaments, as the Navy wanted to see how it handled a full payload. It would be modified for use in the field by adding a tow hook to the back of the aircraft to launch a carrier, but that had not been added yet.

The missiles locked, and she fired.

* * *

Johnny turned into a barrel roll, sending the missile into the distance.

He hadn't expected the attack, so he believed it to be a glitch at first when his warning lights came on. His mind changed as the warnings persisted, getting louder.

He turned the aircraft, trying to shake the tail, but it was no use. He pulled up and banked a hard right to try and get behind the other drone.

Whoever is piloting that thing is good.

He dove to the deck, the drone's wings screaming in the nighttime air. The rain continued, and he worried about how it handled everything. As he pulled up, he wished for a rearview camera.

Bullets sprayed the night as he moved into another barrel roll.

* * *

Gonzalez targeted again, the bullets spraying, but missed, and danced off into the darkness. Her opponent banked hard to the left; she received a lock-on alert and pressed the fire button.

The missile streaked through the sky, clipping the wing. As it spun, she fired another, blowing the drone from the sky.

* * *

Drake watched the drones in a dogfight overhead, and pulled out his phone as the drone disintegrated into a fireball.

Five triggers blinked outside the cabin, where Johnny Milburn started screaming after losing the drone.

Drake had placed them, and when Johnny asked him what

he was doing, he mentioned the raccoon scat. Still, it was fake, and he'd set it there intentionally to divert attention.

Underneath the fake scat lay enough explosives to launch the cabin into orbit and the garage.

He called the number in the burner phone he'd rigged to the explosives.

Johnny, who'd run to the door, only saw a flash of light as he disintegrated in a ball of fire.

Drake tossed the phone over the cliff and into the water below.

He got in his truck, made one call, and arrived at a small airport outside DC. He was the only person other than the pilot on the aircraft.

CHAPTER EIGHTY-THREE

JAX'S EYES fluttered at the brightness of the ceiling tiles overhead.

"Oh, you're awake," a voice said.

He glanced to his left, and Tom and Sarah sat beside his bed.

"Where is Griggs?" he asked.

"She's in another room," Tom said.

"Is she okay?" he asked.

"Her arm is broken, and she has a concussion. So do you, but she's okay," Sarah said.

"What were you doing out there?" Tom asked.

"We were having dinner. He asked us to come out for dinner," Jax replied.

He licked his lips and tried to sit up. His head spun like a carousel.

"No, lay back. Something hit you in the explosion."

"I had a phone in my pocket. Where is it?" he asked.

Tom glanced at Sarah, who stood up and walked out.

"The President is here, and she'd like to speak with you," Tom said.

"She? How long have I been out?" Jax asked.

"A few days," Tom said.

Tom stood up and walked to the door.

"Falcon on the move," he heard from Secret Service agents beyond his door.

Elaine Franklin walked in and sat in the chair Sarah had occupied.

"Hello, Jax," she said.

"Madame President, I hear," he said.

"Yes, thanks to you," she said.

He sat stunned, "Look, I know you want an explanation. All I'm going to say is that Miles Frank was taken into custody. He claimed a few things, but the truth is, I confronted him with that tape. He will stand trial. Last I heard, he was going to be brought in for questioning. He's claimed other things, wild things since his arrest."

"Madame President, I'm sorry I didn't tell you."

"It's fine, I understand. I'm not sure I would have believed you if you'd tried to convince me."

Out of nervousness, Jax tried to spin his wedding ring, only to find it wasn't there.

He raised his hand to look at it.

"Your ring was cut off your finger. It was necessary. I believe Sarah has it." Elaine told him.

"I don't think I'll need it," Jax smiled.

ACKNOWLEDGMENTS

A lot goes into writing a book. I know you've heard that before, but it's true.

I wrote the first draft of this book during the lockdown in 2020. Its first incarnation ran over one-hundred thousand words. I wrote it in April 2020-May 2020. I loved these types of books when I was younger and still do.

There are a lot of people to thank for this one.

To my editor, Gillian Brown, you took this book and made it what it is. Without your help, I'm sure it would sit on my computer for another year.

To the horror and thriller groups on Twitter, you are fantastic, and I love everyone one of you for how much you've supported my writing.

I have to call a few people out for their help. To Gabino Iglesias, you're the hardest working writer I know. Taking your classes changed my writing and made me work harder. To Sadie Hartman, for helping me find Gillian. I'll be forever thankful for that and Nightworms. To T.J. Tranchell, Rami Ungar, Cina Pelayo, Briana Morgan, C.R. Langille, Scott J. Moses, and all the other who I know I'll forget, you've helped me in some way. It could be something online or how you phrased a rejection, but you all helped with this and all the others.

And to my wife and kids. The three of you put up with me writing in the morning. Struggling with rejections and trying to keep my sanity. The latter felt closer than it should have been.

You're my light in my darkness. I love the three of you more than you'd believe.

Finally, to the fourteen-year-old kid who struggled to fit in and found solace in these types of books. This is for you!

ABOUT THE AUTHOR

Brian B. Baker lives in Utah with his wife and kids. He grew up reading Tom Clancy and all the 80s thriller writers. His love of those books led him to write them.

He writes every morning unless he's otherwise detained. He has ideas for books with Jax and Griggs and a few others who wander around in this novel.

ALSO BY BRIAN B. BAKER

The Demon Woods...and other stories. Brian B. Baker also writes horror.